EROS & THANATOS

AN ANTHOLOGY OF DEATH & DESIRE

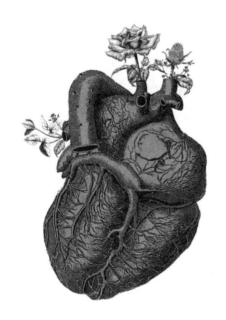

EDITED BY
Cassandra L. Thompson
& Damon Barret Roe

EROS & THANATOS
AN ANTHOLOGY OF DEATH & DESIRE

EDITED BY
CASSANDRA L. THOMPSON
& DAMON BARRET ROE

QUILL & CROW PUBLISHING HOUSE

Eros & Thanatos: An Anthology of Death & Desire
Edited by Cassandra L. Thompson, Damon Barret Roe
Published by Quill & Crow Publishing House

Copyright © 2022 by Cassandra L. Thompson. Featuring contributions by Alexandria Baker, Megan Bontrager, Maddie Bowen-Smyth, Dan Dolan, A.L. Garcia, Rebecca Jones-Howe, Jeremy Megargee, Newton, Ashley Van Elswyk, Melanie Whitlock, Kayla Whittle, and Perry Wolfecastle.

Cover Design & Interior by Marie Casey

Printed in the United States of America

ISBN: 979-8-9851285-2-9
ISBN (ebook): 979-8-9851285-1-2

Publisher's Website: www.quillandcrowpublishinghouse.com

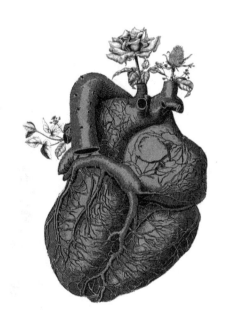

TABLE OF CONTENTS

FOREWORD

A.L. GARCIA

The stories we tell and consume as a society often have the capacity
to reveal our fears, expose our hearts, and represent contemporary
social issues in ways that captivate and inspire us. A brief history of Gothic
literature demonstrates how efficient this genre has been over time at
representing certain facets of society often marginalized or uncelebrated
in other genres. From Mary Shelley to Anne Rice, Poe, Lovecraft, and
so many more, Gothic stories have been particularly well-equipped at
making us contemplate, appreciate, and examine the way we deal with
love, death, desire, mortality, power struggles, poverty, grief, and so on.

This anthology aims to honor that legacy by exploring the
intersections of these profoundly human topics through thought-
provoking, entertaining, and imaginative literature produced with a
diverse perspective we could not be prouder of. In addition to the various
cultures and continents our authors hail from, we are honored to announce
that more than half of the stories in Eros & Thanatos are works of queer
orientation and perspective.

As a perpetual lover of Gothic horror and a queer person myself,
I cannot begin to express how grateful I am to be part of a collection
so inclusive of the underrepresented reality of our society. I was drawn

to, and quickly became obsessed with Edgar Allen Poe's short stories and poems as a youth specifically for their tendency to highlight parts of history and humanity often ignored because they are difficult to think of, grotesque, or terrifying. In addition to being amused, horrified, and intrigued, I also found a peculiar form of solidarity. I felt connected to the struggles present in the lives of the characters, the terrors, the mystery, the longing, the heartbreak. I found solace in these fictional tales because they made these darker sides of our nature into something I could analyze and talk about, unlike explicit hushed truths. I was no longer alone in facing the feelings associated with them.

The concept of experiencing this in a collection with so many diverse voices is, well, like a dream within a dream. I wish I would have had the opportunity to fall in love with stories as a youth that recognized, uplifted, and/or were defined by a variety of perspectives–including those who are openly queer. I hope the stories in this collection can be a small part of changing the narrative for all those learning to accept themselves past the bigotry, sexism, and discrimination so regularly meted out by domestic, cultural, and institutional systems, both in the United States and abroad.

This collection features twelve carefully selected stories, highlighting the intersection of love and death, darkness and desire, devotion and mortality. We hope these Gothic shorts leave you terrified, heart-broken, pensive, and emboldened by the complexities of our humanity, and the societies we create, whose darkness is inexorably interwoven in the very fabric of our souls. Additionally, we hope the unique viewpoints with which these topics are presented continue to encourage more representation of diverse and queer voices in literature and the arts.

CHAPTER ONE

YOU AGAIN

JEREMY MEGARGEE

SALEM, 1692

How do you know which ones are poisonous?"
"Touch and sight. Mushrooms have personalities. They're a lot like people in that way. Some are soft and others are lethal. When we return to the village, look long into the faces of those we live with. People have their poison."

The boy with the turquoise eyes studies the girl with the golden eyes, and he feels his heart quicken. Her hair is woven scarlet, and the wind finds it irresistible. She wears a thick shawl across her shoulders, and her flesh is so pallid it seems porcelain in the weak November sunlight. She has long fingers, infinitely delicate, and he watches as she bends down and adds new morels to her basket. The trees in the forest are dead already, their leaves shed like coats that no longer serve them, and the bare branches reach out, emaciated arms seeking an embrace.

The boy with the turquoise eyes longs for an embrace too, and it's hard not to gather her up into his arms and squeeze her in this grove. His heart is full of poetry when he's with her, and he barely knows how to translate it. He fears if he gives voice to it, the words will not stop, and it'll become a warm torrential wave that takes hold of her and sweeps her away over the hilltops. He's young and inexperienced, and he knows in the deepest fibers of his heart that he's hopelessly in love. There's great vulnerability in the act of love. You give a part of yourself that is easily wounded, and you hope the receiver will bless instead of bruise.

There's something about the girl. She sees him. She doesn't see a lowly farm lad with his pitchfork and his cheeks smudged in mud from the barn. She doesn't smell hay on his ripped garments, and she doesn't laugh at the way his left eyelid twitches when he's nervous. She *sees* the parts of him that matter. Those golden irises cut through flesh, and she glimpses the sparks of his soul. It is like being held, but not physically. It's the warmth of trust unspoken, and he has never felt that before. Not with his family, not with the boys he socializes with after his chores are finished, and not even with his grumpy old gray wolfhound.

She is the person he thinks about when he wakes, and when he dreams, she's always there, forever etched into the framework of memory.

"I worry about you," he tells her. I know without the forest, you'd wither, but it is a bad time to be seen in the woodlands. The hysteria. The trials…"

She comes close, inches from his chest, and reaches up to trace the stubble on his round apple-bud of a cheek. He longs to swoon against her, but doesn't want to seem less of a man, so he simply takes hold of her fingertips, brushing his lips against thumb and index finger.

"Still a sapling, and already you grow hair on your face. I think in a year's time you'll be a big shaggy wolf, and what will I do with you then? Will you still want me when your fangs grow in?"

"Be it beneath sunlight, or moonbeams, or a sky as black as pitch, I'd want you. It scares me how much I want you."

"Why?"

His turquoise eyes flicker over her face, drinking in the features. The high cheekbones, the freckles like constellations on her brow and nose, and the lips so pink you'd think they were smeared in the petals of hollyhocks. "Because you said it best. People have their poison. Many practically drip with it. I want so much with you. I want stars, and children, and to see how your skin will feel when it has a grandmother's wrinkles."

She smiles, a little gap in her teeth, and the sight of it stirs an affection so deep in the boy that he grips her tight to him, digging his desperate hands into her sleeves like she might vanish into the loam of the forest floor if he dares let her go.

"Do you really think we'll become old together? My Nan lived to be fifty. That's a long time. I think I'd like a long time with you."

"As do I."

She looks up, and the wind is once more in her hair, making it wild. There's a blush in her cheeks from the chill, and as the boy touches them, the red deepens.

"When they burn, what do you think they feel?"

"Don't think of that. It's ghoulish."

"Sometimes when I shut my eyes at night, I still hear them screaming. I see them rocking their stakes, and the embers encircle them. I know they didn't do what they were accused of. They were strange, or quiet, or just different. They could have been sisters to me."

"It is madness, but we must tread lightly. When a crowd is hungry for blood, they'll do anything to get a taste. And they're getting brazen in the village. These burnings are new, almost performative, not the normal method of execution."

"When I'm with you, I sometimes feel that I am already burning. Warmth that lasts, the cold banished. I like that feeling. Maybe it is not so bad to burn?"

The boy with the turquoise eyes doesn't have the words, so he just holds her, drawing her as close to his chest as he can. Her chin rests against his clavicle, and he buries his nose in her hair.

He inhales the wilderness within her.

Months after mushrooms and soft words, he's with her again, looking up at her from the bottom of the pyre. He's bleeding from a thousand lacerations, and one of his turquoise eyes is puffed up so badly, he cannot open it. The stones pelt his back and his legs, but he stopped feeling the impact of them a long time ago. She looks down at him, and she does not strain against the ropes that bind her to the stake. Her bare feet must be so sore perched on jagged hunks of firewood, but she doesn't complain.

"This isn't the life for us, but there will be others."

He wants to answer her, but something is broken in his throat, so he answers with his eyes.

"I'll love you as a beggar, or a queen, or even as a mayfly. Whatever comes next, I'll be there, and I'll love you. Will you promise to be there too?"

The boy can barely see her through the haze of blood and tears, but he nods emphatically. His mouth opens, emitting nothing but a weak croak, and he mouths the words: *"I'll find you."*

The stinking behemoth with the black hood shrouding his face approaches, and the boy watches the smoke of the torch twirling skyward. The crowd shrieks and laughs behind him, but they're just ghostly now, not worth even an iota of attention. What matters is her, and he keeps his eyes locked on the golden orbs that soothe him even in his moment of ruin. She is all there is. She is all he sees.

"There's already fire in my heart. You put it there. I won't even feel what they do. It will not compare. What is a strike of iron and flint next to an inferno? I was ashes after that first kiss under the hemlocks."

The boy lifts up the arm that is not fractured, and brushes a trembling thumb across his swollen bottom lip. He remembers, and with the teeth that remain to him, he smiles.

"There's beauty even in a burning. Never forget."

The hooded death-dealer drops the torch, and the flames crawl across the saturated branches, and once the fire reaches the frayed bottom of her dress, she is lit up almost immediately, a silhouette of blazing orange with a backdrop of twilight above her head. The boy watches the porcelain he loved to touch, blister and blacken. His knuckles singe from gripping burning sticks and tossing them from the pyre. He screams wordlessly, his mouth a lion's rictus, and he's numb when hands snatch him up under the elbows and pull him vertically, dragging him in the opposite direction.

She keeps her eyes glued on him even as her hair becomes a halo of cinders, and she breathes in the deep plumes of smoke to keep herself from voicing the agony. The boy is carried, his toes dragging across a splintered platform, and when the noose is drawn tight across his neck, he welcomes the end.

He is thrown from the gallows, his neck too strong to snap, and so he twirls, his face bloating and taking on a purple sheen. His eyes bulge from their sockets, the blood capillaries burst, but each twirl gives him a glimpse of her.

As he strangles, he waits patiently for each rotation. She looks like a fae of the forest dancing in a gown of flame. He stretches forward to feel the ash on his brow, and he reaches for the cinders floating near his head. The rope digs in deeper beneath his chin, and he closes his teeth over his own tongue until it severs. If he cannot speak to her one last time, there is no reason to keep it.

The girl with the golden eyes suffocates at the same moment the boy with the turquoise eyes strangles. Even apart, they die together. Her cremation lasts the entire night, and the hanged boy twirls as charred parts of her topple downward.

Two lovers claimed in the Salem witch trials.

One to the noose, one to the stake.

LONDON, 1854

The man with the turquoise eyes strides along Broad Street, wearing gray cotton trousers, a light overcoat, and a top hat perched on his head, his Brutus curls trailing out behind his ears. His calloused hand rests along the lower back of the woman with the golden eyes, her voluminous bell-shaped dress lifted ever so daintily so the material won't trail in the muck of the gutters. Her light blonde hair is bunned up, a few ringlets bouncing freely, and a bonnet casts shadows across her sharp, olive-toned face. The man presses her palm into his, gripping her nimble fingers gloved in silk, as he helps her hop over a cesspool in the middle of the street. The polluted water stinks to high heaven, but both of them are used to it. Such is life in London. The population is vast in the city, and stagnant places are common.

"It's a filthy old city, isn't it? I'd like to take you away from it."

She laughs, and her voice is music, pedestrians pausing their travels to savor it for a moment. "It's not without its charms. I like the cats that laze about in front of the restaurants. I like how shoes click on the cobblestones, the crowds making orchestras without even intending to do so. And nightfall? Oh, that's the best. The streetlamps all full of gas, every corner lit up with a little sun all its own."

The man twirls his whiskers, and he can't help but smirk. His turquoise eyes glint, and he often wonders how he managed to wed such a marvel of a woman. Only a few months into their marriage, and his wife is a living fantasy pulled up from the ether of dreams. "You're an optimist. I need an optimist in my life. There's too much pessimism in me. I forget the rats in the storm drains when I'm walking with you. I don't even think to smell the sour meat from the beef vendor down Hob's Lane."

"I balance you out. I've always been amused by your doom and gloom."

They walk on, husband and wife, and they try not to notice the bodies wrapped in funeral cloth. There are stacks of them in shadowed alleyways, human cordwood left out to be collected.

"It'll fade out, won't it? No pestilence can last forever, not even the Blue Death."

He draws his wife closer to him, and he wants very much to comfort her, but it's difficult when so much morbidity surrounds them. "I often wonder what came first, the overcrowding or the cholera. There's no place for all the sewage to go here in Soho. It sits in cellars and it festers. Tunnels need to be dug and properly constructed, otherwise the water supply will continue to run with contaminants."

He sees a man sitting awkwardly on a bakery's doorstep, his cadaverous cheeks tinted blue and his arms wrapped around his aching abdomen. The man with the turquoise eyes makes sure to give the sickened soul a wide berth. "I'll get on with a law firm in New York City," he continues. "We'll cross the ocean and get out of London. Don't you think it wise?"

She stops in the street, carriages roaring past her, and she holds his big hands in her small ones. He never ceases to be entranced by her eyes. Flecks of gold in the light, and each morning when he wakes next to her, he mines them, and the wealth of her gaze falling on him is a fortune all its own. "I'll go where you go. We're bound, aren't we? If I don't get to see you twirl these whiskers in the looking glass each day, I'll simply drop dead from despair."

He chuckles, gripping the lace of her elbows, and she reaches up to twirl his whiskers for him.

"Wherever we go, I want a window. I want to watch the people moving somewhere below, living their lives, laughing, and loving when love is offered."

"I'll build you a house in the clouds, and it'll be made of windows. You'll be a vision standing there in all of them. Meadows, hilltops, and not an ounce of sickness to spoil it. How would that be?"

She kisses him, the warmth of her mouth feeling fated, and he tries not to notice when the cough exits her moist lips. He swallows it down and buries it in his sternum, and the two of them pretend it was never there at all.

They clutch each other in bed, their bodies as frail as mummies. Their insides have emptied out more times than either of them can count, the essence of life poured out like rice-water, and no amount of camphor or magnesia able to bring them back from the brink.

She looks into his eyes, the lids heavy, and the turquoise fades to a lost glimmer. "I've been with you before, you know. Before London. Before all this."

"I feel it, something in the bones, but I do not understand."

"Nor do I, but I know it to be true. This time we got to marry. Short, but sweet. Perhaps the next time will be even better."

"Do you fear death?"

"I do not. But I'm afraid of living without love. What an awful emptiness of the heart that must be. If you die first, can I keep you in here? It's a locket inside of me."

She reaches out with weakened hands, grabs his wrist, and places his damp palm against her bare chest. He feels the fluttering of her heart beneath her breast, and each beat seems to come at a cost.

"I wish I could have given you a window."

"In another life, you will."

Cholera is slow, and talking is hard work for the lovers. Sunlight pours in from the little hexagon window above their bed, and it paints the soiled sheets in amber. The man with the turquoise eyes dies first, and the woman with the golden eyes kisses the last breath from his whiskered mouth. She holds that breath within her, and a few hours later, she follows her husband into death.

Rain falls on Broad Street, and London mourns.

POLAND, 1942

"Why do you think they hate us so much?"

The skinny girl with the golden eyes tears her hunk of stale bread in two, and offers the larger portion to the girl with the turquoise eyes. They sit crouched next to each other against the outer wall of a concrete bunkhouse, their attention locked on the horizon. They try to look past the fences, the guard towers, and the razor wire. They both have shaved heads, their thin bodies draped in tattered striped pajamas, and their shoes won't last much longer. The smaller girl picks at a toe that peeks out from a hole in her ruined slipper.

"Because I'm a Jew and you're a gypsy. That's enough for them."

She pauses, munching tiredly on her ration of the bread.

"But look around us. These camps. The hunger and the abuse. It can't sustain itself for much longer. They've built all of this on a foundation of hate, and nothing made of hate can last. It's destined to self-destruct."

"There are rumors the Allies are marching. They're gaining ground. It can't be too much longer before they reach Belzec, right? We met in a cage, but imagine what we can do together outside of one."

The Romani girl with the golden eyes lets her hand flutter into the lap of the young Jewish girl with the turquoise eyes, and they interlock their fingers, relishing the warmth of each other's palms. They keep vigilant to make certain that the SS are not around to see.

"I hope. The first thing I'll do is treat you to a meal much tastier than this."

She lifts up the moldy piece of bread, and both of them chuckle, leaning their shoulders together. They sit there late into the evening, because it is their little tradition to do so. There's a wooded hilltop beyond the western wall, and from their vantage point they're able to see the deer that come out when it's golden hour.

Both girls are fond of a majestic buck and the graceful doe that walks next to him. The deer are just tiny miniatures beyond this horrible place, but they represent a freedom both girls yearn to experience again. They huddle together in the shadows, daydreaming of antlers, soft brown eyes, and endless grasslands.

It isn't long before the Nazis come to herd them into their bunkhouse for the night with harsh words and the gaping bores of rifles.

Once the lights go out in the concentration camp, the two girls crawl into the same bunk and cradle each other, frail hands cupping frail heads. It's hard to sleep with hundreds of other prisoners around them, but they barely see or hear the others.

They only see and hear each other.

Gold locked on turquoise.

The girls awaken to chaos. Orders being barked, bodies being pulled up and shoved in the direction of the door, and a mass exodus of prisoners from the bunkhouse. The girls are caught up in the herd, and still rubbing the slumber from their eyes, they're shambling out into the dawn with the rest.

Single file lines are formed outside, the officers threatening and directing, and soon there is cohesive movement, the prisoners being marched through the labor camp in the direction of that rounded brick building with the corrugated roof. Both girls have seen prisoners taken here before in huge numbers, and they allow themselves to feel a glimmer of hope.

"I think we're being transferred. Maybe they'll take us back to the train and we can leave this place."

"What do you wanna eat first?"

"Goulash and stuffed peppers. If my momma is still alive, we'll go there for supper. What about you?"

"Matzah ball soup with thick dumplings."

"I've never had it."

"I'll make you a big bowl. I'll fatten you up."

The girl with the turquoise eyes pokes the Romani girl in the ribs, and they share a quiet giggle.

The crowd is brought out into a courtyard, barely enough room for people to have any personal space, and the SS force the prisoners to disrobe. There's lots of incoherent yelling, but the girls are able to hear that they all need to bathe and be disinfected before boarding the next train leaving Belzec. They let their striped pajamas fall to the muddy earth, and the girl with the golden eyes crosses her arms over her wasted breasts, ashamed of how her ribs jut sharply out from her starved frame.

"Don't be embarrassed. You're beautiful."

She blushes at the compliment, and both girls cling to each other as they're pushed into the interior of the building. The Nazis seem to be rushing, eager to get this business over and done with. The space is terribly dark, a giant circular area, and once the doors are shut and locked behind them, there's nothing to be heard but hundreds of people all whispering and murmuring to each other, shivering in their nakedness.

This doesn't seem like a shower, and there are no officers inside to disinfect them. They sense deep in their young hearts that something is wrong.

"I don't think we're going on the train. I think we're going somewhere else."

The golden eyed girl begins to sob, and the girl with the turquoise eyes takes hold of her arms and draws her into a tight embrace. "Don't cry. They only have their hate. Hate is a pitiful thing to cling to. We have something better, don't you think?"

"Love."

"That's right. I think I've loved you before. I think I've loved you in other times and other places. I'll love you again, if you let me."

The girls cannot see each other in the blackness, but they nod against each other, hands rubbing at cold goose-pimpled skin to give comfort.

"I'd like that."

"The soul goes on. The love goes on. They can snuff everything out except for that. It's all we need."

There is a deep hissing noise as the Zyklon B gas is filtered into the chamber, but even though the girls are blissfully ignorant to what it is, they do not panic like the others. They hold tight, and they press brow against brow.

There is the surging of terrified men and women all around them, screams rupturing throats in this manufactured Hell, but the girls do not listen. "Close your eyes. It's late evening, and we're on that hill. No fences. No gates. Just grass and trees."

"I'm there."

"I know. I'm with you."

The gas kills quickly, prisoners falling into kneeling positions, choking on their own fluids, and soon the screams give over to stillness. The girls are found holding each other, their skinny arms and legs entangled. Their bodies are incinerated in the crematorium, and what is left of their bones is ground down into a fine powder.

The dust is strewn into a field near the labor camp, and vines grow up from the fertilized soil, the growth of them all tangled up in duality.

WASHINGTON, 2021

The centenarian stands in her giant bay window that overlooks the wooded acreage of her property. The redwoods tower over the yard, and the rustic cabin-style home seems like an oasis among them, a little settlement in the center of the primeval. Her golden eyes are watery these days, but even though she's a hundred years old, her vision remains as clear as ever. She holds two mugs of steaming coffee in her liver-spotted hand, and she takes her time heading out to the porch to sit with her spouse.

She moves slowly, because all things slow down with age, but her man doesn't mind. He rocks in his chair, his wrinkled face draped in shadow, and thick spectacles over his light turquoise eyes. He's watching his grandchildren play in the yard, running around their parents in a mock sword fight with twigs from the forest. He's younger than his wife at the age of ninety-eight, but he feels his age. There are aches and hurts that bedevil when the cold weather blows in, but it doesn't matter, because the old man is happy.

"What are you grinning at, old fella?"

She hands him his cup of coffee, then negotiates herself down into the wicker chair beside him. Her hair is spun up into a messy bun of pure white silk.

"Grinning at them. Grinning at you."

"How in the hell have you been around for almost a century and you still have all your teeth? You're a marvel to me. I'll never understand it."

"These pearls hold no candle to yours."

"Flattery will get you everywhere."

The couple sits in silence, sipping their coffee, watching their children and their children's children. An entire generation at the homeplace for a visit, and it feels right.

"It's a strange thing to get old," he remarks. "I feel like we've lived for a thousand years."

"Maybe we have."

He leans over and takes her hand, lovingly tracing the veins that stand out from her parchment-thin skin.

"Do you believe in reincarnation?"

"I don't rightly know. What's got you talking this craziness?"

"I read about it in this science fiction novel I got at a flea market in my twenties. I can't recall the title because the cover was torn off. But it was all about the lives before, and the lives yet to be. How people are never really gone, just changed. The idea that we keep on coming back with new bodies and new faces, and sometimes not even as people."

She reaches up and pinches one of the wrinkles on his face. "How am I gonna recognize you without this mug?"

"I can't say. You might just get a funny little feeling in your heart. Maybe our hands will brush together on some crowded street, or in a subway car, and you'll just know. Not just strangers passing, but the start of a story."

"Well, if life is just a story, I'm glad I got to have this chapter with you."

There's a cataract in his left eye, but it blends perfectly with the turquoise iris, and her gold-flecked eyes gaze as deeply into her spouse as she can. She reads him like a book, the pages trusted and familiar.

"We've lived longer than most people get to live. We fell in love young. We built this home. We saw this world from end to end. We made memories, and we made children. I have this feeling that I can't explain," he says, eyes twinkling. "I feel like this time, in this life, we finally got it right."

He squeezes her hand tighter, and she returns the gesture.

"We got our time. We got our happiness. We danced together, and ol' Death didn't dare take us early."

"You're wild this afternoon. Your eyes are full of fire like that week we spent in the Mediterranean when we were just babies. Did I accidentally slip some whiskey into that cup of joe?"

"Just drunk on you, old woman."

She rises, hoarse laughter in her throat, and she swats her old man behind the jug of his ear.

"Come in after a while, your arthritis will act up if the temperature keeps dropping."

She stoops her way forward, but he awkwardly leans his body out from the rocking chair and catches her elbow.

"I love you."

She bends down and rubs the wisps of charcoal gray hair from his bald spot, and she plants a kiss on the top of his head. "Love you too. And if that wild talk of yours has truth to it, I suppose I will again, in all the lives to come."

She leaves him there to return to the kitchen, and the old man settles deeper into his chair. He watches the great trees that tower above him, and the birds that make homes of them. He watches his son lifting his little granddaughter high into the air. The sun shines down on him, and it feels especially warm against his skin.

The old man closes his turquoise eyes.

A FAR AWAY HILLTOP, 2250

The buck emerges from the pines, his shoulders tight with muscle. In the prime of his life, his antlers are majestic, stretching outward to crown his head. He digs his hooves down into the soil and looks to the remnants of the human city that crumbles on the horizon. Nothing is left of man but dark broken towers, and the vines that encircle and overtake them. He grazes fearlessly, munching on grass as he goes, and soon a gorgeous doe emerges to join him, her coat as soft as satin. They touch their wet black noses together, and walk down the hill, savoring the scent of the wildflowers as they go.

It isn't long before a little spotted fawn joins them, her legs wobbly as she struggles to negotiate her way down the game trail. She bleats to her parents, and they pause, giving her time to catch up.

The fawn chases the big fat bumblebees, bopping them playfully with her nose and sneezing as the pollen from all the growing things fills her with mirth. Everything is new to her, and life seems full to the brim with possibilities. She will never know hunters, and she will never know highways with rumbling metal machines that strike and kill.

She will eat, she will drink, and perhaps one day, when the time is right, she will love. That is all there is, and that is enough for the fawn. There are no clouds on this day, and the sunbeams are at their most powerful.

The sun catches in the fawn's eyes, and the light reflects. She was born with heterochromia, her eyes two different colors.

One gold, one turquoise

CHAPTER TWO

HEART SONG
KAYLA WHITTLE

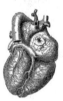

Sometimes the notes of her music came from the trees, or the wind, or the sigh of wilting flower petals. Always, the rhythm came from her heart. The magic demanded it be so. Each dawn, Mae stood in the garden, toes pressed into the moon-cooled earth. Tucking her violin beneath her chin, she played her music for herself and the rising sun, the black beetles flying between what little managed to grow beside her home. Mostly, she played for the witch's bones, so they would stay quiet and still and dead.

Enough power rattled within the skeleton to make good on the witch's vow to return one day and raze the nearby village that had conspired against her in life. The magic in Mae's song helped the bones sleep, and kept the village prosperous. But all magic, even when used for good, required sacrifice.

Each morning, when the sun grew stronger, rising higher, claiming life once again, Mae's music faded. Skin warm, fingers tingling, she'd slip her instrument beneath an arm and go in to have her breakfast. Bright jam spread over stale bread. Wincing over the sharp tang of berries, vivid and red as the roses that struggled and died in the garden. Her meals arrived irregularly with whispered thanks and averted eyes, donated by the villagers who lived over the hill. Just out of sight. Mae ate alone. She had done so ever since Adelaide had kissed her softly, lips sticky from their breakfast, and declared she couldn't do this anymore. This meant Mae, or at least, it did in her memory. Whenever she felt more rational, in the long, inky nights before her work began at sunrise, Mae knew there'd been more to Adelaide's leaving. It'd built in and up and over itself like the snow that trapped them in over the winter. It'd been the tiny cottage with the roof that leaked during spring. It'd been the withering flowers and the fence that never sat upright, the wary stares of the villagers bearing food or soap or other necessities that would, at the very least, keep Mae alive.

Most of all, Adelaide left because Mae couldn't.

The witch had been strong enough to cast a final curse, keeping her violinist trapped alongside her. The magic refused to let Mae leave the property, ignored how she'd begged and screamed and clawed at the fence until her nails bloodied and her hope sank like a stone thrown down a well.

Seasons passed and nothing changed. On one sticky summer morning, Mae stood to scatter the remnants of her meal by the back door. Sometimes the birds would visit her, sparrows and robins. The crows, too, but they preferred to sit along the fence by the road, attracted to the shining metal stabbed into the small trees. It was the road she walked toward, following the little path leading from her cottage. The stones were smooth beneath her feet, worn by persistent pacing since the place had been built dozens of years ago.

A burning need settled in her chest, one that reappeared every few weeks. The urge to go, to run. Muscles restless. Blood unsettled. Mae wanted to race the wind and lose and look up to see a different scattering of stars. Even then—always, and maybe, especially then—she wanted to glance toward the garden. The grave. The magic inside Mae was selfish, and it held a short tether.

Grinding her teeth, nearly relishing the twinging protest of her jaw because it was a new ache belonging wholly to her, Mae opened the front gate. It swung with a creak, a protest, because it wasn't often forced to do its job. The wood had been battered and worn by the elements. Lifting her foot, Mae wriggled her toes. They were dirt-stained on the bottom, calloused, too. She did ask an awful lot of them, even then, as she stretched her foot between the gate posts.

The fool within her hoped one day, her curse would fade.

It was midday. She'd already played her song for the bones. But it returned, the hook in Mae's gut that woke her each morning a handful of minutes before dawn. The press at the base of her spine that hurried her toward the garden. She withdrew her foot and spun back toward the sticks and dirt and broken stems that were meant to be beautiful before her thoughts caught up with her. The gate swung shut with a sharp click and she swallowed back the rage that threatened to consume her, the useless desperation that left her hands shaking. She was stuck. Trapped. Cursed with a life that wasn't terrible, that could have been so much worse. It only ached so persistently because it wasn't the life she'd wanted.

Tucking her arm around her waist, she remembered when Adelaide would hold her close. Together they would whisper of running off and seeing the world. The tang of salt water on their lips; sunrise blinding them with all the colors that refused to grow in the garden. She wondered where Adelaide was at that moment, what she'd already seen. If she ever regretted leaving Mae to this cottage with only the birds and the dead witch and the occasional villager for company.

It didn't matter. Even if Mae had never loved anyone the way she'd loved Adelaide.

She was Mae, and this was her land, and there would never be more to her story than that.

Life had a sense of humor, or at least a feel for ironic timing, because just as Mae thought her life would continue forever at its same tired pace, he arrived.

Leaning against a fence post that bowed with her weight—swaying, intoxicated wood—Mae listened to the jingle of reins, the methodical clip of hooves against dirt. She waited for the rider to crest the rise, matching the music of his arrival.

It'd been a long while since she'd seen a horse. The villagers never brought theirs. Other travelers preferred to take the King's Road. This one passed by her cottage and then petered off into an unsteady track by the mountains, leading nowhere safe. Stories came from those peaks—stories, the witch buried a few dozen feet away, and not much else.

The horse, when it appeared, was tall and restless, like his rider. Not so much walking as lunging, throwing itself eagerly down the gentle slope. Propelled by an urgency that lit Mae hot with envy; the fence creaked beneath her grip. With the sun framing the back of his skull, it was difficult to assess the rider until he was kind enough to come directly to her gate. Then she gave him a proper stare.

"Is this the witch's cottage?" he asked, peering down with wide eyes, blue like the sky behind him, bright as forget-me-nots. Hair dark and rumpled, frizzed on one side when he ran a strong hand through it. Everything about the stranger spoke of impatience, from the half-mumbled edges of his words to the misaligned buttoning of his vest. Still, his clothes were well-made, especially his pretty, polished boots.

"I suppose it must be," Mae replied, smothering her interest beneath a frown. No one accidentally found themselves beside her home.

For a moment, his flower-petal gaze caught on the trees beside Mae. The overbearing sunlight flashed and sparked, reflecting on the innumerable spikes embedded deep in the wood.

She disliked the way he looked at her afterward, like she was a puzzle to be solved. Mae wanted to follow the stinging heat within her and kick through the gate, race down the road, leave him in the dust. Swallowing back the urge to try again, to see if the curse would relent this time, Mae shifted uncomfortably. Her hands knotted in her skirt; once upon a time, maybe, one of the villagers had worn it to a feast, head thrown back beneath the stars. In the sunlight, the pink was faded, a memory of itself.

From a saddlebag, he removed a bundle Mae recognized; inside would be more hardened bread and a tiny pot of scarlet jam. Perhaps a few other bits to tide her over, as it was summer and the villagers weren't so gaunt and desperate. Shades clinging to the promise of a better season.

"They asked me to bring this to you," he said, and then it was his turn to frown because she did not step forward to accept his delivery. "You are the witch, aren't you?"

"No," Mae said, resting her elbow on the gatepost. The old wood bit into her skin, and she bit back any ill-tempered words that might scare him away.

He and his horse remained a few feet from the gate, well out of her reach. He didn't know, then.

The iron embedded in her trees usually warned stray passersby about the magic that lingered here. Superstition warding off the curse that'd caught her up in its jaws and swallowed her whole. For a dark, terrible instant, she wanted to see it, the moment when he'd hear of the curse and thought that meant he could understand Mae, too, all in the same breath.

"They didn't tell you much, did they, when they sent you here."

"Well, no," he admitted, and then he faltered, arms hanging limp by his sides, expression falling, too. "I've only just arrived this morning to see to my uncle who lives in the village. His neighbors asked that I bring this to you, and it was the least I could do, for all they've done for him. Is—is there something more I should know?"

Glancing over her shoulder, to the cottage and the garden and the little ground found in-between, a breeze slipped across the back of Mae's neck. A warmth like the caress of soft fingertips. It didn't mix well with the eagerness in her blood and the darkness in her mood. It was something different, in a place where each day was the same. It helped her to decide.

"I could introduce you, if you'd like," Mae offered, nodding toward her gate.

Hesitation turned his expression, drew his thick eyebrows downward, scrunched his sharp face into something ugly. Then he looped the horse's reins around a fence post that wouldn't hold against the gentlest tug, joining Mae on her land with the sort of determination usually found in untried young men, or crows who'd grown too curious.

She took the bundle from him, watching the way his hand shifted, clenched. It'd been so long since she'd had someone stand so close beside her; she could nearly feel the heat of him, cutting through the summer air. They went around the cottage, back to the garden. She lifted the cloth bundle, dipping her chin close, sneaking a delicate sniff. The thick, rich scent of chocolate hit her, weakened her grip. Mae silently thanked whichever villager had taken enough pity on her to send the treat.

The stranger's footsteps were loud but careful, only crunching stems that'd already withered, withdrawn by the garden's edges. She wondered what it looked like to him; for her, it was a patchwork of unfulfilled hopes and promises. A memory of Adelaide and dirty knees, slim fingers meeting between furrows. Daffodils struggled for life in one corner; a cluster of lilies thrived by the back fence. Scattered seeds that would have lived better lives elsewhere.

Mae stopped in the center of it all. The grass had worn away to brown earth; she dug in her toes. It felt like her skin sighed—an exhale, and also, a beginning.

She pointed downward.

"Here is the witch."

It looked like ordinary land where life refused to grow. There was a sharp tremble of magic, though, a rhythm that beat against Mae's toes. As if the witch's bones knocked gently, asking to be freed. Waiting for the moment when the violin would fail, the music would stop, and the witch would rise. The echo of long-spent spells grew stronger, shaking the garden as if the grave understood someone new had arrived.

The stranger came close, looming in the way tall people did without seeming to recognize the consequences of their height. The ground shifted, and he startled backward. Boots, sturdy and thick and destructive, stumbled through the flowerbeds. Mae laughed, loud and light and freeing. It surprised her. It made her want to laugh again, because she hadn't done so since that gate had snapped shut behind Adelaide. That decided for her what she would do next.

"Don't worry," she said. "I'm only the one who tends to her land and the cottage."

Then she invited him to come in for some tea.

The stranger had a name, which was Calan, and an uncle, who was ailing in a way that meant dying. His hand was unsteady when he accepted a cup from her. He was all knees and elbows, folded over on himself in the only other chair at her table.

"His wife passed away a few winters back," Calan said. "They had no children, but my parents have plenty. I'm the one they can spare."

Calan's smile was one part rueful, one part careless, before he hid it away behind his cup. She saw the way he watched her carefully, and tried to pretend he didn't. She liked it.

Mae had never had a visitor all to herself. Dust lingered in the cottage's corners. The kitchen window was smudged, fingerprints tracking the days she'd strained to catch a glimpse of any travelers on the road. The room no longer smelled sweet, like scattered petals and crushed berries. Calan had carried in the scent of someone who might have seen a bath or two while traveling but, in the end, the dirt had won out.

The villagers had paid him a few coins, he sheepishly admitted, to make his delivery to the witch's cottage. They'd caught him at the market, buying a few things for his new, temporary home. Anyone, in their first assessment of Calan, could think he'd be useful. All that height and those arms, that wrinkle of curiosity caught between his brows.

"If you were hoping to get a glimpse of magic, I'm sorry to disappoint you," Mae said, smiling wryly through the lie. "You've only found me."

Calan found amusement in that somehow, shaking his head and then draining the rest of his tea. A droplet escaped his lips, snaking toward his chin—slow, steady, just like the press of his knee inching closer to hers. It could easily be accounted for because of his height, taking up space she hadn't anticipated. She didn't move away because she knew it wouldn't last; after Adelaide, nothing good lingered for long.

"Will you tell me how you came to live here?" Calan asked, turning his cup over and over in his hands. Carefully, as if he wished he held something else. "If you're no witch?"

Mae had set her teacup aside several minutes ago and turned her attention to it then. Something had spilled onto the tabletop, staining the wood darker, and she rubbed her thumb uselessly against it. Over the months, she'd scrubbed and scrubbed at the spot with only cawing crows for company.

"I came to the village searching for work," Mae said. "Then it didn't matter any longer." Didn't matter to the village, anyway, because they had someone to tend to their witch, someone who didn't need much to stay alive.

Mae's legs ached; she stretched them beneath the table and spotted the question in his eyes before his lips even thought to move. "How much do you know of curses, Calan?" she asked.

His knee shifted, pressed against her skirt when she said his name.

"As much as anyone else, I think," he told her. "I've heard stories."

People loved to tell each other memories until they no longer felt like truth. Tales became legend became myth; warnings of curses and magic grew vague. Don't go into the forest at night. Don't take candy from strangers. Don't follow the light that will lead you anywhere or nowhere or leave you stuck in a witch's old cottage.

That was all she and the bones were to the villagers, after all. A myth they tried to forget. A story Adelaide had removed herself from, striking her name from the pages so she could flee.

"I could show you mine, if you'd like. Then you'd see real magic," Mae said. "You'd need to return at dawn. I wouldn't pay you for the trouble."

She smiled, and he grinned, still folded over in his chair like a rabbit caught in a trap.

The next morning, so early the sky remained a bruise only remembering the sun, Mae stood in her garden. Though she'd done so day after day after day for what easily amounted to years, still her eyes stung from want of sleep. She hadn't been able to rest after Calan left her, riding up and over the hill. Something stirred within her, something dusty as the eaves of her home, and she wasn't sure she liked it.

Sometimes it was difficult to recall a time before, when she'd been more like Calan. Finding her own path. Trying to do right by her family. Associating too closely with women touched by magic. Before she'd fallen for Adelaide, so hard it'd felt like her chest had cracked open, and no matter how often she paced the cottage she couldn't find the means to patch herself together.

Yawning wide, Mae's jaw cracked. Her toes were cold, the earth chilled despite the season, and her fingers were stiff around the neck of her violin.

Calan waited, propped against the fence by the lilies. She caught the flash of his heated stare when she nestled her instrument beneath her chin, lifting her bow. Her fingertips pressed hard against the wood, feeling the thrum against her skin—steady, beating, grounding.

Before—before the cottage, before becoming well-acquainted with the witch beneath her feet—Mae had never learned to play. She'd worked hard and had little time for anything else. She'd liked pretty dresses and quickening heartbeats, kissing the wrong men and women, running fast and far and wild out into the world. Still, she knew her way through this song. That was the magic of it.

Shutting her eyes against the garden and Calan, with the rising sun above and the grave below, she played. It began as an accompaniment to a pounding beat only she could hear, a coerced solo, a hook within that both held her fast and shoved her forward. Nudged her to the next note, the next slide of the bow, continuously picking her way along the edge of a precipice. One wrong movement, one discordant note, could send it all crumbling down. Could break the instrument, break her, wake the witch. The music, the curse, refused to let her fall.

Magic spiraled from her hands, or the bow, or both, spilling into a pool on the ground beneath her feet. A glimmer that could have been mistaken for sunlight, if the world hadn't been wrapped in so much shadow. A spark that kept the witch in her grave and kept Mae trapped between the fence posts. It made the village safe, made Calan's eyes widen, and left Mae energized, a strike from a summer storm caught within her chest.

It was important work, and good work, but she hadn't freely chosen it.

When Mae lowered her bow, the music faded. Something new hummed in her veins, making her sharply aware of the world for the first time in a long while. The sun continued its steady climb; the witch slept, bones calmed by her dawn lullaby. Calan stepped forward from where he'd leaned so heavily against her fence.

She looked beyond him, eyeing the road she itched to touch before she forced herself to glance away.

"You'll come in for tea?" Mae asked, and Calan nodded. They went in together, the violin held loosely by its neck between them.

Summer turned to fall. The last of the flowers died, but Calan brought her cloth ones from the market that sat nicely in her vase and never wilted. He brought himself, too, more and more often, and never again mentioned payment from the villagers for any of his deliveries. Mae pressed herself close to the kitchen window each day after dawn, peering down the road and listening for the sound of hooves and reins and Calan beaming, swinging himself down from the saddle.

He was useful, even if he did spend an absurd amount of time looking at her when he thought she wouldn't notice. Calan was tall enough to chase the last eddies of dust from the cottage. Curious enough to stand by her side as superstitious travelers paused to nail more iron spikes into the trees by the road. Gentle enough to lure the crows closer with seeds and leftover bread.

Mae's skin warmed, the whole of her flushed, whenever she spotted him cresting the hill. She spent more time reminding herself not to think about Adelaide.

Calan told her his uncle had become too ill to leave his bed. The village felt large and sprawling, nothing like home to him, and Mae found herself nodding without really relating to his words. He missed his family, but she could hardly sympathize; she would kill to experience life once again in an unfamiliar place. She felt better when he arrived with stories borrowed from visitors who passed through the village for the market or a festival. A coven was rumored to be hidden in the mountains. A curse had been broken in the King's own home. Wild and brilliant stories of magic spilled from Calan's tongue as they huddled together over her teapot. Tales that had nothing to do with Mae, but still lit her bright as the stars chased away each dawn.

In turn, she showed him where she planned to try again with her flowers when spring arrived, although speaking of that future felt bitter on her tongue. She took his hands and pressed them against her instrument so he could feel how it thrummed, humming with energy even at midday. She showed him gifts the crows left her: pieces of fabric and string, beads and glass polished so bright and blue it reminded her of waters that'd faded, dulled in her memories. Deep waters meant for sails and strength and boats large enough for two.

One day his hand brushed against hers as she handed him his tea, and she saw the way the contact made him shiver. Mae had to turn to hide how her stomach twisted. Pretended not to notice when he sat a little closer, sending flutters like wings brushing up and over and around each other in her chest, ready to burst free.

Together, they searched for a way out. Calan tried lifting Mae over the gate. Dragging her beneath the wooden beams of her fence. Coaxing her out at midnight, or after her song finished at dawn, or as soon as dusk fell. He collected stories for her, magical, wild ones, each heavy with a curse. A man forced to walk backward during daylight. A person who could only speak words beginning with vowels. A cow who'd sprouted feathers and threatened to fly away. Sometimes Calan knew how those curses had broken. Someone found a counterspell. Someone else bathed in gems and milk and honey.

"True love's kiss," Calan mentioned one night, quietly, the tips of his ears flushing red.

Mae wanted to dismiss it, because she'd loved Adelaide enough to give up the rest of the world. But was it true love, if Adelaide could break Mae's heart and leave her with the remnants, never looking back?

Mae's skin itched, ill-fitting with each day that passed. As often as Calan watched her, Mae stared at the fence, and beyond.

They tried dousing Mae with salt, but it only stung her skin. Whispered clumsy, unfamiliar words together over candlelight, but she was left breathless and disappointed.

Tears welled, startling her—startling Calan, too, setting him into motion. His arm went around her shoulders and for a moment, Mae allowed herself to lean against him. He smelled like the road, of places she couldn't touch, and it hardened something in her chest into a heavy weight.

"It will be alright, Mae," Calan whispered. He tried to dry her tears, and tried to warm her to stop the shaking. "You'll be alright."

She knew only one of those things could be true.

Their final attempt to break her curse kept Calan with her at the cottage late into the night. They'd dipped Mae's fingertips in blood, but even with ruby-stained skin, she still couldn't push past the front gate. She'd insisted he stay afterward to patch himself back together. Her emotions flashed between despair and anger, sheer determination thrashing against hopelessness.

"I don't want to try anymore," Mae said, eyes lowered as she wiped the last smear of scarlet from his skin. "It hurt less when I accepted that this is where I belong."

He'd cut himself too deep, too hastily—too eager to have her outside her home, away from this place. His blood, in the end, had been useless. Winding bright white cloth around his forearm, she felt the heaviness of his exhale, curled around his resolve.

"Mae," Calan started and then hesitated, as if despite her tether, the wrong words could still chase her away. "We can't give up. You deserve the world, even if it might not deserve you. I—I—"

His hands trembled so she allowed him to take hers, his skin a warm flush against the chill that'd stolen over her. She held onto him tight, steadying herself. There was nothing more to try; this had been Calan's last, futile idea.

"There's little left for me anyway, outside my gate," Mae said. "Even if the curse was broken. The villagers wouldn't ever accept me."

"I would have you," Calan said. A too-large presence in her cramped cottage, ruined only by the way he seemed to fluster himself with his own boldness. "If you would have me, that is. My uncle is not long for this world. Let me come for you when he is gone."

"You, come for me?" Mae asked, not knowing quite where to look. At their fingers laced together or the worn tabletop beside them, stained and cracked and just big enough for two. The way he looked at her, like she was some shining thing, made her skin flush, her grip tighten. The way he offered to stay. Bitter hope lifted her gaze, pulled her closer to him.

Leaning forward, a lock of dark hair shifted, nearly falling into one of his eyes, crinkled with earnest desire.

"You're beautiful, Mae. Wonderful. I never expected to meet anyone half as brilliant as you," Calan said. "I can't help but love you, Mae. It always—I always—will come back to you."

Love. He loved her. Her breath faltered; the cottage unsteadied around her.

She thought of Adelaide, long hair and soft skin and leaving, refusing to stay. The pain that'd settled in Mae's chest. She clung to the burning joy that laced through her veins and knew then that she would do anything to feel this happiness always, to keep the gloom from crawling back in. Her breath steadied, and she smiled.

Shifting, her chair creaked beneath her. He came closer—suddenly, startlingly closer—and then their lips touched. His were chapped with winter's chill but eager, parting around a sudden gasp.

"Oh, Calan," Mae said, a pang of remembered pain reverberating inside her. "It'll only hurt for a moment. I promise."

She sat back and he slumped forward over the knife he'd used to spill his blood for her. The knife she'd stabbed him with, above his heart. When he gasped again, those chapped lips speckled red as an orchid. Blood tapped arrhythmically against the floor. Mae waited for the shock to hit her, or regret; instead, it felt like after months of living in a blur, the world had come into focus. Her hope had sweetened, grown, like fresh blooms after a long-awaited rainstorm.

"Thank you." Mae said. "Hold still. I'll be quick."

Her chair creaked again when she stood to fetch the violin.

It wasn't easy to cut out a heart. So many bones in the way; so much blood and ooze and tissue. She'd experienced it personally, once, but then she'd been distracted by other things, like the blade plunging into her chest.

Carefully, she laid out the violin beside Calan. The back of her instrument wasn't smooth; she flipped a small latch, feeling the thrum in the wood beneath her fingertips. The steady beat that hadn't pulsed through her veins since the day she'd been forced to replace Adelaide. The witch always needed her violinist; the curse never said the musician couldn't change.

Slick with blood and torn tissue, Mae's hand pressed into the opening—pushing, squeezing, until Calan's heart was shoved into the small space in the back of the violin. It was a tight fit, but it worked. It worked. Shutting the panel, Mae shivered.

Her heartbeat returned, thumping over and over beneath her skin. She slipped a hand beneath the faded pink collar of her dress, inching past the raised line of scar tissue. Her pulse felt like the embrace of an old friend who'd never meant to leave her.

Then she stood, washing her hands until the water in her basin turned scarlet. Misshapen chunks tumbled beneath the surface. He hadn't held still, in the end. It'd been messy work. With her foot, she nudged the violin until the neck sat on his palm. Waiting.

Calan's eyes flickered open. They were dark with confusion, and maybe the memory of pain, though Mae knew he wouldn't feel the hurt any longer, only an echo. She wondered if he already felt the song stirring in his veins. As she rubbed her arms, they filled with the rush of blood and life and freedom.

"You'll live as long as you'd like, until you grow tired of this," Mae said, crouching by his feet. "The first violinist played for years before he no longer wished to look after the bones. He was the one with the real magic, leaving some of it behind in his instrument for his replacement. But there needed to be a guarantee someone would always be here to play for the witch. A heart freely given can take over the responsibility, and borrow the magic."

In those first days after Adelaide, Mae had been certain she'd never hurt anyone like this. But immortality was daunting in its loneliness, and she didn't know if reaching her breaking point meant strength or weakness.

Her fingers made quick work of the laces on his fine boots. Mae slipped them onto her feet, tied them tight, and then stepped over him to gather her things from the bedroom. The villagers would provide for him once they realized someone new lived in the witch's cottage. They wouldn't remember Calan's name. They wouldn't remember knowing him, or that there'd once been a girl playing for the witch's bones, or realize the power trapped inside that violin could stretch far enough to brush against their homes. Otherwise, they would know enough to stay away, and none would be left to look after the witch's keeper.

Mae paused after she'd stepped over Calan.

"If it helps, I don't think you really loved me, Calan. Think. What do you know about me? You know my life here and that I want to leave it. Do you know who I was before I came to this cottage? Do you know who I want to be, after?" Mae shouldered her bag, thrilled at her climbing heartbeat, ecstatic and nervous, a little bit angry. "Perhaps you feared that if you asked, my dreams for after wouldn't include you."

His dark eyes were so wide. Adelaide's had been narrowed, hidden, when she walked through the front gate.

"The magic doesn't care if you only loved the idea of me," Mae said. "You still gave me your heart. When you're tired, and you're ready, you'll know the way to break your curse."

She left him there, groaning and trying to sit upright.

At dawn, his music would be beautiful. She refused to stay to hear it.

Mae went to the gate and strode through it with a confidence that left her gasping, laughing up toward stars that looked no different on this side of the fence. Calan's horse waited, familiar with her by then. She no longer had the privilege of all the time she could want, but now, she had the world.

CHAPTER THREE

MOMENTO MORI
MELANIE WHITLOCK

Death was here. You could smell it.

Its scent clung heavily to the air like sulfur, rotting the core of those it wished to take, and stifling the breath of those it left behind. The crimson sky reeked of its arrival. Its shadows swirled, tainting the rouge and burnt orange with inky tendrils, like clawed hands grasping at the light, ready to pull unsuspecting souls into the harrowing depths of Tartarus.

A lone figure stood watching the beginning of the end from the hill crest of town. The tortured artist of this haunting masterpiece. Fingers elongated and tipped in ebony, shrouded in wisping matter of the same color. All features lost to the void of the night that followed him, until he could take the form that this plane desired. Only as the dying sun set, under the cover of darkness, could his work finally begin.

Impatience bristled its way through his veins, pulling his lips taut and narrowing his eyes. This was a skill he had refined; his features usually impassive and cold to all that stood before him.

But this time was different.

For within the sulfur, came the taste of summer's end. Memories of sumptuous, ripe pomegranates and bittersweet damson exploded on his palate. The promise of what accompanied such fine tastes made him shiver and groan. Yes. He was agitated and impatient now, swallowing the saliva that pooled in his mouth.

Cobalt blue now threatened to swallow the sky whole, and he knew the time was upon him. A thick, contented sigh escaped his throat, eyes sweeping the valley beneath him. Roving over every roof, tree-line and road, over the humans going about their evening tasks, their menial existences of no interest to him.

Apart from one.

Auburn hair fluttered in the wind, lilac dress billowing behind. Not a care in the world this woman had as she almost skipped her way down the main street. Dancing between other townsfolk and into the iron-fenced graveyard...*the* graveyard.

He smirked. *How fitting.* Pulling the surrounding shadow into himself, his features and appearance took the form he required. Statuesque Adonis and adorned entirely in black no less, he stalked towards the town. Death had a debt to settle, and as autumn began to call summer home, it was time to collect.

Auspicious clouds hung over the town of Asphodel Square. A damp and heavy heat had settled in a week prior and showed no signs of moving. Highly unusual weather for the end of August. Normally, the ground was scorched, and the trees fit to burst with ripening harvest whilst the town prepared for its end of season fair. But the townsfolks' good moods had dissipated with the weather.

Deus smiled to himself as he watched the people mutter between themselves, frown, and hold their hands up to the air as if the act would simply shift the weather on. No such luck, not that there was such a thing to begin with. The weather would remain as long as his presence did. Perfect conditions for decay to set in. Working its way within every fiber and root of this prospering settlement. Whilst he didn't have the flair for dramatics his eldest brother had, he knew how to put on a show.

He'd taken the human surname 'Deus' for ease. A play on words if one was intelligent enough to look closely. Not that anyone had questioned him so far. Far too wrapped up in their own meek existences to question lineage, simply settling on the idea that he was exotic, perhaps

Mediterranean, or at the very least eastern European, despite his deathly pale complexion. That assumption however, allowed him enough of a wide berth to continue his task. Prejudice has always been human failing.

Deus idly inspected the bluish, grey skin around his sharp fingernails whilst he waited for the next piece of his intricate puzzle to fall into place. All in the hands of a beady-eyed, short, plump woman whose fashion sense predated the 1950s. Her greying hair was pulled taut in an updo that had her wrinkling features working overtime, as she punched in the information into the computer in front of her. Her brow creased. "We're not due an inspection from the state government for another couple of months…" she trailed off, narrowing her eyes at him as she looked up from the ancient machine.

"It's hardly a fair inspection if one anticipates it," Deus crooned easily.

"Yes, but—"

"Mrs. Jenkins, the sooner we begin this, the sooner I can be on my way from this stifling small town and, therefore, out of your hair." He sighed loudly enough to put his point across. "You are merely delaying the inevitable," he stated with a shrug and a pointed look.

Mrs. Jenkins pursed her lips but nodded, turning back to the screen for a few moments before shuffling out of her chair and around the desk with difficulty. Fetching a set of keys from a hook by the side door, she huffed, shimmying them in the lock. "I won't be able to take you around the entire plot. Knees aren't what they used to be." She muttered over her shoulder to him, "But I can give you the plans to the grounds and you can go off those. They are simple enough. Ain't that much ground to cover when you're fit young things like yourself." She tutted as if this was somehow a great agitation.

Deus smirked again, "Distance is of no issue for me. I assure you I have travelled further than a few gravel paths to be here," he assured, raking a hand through his hair. A habit he'd never been able to shake from his days of impatient youth.

"Yes, well." She grunted, and the lock finally clicked open. "I'll be here to show you around the office and parlor rooms when you're finished." She pulled the door open wide and gestured for him to leave. "You'll require the mortician's presence to visit the morgue, of course. Is that on your list of requirements for today or would you be happy to come at a more convenient time?" she inquired, smiling condescendingly.

She was grating on him. "Have you ever known death to be convenient, Mrs. Jenkins?"

Her smile dropped and the frown returned, "No but—"

"Then you'll be more than used to tolerating inconveniences by now, won't you." It wasn't a question, rather a statement. One that he left her to choke and splutter on as he stepped through the door, out into the graveyard and onto the first row of plots.

Eyes scanning from copper birches to ageing willows, and perusing the differing headstones in between, it didn't take him long to find exactly what he was looking for. "That woman over there," he called back over his shoulder before Mrs. Jenkins could close the door on him, "Does she spend a lot of time here?" he asked casually, looking between the women.

Mrs. Jenkins laughed unkindly, hand on the door jamb. "You could say that."

Deus raised his eyebrow, making it clear he was waiting for her to elaborate.

"The girl isn't right in the head. Spends most of her days here tending to the place. Muttering to herself and the wind," Mrs. Jenkins spat, folding her arms across her chest. "If the place ever had a vermin problem, you're looking at it. Can't get rid of her. Though I suppose it keeps the townsfolk happy if she's in here and out the way of everyone else."

Deus's jaw locked, fists clenching at his sides as he swallowed back the shadows threatening to spill from his being. He smiled unkindly. "Do you believe in the soul Mrs. Jenkins?" he asked, his voice deadly.

"I, well, yes I do, Mr. Deus."

"As do I, Mrs. Jenkins…only, I view souls to be a bit like apples."

Mrs. Jenkins opened her mouth "Come again Mr—"

"You see, when an apple falls to the ground, people think its days are over. No good anymore. The end of its short-lived life. But what people fail to take into account is that merely the vessel is bruised on the outside, perhaps even battered, but it's the core that decides its fate."

Mrs. Jenkins remained silent.

"You see, often, if the apple has been nurtured, it can stay pure and sweet. The core is untouched by the elements despite how harsh they can be, and the apples that haven't been treated right grow sour and wither quicker than the rest. But—" He paused, looking from the woman tending to the gravestones and back to the elderly lady who watched him with a sense of unease. "Sometimes…sometimes even the most beautiful apples from the best farmers are rotten to the core. And *they* are the ones that need to be discarded. Because *they* choose to be bitter when they could be sweet. They are the ones that poison the rest of the crop." His lips curled. "Only fit for the fire, you could say, and I do love to see things burn, Mrs. Jenkins."

A weighted silence descended between the pair.

"I think I'll take the rest of my inspection in solitude. Better to make the correct evaluation of things that way. Enjoy the rest of your time, Mrs. Jenkins." He nodded, giving her a bright charming smile.

Mrs. Jenkins shivered, clearing her throat and moving to close the door. "I think you mean 'day,' Mr. Deus."

"I meant exactly what I said, Mrs. Jenkins."

Another laborious two weeks had passed since his first appearance at the town mortician. Asphodel Square had suffered the untimely loss of the prominent town gossip, Mrs. Jenkins. Found asleep in her rocking chair by the fire at home, a half-eaten apple on the table beside her. Some of the townsfolk twittered that it was because the apple was rotten that she'd fallen ill in her sleep and passed. At her age, anything was possible, of course. Most accepted that she was in the twilight of her life and these things happened. Death worked in mysterious ways, after all.

Meanwhile, the weather hadn't improved, save for the late evenings when the copper sun burned through the cloud in a last stand against its murkiness. It was as though the town was under a permanent shadow, one that refused to move until whatever needed to be done had transpired.

Deus leaned against the cracked limestone of a once admirably sculpted angel. He watched the young woman like he had done every day for the past three weeks, weaving between the headstones, with unearthly grace. Auburn hair burning beneath the setting sun, cerulean eyes set on her task, shoulders relaxed under the worn shift of her sage dress. He stood enraptured at her performance. How she took to every grave with as much care as the last, cleaning the aging stone and laying differing arrangements as though each individual flower had been selected with purpose. With intent that the shallow earth's occupant would delight in their new offering.

How peculiar. How morbid. How fascinating.

The corners of his lips involuntarily curved upwards as she conversed with herself, unaware of her silent audience. She had come to a stop by a section beneath a large withering willow. A crease formed between her brows as she looked between one headstone and another. Deus frowned too. *What had wiped the elegant smile from her face? Was she confused? A frown marring her elegant features? What had caught her eye and taken her smile?* His black coat tails whipped in the early evening breeze as he stalked towards her in pursuit of the answer. He'd watched her in silence as summer breathed its last, but he'd never approached, never felt the desire to.

Until now.

Deus had to be stealthy in his approach so as not to disturb the moment. Nor did he wish to frighten the poor wraith away. He'd never risked being seen by her before, but time was of the essence. He could kill two birds with one stone.

He was also painfully aware of his imposing and threatening all-black attire and blueish, pale skin. His appearance was a black shadow on the earth. In more ways than one. He stopped just behind her, straight back and senses on high alert as her floral scent permeated the air. Hands clasped behind his back, he watched as she kneeled between the two headstones, gaze filled with sorrow as she lingered on the unkept and decaying sandstone of the one to her left. She sighed aloud, reaching for her basket of flowers and he almost…almost reached forward instinctively to comfort her. He shivered at the onslaught of emotion. *Ahh, to be caring for another once more.* It tasted bitter on his tongue and made his muscles ache. But this display was beyond mournful. Painful even to him. He never wished to hear it again. Still, he did not move. He must be patient in order to understand and patience was something he had in abundance. Playing the long game was his forte. A skill he'd developed early with nefarious brothers like his.

"Are you just going to stand there then? Or are you going to help me?"

Deus froze.

She knew he was there. *How?* She hadn't even turned to look at him. There was no way she could have heard his approach; he moved within the shadow itself. *How did she…*

"Tell me, who do you suppose is stranger, the girl who spends her days keeping the dead company?" she whispered, pausing to select some daisies from her basket before finally looking over her shoulder at him, eyes meeting his without fear but narrowed in curiosity. "Or the man watching her?"

Deus frowned, lowering to the gravel. This was unexpected. Her nature appeared so frail and withdrawn, yet here she knelt, addressing him like no other had before. Demanding information from him as though that wasn't his area of expertise normally. It was wholly unexpected, and he hated being caught off guard, but a small part of him, deep within his chest, flickered with excitement. He was still frowning when he looked up at her again; annoyance crossed his features when he noticed she was struggling to withhold a smile.

The young woman giggled at his silence and perplexed expression. "I'm sorry. I really shouldn't tease. But...you're making it incredibly easy right now." She shrugged her delicate shoulders.

Deus growled low under his breath, rolling his shoulders, and looking away from the nymph's mischievous eyes. He needed to focus and remember who he was dealing with and why. "Forgive me..." he muttered, clearing his throat. "I guess you could call me curious as to why a young woman was tending to graves so close to nightfall?"

"And you thought it would be okay to approach a lone woman in the middle of a graveyard?" she asked, raising an eyebrow and flicking her auburn hair from her eyes. "So close to nightfall and all?"

Deus huffed. "See my previous statement. I think any woman who's brave enough to find company between the dead of an evening fears not a lone gentleman."

"The dead are harmless. It's the living who are dangerous."

Although he was incredibly surprised and impressed at her ability to hold step with him, he needed to regain control of the situation. An unexpected flirtatious gaze would quickly restore the balance in his favor; Deus smirked "Touché." He nodded, enjoying the color rise in her cheeks. "Perhaps I should have been clearer." He continued, "Whilst I agree the dead are harmless, death itself is not so."

The woman nodded absentmindedly, glancing around her. "Well, I'll let you know my thoughts when I meet him."

That was the second time she'd frozen Deus in his place. The eerie feeling of unease settled deep within his veins and made him shiver. *She couldn't possibly know...*

"Plans to meet him soon?" he inquired.

"If I have, they are not my own. But who knows what fate has in store?"

"Religious? Or a fan of mythology?"

45

"Neither," she scoffed, rolling her eyes and wiping her hands on her dress, turning her attention away from their verbal sparring to the daisies beside her. "But I don't hide from the truth. And if two things are certain in life, then it is that all stories are born from an element of truth," she muttered, turning her back to him.

"And the second?" he pressed almost desperately when she trailed off to start the bouquet.

"The second…is that death comes for us all." She frowned slightly again, peering over her shoulder, her expression curious as she looked up at him. Taking every inch of him in. Eyes narrowing as though she were looking for something. A chink in his carefully constructed façade.

Silence descended again, the last of summer's stale breeze shifting around them. But that is not what had them shivering.

A crow called in the distance, breaking the spell. The young woman shook her head, but Deus kept his gaze steady on her back, clearing his throat.

"So, what are you doing then? If I may inquire?" he asked, inching towards her. She hadn't yet dismissed him, and he was going to monopolize on that in every way he could. Perhaps this would all be over a lot quicker than he had anticipated.

The young woman huffed, looking left and right as if suddenly nervous. *Interesting*, she was nervous receiving attention but not discussing death. Now she really was in danger; his fascination always came with a hefty price. "I'm sure you've heard the townsfolk discuss my daily routine." She wiped her hands down the front of her dress again. Her nails were short and caked in mud. "Yes, I'm sure they've delighted in sharing the stories of the weird girl who talks to the dead," she continued, a faraway look in her eyes and resigned note to her voice. "Not that I'd talk to that Mrs. Jenkins if she could hear me. Old bat," she mumbled.

Deus stifled a laugh, raising an eyebrow. "You talk to the dead?"

"I get lonely." She shrugged. "I'm sure they do too. Not a lot to do when you're six feet under. Half of these souls don't have any living relatives either. Town's so old, most have either passed on or moved away. Somebody has to come make sure they're okay."

They stared at one another again, but this time in challenge. Deus kept his gaze narrowed, focused, waiting for her to back down first. And she did, but it took longer than he was used to. It had been a while, anyway.

"Fine! I don't talk to the dead. Well, I do…but not because they're lonely or not okay. Of course, they are not okay, they're dead!" she rambled, throwing her arms in the air. "I merely tend the graves. Lay flowers down that I think they would have liked and keep the headstones clean. It's respectful and it's kind." She explained, eyes sad. "There isn't enough kindness in the world anymore."

Deus nodded; she was right but wrong, too. There had never been much kindness in the world, but he supposed it was a matter of perspective and what side of history you were on. The woman's features were unsure now, shoulders slightly curved in. She was no doubt expecting the same treatment she received from her neighbors when they asked about her peculiar behavior. Whilst he wasn't here with the best intentions towards this fragile little being, he could relate to being treated like a pariah. He offered a tight smile, hand raking through his raven hair as he stepped further forward. They were almost level with one another now, side-by-side amongst their deceased audience. His arms fell slack at his sides to make her comfortable once again. But it wasn't working. Her features were still pinched and so it was time for him to use a skill he'd neglected, but one he was certain he still had. He turned on the charm. "So, how do you decide what flowers the deceased would have liked?" He offered a small smile. This hadn't been how he intended this whole thing to go.

The woman gasped so quietly, he almost missed it, her gaze incredulous "I..I, well, I read their headstones. Then research what I can about them in the local library or by attempting to chat to their remaining family in the town." She played with a loose thread on her dress.

Deus couldn't stop the smile this time. There was very little beauty like this that remained in the world. Shame he would have to pluck it. "And what had you frowning so fiercely before I interrupted you?" he inquired.

"Gods! Been watching me for a while, have you?"

"Yes."

"Usually people don't admit that."

"Oh, but I am completely unusual."

The woman sighed, shaking her head with a smile, fixing the daisies so that they sat neatly before the two graves. "I'm sad that not as much care was taken when selecting this woman's headstone in comparison to her husband's."

How utterly odd. "And why would such a thing be sad? Headstones are for the benefit of the family, not the deceased. Perhaps the family merely ran out of money when the woman passed."

The woman shook her head. "She passed first."

Deus still wasn't entirely sure what the fuss was about. The woman continued.

"I researched this particular couple a while ago. They were like Bonnie and Clyde to the town back in the day. Though, small petty theft in comparison to those two heavy-weights. The woman appeared to be the mastermind, the brains behind the duo. They were eventually caught and hanged by the town council. A month apart, as she was caught first. Yet, after all his wrongdoings, the gentleman was given a proper burial and the woman was left unmarked for a while. The headstone only applied to hers when a later council took pity on her remaining family."

"They were both undeserving of such treatment." Deus scoffed. "Perhaps it is slightly unfair…"

"Slightly?!" the woman exclaimed, turning on him, her eyes fierce. "We women constantly mold ourselves to the men around us, to the ones that supposedly love us. Doing things we'd never do, no longer recognizing ourselves until we are on the same level as the person we are with. That's how men justify breaking us, by tricking us into becoming the same as them in the name of affection." When she finished, her breathing was harsh, chest rising and falling with her outburst as pain flickered in her features.

Deus remained quiet. He allowed her this moment, agreeing with everything she said. Even if her words twisted like a blade in his gut.

"Sometimes I wonder if that's what happened to me," she whispered in a small voice, averting her eyes to the headstone behind her.

Deus clenched his jaw. "Meaning?"

"I don't remember anything. Memories are fragmented and nonsense at best…" she shook her head. "That's why I'm the town joke. Well, that and because I spend all my time here." She laughed humorlessly, pushing the hair from her eyes once more. "Maybe I have the life I do because I did something for someone that broke me."

Agony wound its way around Deus's heart, like vines of ivy strangling a cypress tree. The primal urge to roar choking his throat, stealing his breath as he watched a lone tear track its way down her cheek.

"Maybe that's why I find solitude in the dead. Some twisted way of reckoning." She laughed again, shaking herself, and bending down to pick up the basket of daisies. Wiping the tears from her cheeks, she managed a small smile when she looked back up at him. "Anyway, I'm afraid I must take my leave. Apologies, my company has been rather morbid, shadow man."

Deus let out a strangled sound between a snarl and laugh. "Shadow man?"

She nodded. "Well, you do keep appearing out of thin air. Don't be thinking this is the first time I've noticed you."

Deus's mouth fell open, but quickly shut as he tried to desperately think of all the ways he could keep her here. To talk to her more. To see how close she was to finding the truth of why he was here in the first place. He watched as she made for the gate, swinging the basket behind her. Just as she got to the last headstones, she turned, meeting his eyes "My name's Cora, by the way," she offered with a small smile. "But I bet you knew that already."

He did but it sealed her fate entirely when she uttered it herself. The threads pulled taut and his higher being within stirred; ready to pour out and consume what it desired. All he needed was one last assurance. One last incantation from her lips. One last coin to toss for the boatman.

"What's your favorite season, Cora, do you remember that?"

Cora smiled, looking up at the trees. "Autumn. Because it reminds me that change is good and that death comes for us all, eventually, and it's beautiful."

Deus smiled.

So, it would be done.

September settled in Asphodel Square with as much grace as Zeus hiding his infidelity from Hera. Another fortnight had passed, and Deus had spent many an evening with Cora. They talked of the buried people she tended to, about her favorite books, and what she wished to do with her life. Which, apparently, was nothing more than what she was already doing. It was almost too easy. *Much easier than normal,* Deus thought one lazy afternoon as he handed her crimson roses for her latest floral arrangement.

That was until she became sick. Then everything changed.

The sickness, of course, was expected. Deus had planned the timing of every turn of events down to the final second. One could not spend so much time in the company of death and remain the same. Often, it was a sickness that ate away at the brain, but this time it had seeped into the body.

He'd watched as sweat gathered on Cora's brow, and a flush developed under her cheeks even in the cold wind that had taken up with autumn's arrival. He'd noted her breathing growing labored—despite little effort—and her general appearance becoming more and more disheveled every time he saw her.

Until he didn't.

Cora was evading him. Even she had sensed that something was amiss and had been avoiding him and the graveyard like the plague. From their first conversation, he'd known that this time was different from his previous encounters when claiming a soul. She was the perfect balance of aware but naïve. But even he hadn't prepared for her ability to evade him. At night, he stalked the streets, his shadows constantly swirling and guarding the cemetery, ready to alert him of her arrival. His days were spent mingling with the townsfolk, trying to garner information about his fixation. All they could talk about was how nice it was not to have to put up with her unusual behavior. Better to everyone that she was out the way.

He had learned that she wouldn't be missed on this plane.

Her mother had long-since deserted her in favor of a landowner upstate. Followed farming and money instead of motherhood; her responsibilities, along with Cora, left to the wayside at the flutter of cash and status. Some things never changed. But Cora being missed would never be one of them. Where she would be going however, she would always belong. He just needed her to show herself first. It had been a long time since he'd enjoyed a hunt. They were almost tedious now and he had to be careful when it came to Cora. She was different. Her soul was different. It always had been.

Since the very first moment he'd tasted it.

Anger ebbed from his form and erupted in shadows the more he dwelled on it. The more his mind conjured up her image. It had been a while since he'd spent so long on this plane and it was starting to sting. He craved darkness and solitude. Everything about this place screamed at him. He didn't belong. He needed to finish what he started. What he came here to do. To collect what was rightfully his. Frustration knotted his shoulders, his jaw locked, and his teeth ground tightly as he paced the trees on the outskirts of town. Thunderous clouds loomed tauntingly overhead, and he couldn't stop the fury bursting from his chest with a snarl as he grasped a nearby fir and ripped the bark from its trunk like skin from a corpse.

"Deus?"

The strangled moan of his name halted his destruction. Eyes as black as charcoal turned to find the source, his shadows still swirling, unable to be contained anymore. He spun on his heel, shoulders back, stance defensive.

Cora stood between the trees before him, death written plainly across her features. Deus sighed in relief.

"Am I dying?!" she demanded, hunched in on herself.

"We're all dying."

"You know damn well what I mean, Deus!"

"Yes, Cora."

Cora gasped, her breath catching and making her cough. "How long?" She winced.

"You've been dying since the moment I laid eyes on you."

"Of course," she whispered, nodding her head in resignation.

"I must say though, now, you look like death," he murmured, voice strained.

Cora gave him a small smile, though it looked as though it pained her to do so. Her eyes widened and she wrapped her arms around herself protectively as she watched the shadows form behind him. "That's funny." She chuckled softly, but uncertainty laced her voice. "I could say the same to you."

Deus grimaced. *No hiding the truth now.* But as he took in the look in her eye, there wasn't a trace of fear to be found. Acceptance but not fear. Deus laughed viciously. "How long have you known?"

"That you were Death?" Cora asked, slowly walking towards a boulder. She perched herself on the rough stone, holding herself as though her bones may shatter if she were not careful. "Oh, only for certain when you just admitted then. Don't get me wrong, I had my suspicions." She paused, looking away thoughtfully. "But yeah, I don't know. I guess I just wanted to dismiss it."

"I thought you weren't afraid of death?"

"Oh, I'm not afraid of it. 'It' or 'you,' I should say," she corrected herself with a smile that made the corners of Deus's mouth lift too.

"Comes for us all, as I am sure I've already said. I guess I just meant that if I admitted all...all my thoughts out loud, it would all be true."

The smile fell from Deus's face. "What's all true?"

"That my dreams of the god of the underworld were real." She focused intently on him. "That they're not dreams but memories locked away and fractured upon returning to this life, or human life, however you wish to put it." Her voice shook then. "That I once walked beside you, in gardens beyond my wildest imagination, and sat by your side as you dictated where lost souls rested eternally." She whimpered.

Deus swallowed hard, looking away and out onto the horizon. *Shit.* Usually, his brother's bargain dealt with this better. He would have to consult the queen of magic herself in future. Semantics were tedious, but she'd always had a soft spot for Cora's soul and his...tie to it. His mind felt free, thinking openly about it all again. It had been a long summer. Unusually long in fact. But it had been so at her own request. Not that she could remember that now.

He would have to be careful and claim her delicately this time. He may be Death himself, but he was also the keeper of treasures, and Cora's soul was the finest of them all.

"What am I to you?" Cora asked pleadingly, pulling him back to the present. He turned, taking her form slowly. The sickness was spreading fast, her frame shaking and thin. She was already so wraith-like this time around. "What am I to you Deus?!" she demanded, her voice steadier than before.

"You are my autumn."

Cora shook her head. "I don't—"

"And I am your winter." He declared, cutting her off as his shadows moved to surround them both. "And I'm afraid I must be your death for you to blossom again as my spring."

Tears slipped freely down Cora's face, head bowed as she accepted her fate. "No need to be dramatic about it." She sniffed, trying to chuckle and smile but failing. "Will it hurt?"

"Every time," Deus whispered, his true form taking over. Fingers elongating once more, the ebony tips brushing against her cheek tenderly in a lover's caress. Shadows erupting and consuming the world around them. Nothing could stand in their way now that they were before one another, and fate had sealed their path once more.

Cora nodded, biting her lip. "Death is easy right? It's living that's dangerous."

"Oh, Cora." Deus hummed, his own voice rasping with emotion. "There's nothing more dangerous to me than you, and death, my dear, is only our beginning."

Pain erupted in Cora's chest and the world fell away.

CHAPTER FOUR

INBETWIXT

DAN DOLAN

My grandfather once told me the story of Will O' the Wisp, also known as Jack of the Lantern. Made famous by garish Halloween decorations, he'd originally been just a man who managed to outsmart the Devil but, when he died, he found he was unwanted by Heaven *and* Hell. So, he took a piece of smoldering brimstone from the infernal pit and placed it in a turnip—not a pumpkin, as would later be told—and wandered between worlds instead. Grandfather warned to be careful of lights in the fog, for that was Will trying to make you lose your way so you'd wander forever, like he did. There are so many worlds. The feeling of not belonging makes so much sense once you know that.

Unfortunately, I, Sean Guilfoil, am forced to live in this one.

What I know of being caught in between two worlds is limited to more mundane realms; being too old to be young and too young to be old, for one instance.

Currently, I find myself transitioning between two worlds, two versions of myself. My family, mainly my mother and *dear* Uncle Roy, talk about things they don't want to happen; they don't *want* to send me away to a monastery or kick me out on the streets. They even say they don't want to have me exorcised, but the way they say all these horrid things makes it clear that's what they really want. They're just waiting for me to give them an excuse.

On the other side of it, so many things that had previously been taboo were now encouraged. "Stop reading so much," they'd say, "and go on out with those old school mates who hang out with the *wrong young girls*."

So that is what I found myself doing on All Saints' Eve. The blasphemous few in town who practiced more traditional, secular Halloween festivities had their turn, but now the Catholics erected their bonfires, and the faithful youth were using this holy day of respecting the dead to live a little.

We'd gone to the local church for the lighting of one such fire and, gradually, the piousness of the gathering had eroded with the presence of alcohol.

Fitting the macabre nature of the holiday, our group finds its way to the church's cemetery, just past where they'd lit the bonfires. The rows of gravestones serve as our dance hall as the fires burn behind us. The bonfires are, of course, meant to be a barrier to keep these deep dark things at bay, but this crowd ran *towards* these things. The thrill of it was as much fuel as the whiskey in our guts.

Liquor is also liminal, a gateway. I feel it the more I drink, the more I cross over to that other person they don't want me to be. That person who knows the poor young lass who they shove my way does nothing for me.

"Not having fun?" Kinney, the ringleader of the little gang I've fallen in with, is suddenly by my side after I'd finally chased that girl off with the most tepid small talk I could muster.

I shrug and take another swig of my drink. "Not my scene, I guess."

"All Saints Day isn't just Catholic Halloween, *boyo*. You know what my nan used to call it? *Samhain*. They say it was the Witch's New Year." He laughs between coughing. "You see, the church lives in fear of it, but those damned pagans? They celebrated it—they reveled in it!"

"Ah, shut your hole, Kinney," Colin slurs as he and the others gather around me. "You going on about the ghosts again?" They all laugh.

"Not just ghosts!" Kinney continues, using a childish, spooky voice like he is telling stories around a campfire. "They thought all sorts of stuff came out when the veil thinned: demons, fairies…you'd like to see a fairy, wouldn't yah, Seaney?" He sneers at me, and my blood runs cold at the threat underneath. For a split-second, I become very aware of how we are seated—all three of them huddled around, facing me, alone. I laugh it off and the tension dissipates…for the most part.

"Anyways," Kinney scoffs, "they come out around this time of year when the veil thins and try to drag the living back with them. That's why people started dressing up in the first place. Disguise themselves to be safe…"

A concept I can definitely relate to. I make a show of nodding along but say nothing else and, one-by-one, they wander off again, either to get another drink or find a girl to swing around the fires. Once the last of them finally finds a flimsy excuse to abandon me, I try to covertly distance myself from the lot of them. I find myself alone in the darkest corner of the cemetery. The bonfires do their job of keeping anything strange and unholy at bay, it seems, even me.

"What brings you out here?" A voice startles me.

I swing around to find a handsome but unfamiliar young man about my age, floppy, dark curls falling into his face, in somewhat formal clothing for such an informal event. He holds a white rose in his hand. He's smiling at me in a more genuine way than anyone has in a long time.

"My…uh…friends." I look back at Kinney and the others and the word almost refuses to leave my mouth. "They thought I needed to get out more and meet…people. What brings you out here?"

"I wanted to find something beautiful." He smiles with a bit of a blush. A look crosses between us, a recognition of sorts, but also an *invitation*. I return his smile.

He holds up the rose and, despite how comical it should feel to take it, take it I do. I hold it up to my nose, and all I remember is the scent of this other man being so close to me, allowing myself to enjoy that feeling for once.

"People will see," I say suddenly, letting the world rush back in. He nods but smiles, backing further into the shadows, beckoning me to follow him. We make our way just outside of the cemetery, and find a discarded hay bale half-spilled by an unmarked stone. He lies down on the hay and, after a moment's pause and my stomach doing somersaults, I join him, careful to keep hold of his rose.

"How'd you know I was…that I liked…?" My words fail but he seems to understand me.

"Same way you would. We always have our ways of finding those who…understand us." He smiles, running a hand up and down my arm. I blush and turn away to smell the rose.

"It's a white rose for you, not red..." he spouts lyrically all of a sudden, leaning his head back and closing his eyes. *"For red is blood and white the dove. We will always live, even if dead. Accept nothing but life and love."*

"That's beautiful," I say, leaning towards him, a tear in my eye.

"So are you," he whispers before our lips meet.

It feels like a dream, like a fading memory of something that might have happened to me rather than something happening at this very moment. The more I try to focus, the more the sensations blur. At the same time, I curse myself for drinking so much, wishing I had a clear head to experience this, but knowing if I wasn't half in the bag, I never would have acted on this in the first place. It is surreal in a way I'd only experienced in dreams, where nonsense makes perfect sense until you wake. Somehow, we are having the deepest conversation I've ever had and making love in a way so passionate, it erases my sordid sexual experiences entirely, as though I were a virgin once more.

I move on instinct alone, my limited experience having been with young women who took pity on me, and those stolen moments had been over just as quickly due to shame, self-hatred, and my own innate disinterest.

This is entirely something else.

I feel every kiss, caress, and thrust, and the heat beneath my skin mingles with his; our very own bonfire of flesh and passion.

I wake alone with no idea when sleep even took me. No sign of the other boy, my clothes are on—rumpled a bit but still firmly in place—and, worst of all, the white rose he gave me is nowhere to be seen. I assure myself last night happened, I know it happened, I won't even entertain the thought that it didn't.

Sitting up, I take in the stone marker behind me for the first time, undistracted. It isn't a tombstone, isn't even inside the cemetery gates, just a large rock that was placed very intentionally. I push the hay aside to see a crudely carved cross at the base of the stone, its only marking. Suddenly, I hear a sharp intake of breath and my pondering is broken.

I turn swiftly to see a young woman a little older than me, refusing to make eye contact as she awkwardly walks up to this spot, picnic basket in hand. I step aside just as awkwardly, trying to make myself less conspicuous but likely achieving the opposite. After one last look from her, I back into the cemetery and make a show of mourning at a random grave. This seems to placate her.

She totters up to the stone and kneels, laying her basket to the side, producing an open bottle of wine and several assorted foods. She lays them around the stone, almost like an offering, praying as she does. She slips a small piece of paper from her pocket, laying that down too before rising, crossing herself quickly, and leaving. I walk back over and—casually as I can—pick up the paper.

What I read nearly makes my heart stop.

> *It's a white rose for you, not red,*
> *For red is blood and white the dove,*
> *We will always live even if dead,*
> *Accept nothing but life and love.*

I return the note and consider running after the woman, no matter how crazy that might look, though being seen running after a woman could really only help my reputation at this point. When I turn, I find the woman has snuck up on me. I nearly jump out of my skin but manage to stifle myself. "I'm sorry, I didn't mean to pry…" I say, almost whispering, her teary eyes narrowing at me. "I'm very sorry," I repeat more strongly. "I'm just curious. That marker back there. What is it?"

She looks at me for a moment and I feel the nerve leaving me.

"I don't mean to upset you…"

Her expression speaks of an immeasurable sadness. "That's…" She hesitantly opens a locket and shows me a faded photo of herself, as a young child, in the lap of the young man from last night. "That's where they buried Thomas."

Days later, the encounter is still fresh in my mind. That young man, Thomas, is all I can think about. I learned later that the young woman is his sister, Deirdre Flannery, and the poem was one of many he had written in life. She was only seven when he died—almost three decades ago—but she remembers him, and implies that she is the only relative who mourns his passing.

According to Deirdre, Thomas had not only been quite the poet, but also a lyricist and composer. She told me a few stories about his life but next to nothing about his death, and, as understandable as that is, it is frustrating all the same.

I cut a piece of bread for myself as I read through a book of poems from the library, hoping to feel some connection to this specter who had visited such an experience on me. Then I hear the disapproving cluck of my mother's tongue.

"You're supposed to be fasting right?" There's a hint of mania in her voice. "That's what Father Douglas told you?"

I don't even question how she knows what we've discussed in confession anymore. I'm quite sure the parish feels ridding the town of sin far outweighs keeping a poofter's confidence. My *condition* has been quite the topic of conversation ever since I'd been caught in a compromising position with another lad, even though we were too young to understand the aberration of it all.

"Yep." I nod. "'Skip one meal a day,' he said." I sigh, buttering the bread.

"Still…" Her breath quickens, the mania reaching her eyes. "Can't hurt to pay a little closer attention to your spirit than your base desires."

I sigh again and abandon the bread, book in hand, and make leave to find some work for the day. What little money I could save—that wasn't going towards the family coffers—would still be of help in freeing me of this place.

So many of these poems speak of freedom and part of me wonders if that's what Thomas died for; did he just want to be free? A dark thought, perhaps, but one I understand all too well.

Over the next few weeks, I meet with Deirdre Flannery to talk about her brother. I insist that my interest is pure curiosity, but I sense she suspects otherwise. I'd tell her I found another of his poems on his grave on a past All Saints' Day and just wanted to know more. She is eager to talk about him, but her family is happier pretending he never existed, so she doesn't question my interest.

My family is quite happy to learn I am meeting regularly with a young woman of *decent reputation* in the town. That she is a bit older than myself is something they are blissful to overlook.

On one such occasion, she shows me letters written to Thomas by a boy with whom he'd shared an intimate connection. The other boy does not name himself, signing his letters, "From your friend." In one, he says Thomas is a dreamer and needs to live in reality. One line nearly stops my heart: "*I want you to be happy, to get what you want. But you keep saying you want "to find something beautiful" and I don't think you realize how foolish that sounds. Find a young woman, as I have, and live your life properly by day, and find what comfort you can by night. It was always going to be this way.*"

To find something beautiful. That was what Thomas said to me. Something he apparently never found while alive.

"I know this may sound crazy," Deirdre whispers to me during our latest meeting, "but sometimes I think I see him out of the corner of my eye, looking at me. I bring him offerings on All Saints' Day the way everyone else does for the consecrated dead, who died with the Lord in their hearts, and I hope that somehow he finds his way...as he never did in life."

"Deirdre...how did he die?" I ask quickly before I lose my nerve.

"Our father," she pauses, choking back a sob. "Our dear departed father gave him plenty of chances," she says, as though she's trying to convince herself rather than me. "He just wouldn't listen." Her face contorts; it is the most agony I've ever seen without the aid of a mirror. Something in it breaks me. The desire to comfort her is strong.

"Well, since we're talking about things that *seem* crazy," I blurt out, "he appeared to me, too, not just in the corner of my ey,e but fully appeared. Last All Saints' Eve. He talked to me, he—"

But she cuts me off before I can continue, her agony transforming into *something else*. "Why would he appear to you instead of family?" She seems insulted, defensive even. "Did he seem sorry? Repentful? Do you think he's been saved?" Her desperate eyes hold a danger as well. Yes, she may mourn her brother, but that doesn't mean she is innocent of her family's crimes against him.

Before I know it, I'm standing up. "I have to go, Deirdre. Thank you for the talk."

She cries, but says nothing.

I walk away from the table and keep in my heart the answer to her questions.

As the months go by, I find myself filling up my life with places to be and things to do; how odd that a nascent obsession with a dead man has caused me to truly live a bit more. It didn't hurt that every interaction with my family is more of a chore than the actual manual labor I'm reduced to taking for even a few coins. Better for me and for them if we just keep to ourselves, I tell myself. They seem to feel differently.

This morning, I aim myself at the front door like a bullet—as has become usual—but they're a bit quicker on the draw than I am.

"Where have you been going lately?" my mother asks, finding a reason to stand in my way.

"Oh, you know." I roll my eyes and I know she's picturing plucking them right out of my skull. "Working, studying, reading—isn't that good?"

"You're worrying us, is all," she replies but my uncle, towering over her shoulder with an angry gaze, tells a different story.

"Oh, I'm worrying you?" I force down a laugh.

"You show your mother some respect!" Uncle Roy scowls, seemingly the only expression he can muster.

"I'm sorry, you're right. I guess I'm just confused. A short while ago, you were all about to throw me out, and now? I'm not home enough... So which is it?"

"For the moment, you are still a part of this family, Sean."

"Maybe I don't care if I don't get to be a part of this family anymore, Ma."

Then I see him, in the corner of my eye, just like Deirdre said. Thomas seems to be giving me a warning look and, when I turn back and accidentally lock eyes with my Uncle Roy, I see why; no mistaking the violent intent written across his beet-red face.

"That's it!" Uncle Roy seethes. I watch his raving gestures...I know all too well the sting of those hands. "You want to go somewhere so badly? Go to confession or never come back!"

In the millisecond I have to respond, I briefly consider the prospect of homelessness, but I see those worried eyes in the corner of my vision. I nod at my uncle and mother; swallowing down my pride seems a small price to pay when compared to a beating...or worse.

Father Douglas is not a wholly bad man, you know, besides him telling my family almost everything I say in this booth. He, at least, managed to discuss my *predilections*—as my mother calls it—without dry-heaving, even bringing a sense of understanding to some of our sessions.

"Your mother tells me you're having a bit of a crisis again, Sean," he gently says through the partition.

"You could say that." I'm hoping this will be over soon.

"She was more hopeful lately, so this is disconcerting. She was quite happy to hear how much time you've been spending with Deirdre Flannery."

"Yeah, that…" I pause. *What does it matter? Not like she'll cover for me now.* "Wasn't what everyone thought it was."

"What was it, then?" he asks with a hint of concern.

"I wanted to know more about what happened to her brother," I say quietly.

For a long, tense moment, Father Douglas says nothing at all. Then he asks, "W-w-why would you want… H-how would you even know to ask about that?" It is the first time I've ever heard him so hesitant, so unsure.

"I had a dream about him last Hallowee—er—All Saints' Eve." I await his response, only to be met with another pregnant pause.

Finally, he clears his throat and forces himself to speak. "Sean, have you been talking to Matthew Doyle? You can tell me if he's approached you."

"Matthew Doyle?" I think back to the middle-aged man sweeping up as I came into the church just moments prior. "The caretaker? No, why?"

"Sometimes…" He stops, thinking about his next words. "When people are lost in the fog, they often try to get you to stray from the path as well. Partly, they want the company. It's a human thing to do when we are afraid, but they know deep down they are sinning, and it's only through spreading this sin that they feel the weight lift off them. A friendship can seem sweet but it can be a dangerous bargain. Sean, you need to be careful who you trust. Your very soul could be at stake." In the good father's defense, by the look of mild embarrassment on his face, even he seems to think this last line is a tad melodramatic.

What does Matthew Doyle have to do with any of this? Why would Father Douglas automatically jump to that connection? I can't fathom the reason, but then something the good father said sparks my memory: friendship. The way the boy Thomas was seeing signed his letters: *From your friend.*

"Are you listening, Sean?"

"Yes," I answer truthfully; I am listening, just not to him. My gut instinct and Thomas Flannery's bittersweet face in my peripheral vision are higher priorities, and they came to the same conclusion.

"Say ten Hail Marys, continue your fast, and I'll see you again next week, yes?"

"Yes, I'll see you then, Father."

"Good, kneel and be absolved."

I kneel reluctantly, wishing instead to run out and confront Doyle, but I cross myself dutifully and recite my practiced prayers. Once done, I race from the confessional, hoping to catch the caretaker. To my surprise and frustration, Father Douglas has beaten me to it. I watch fruitlessly as the priest guides the other man out of sight.

A few days later, I am still forming a plan to approach Mr. Doyle. As per usual, I hear people whisper about me but now, quite oddly, they whisper about me and Doyle. This is how I discover the church has fired him. Any plan I had conceived becomes invalid when, one day while deep in the back stacks of the library, Doyle finds me instead.

"What the hell did you say to Father Douglas, boy?" The man somehow yells and whispers at the same time, his eyes bulging in desperation and rage.

I back up, memories of my Uncle Roy momentarily flooding my mind. I take a breath and steel myself.

"He's the one that brought you up! Not me," I snap as quietly but firmly as possible, hoping not to draw any undue attention.

"Why would he do that? And why does he have it in his head that I've done something inappropriate? Do you know how long it's taken me to build any kind of decent reputation in this town?"

"I have my suspicions," I mumble. His eyes narrow at me but then drift to the pile of books stacked by my side: *The Poems of Katharine Tynan, The Collected Works of Oscar Wilde,* and a detailed history of the Celtic ritual of Samhain.

"You've seen him, haven't ye?" He exhales deeply and all the wind goes out of the sails of his anger. "Thomas?"

"Have you?" I ask before the implications of the question wash over me. "I mean, since he..."

"I know what you mean, lad," he grumbles. "Yeah, once or twice. Most everyone in this town has an All-Saints' story. Flip through that book there." He jerks his thumb at the third. "It'll tell you something about what they call *ley lines* and why our dead never seem to rest as comfortably as others." He rolls his eyes as he picks up the book, turning it over in his hands.

His wrath shifts to something like melancholy. I start to speak but my words die as he picks up another of my books; underneath, he finds one of the letters Deirdre gave me. I'd forgotten I brought it.

I wince as he turns back to me. "I'm sorry you lost your job. There had been something I wanted to ask you but I suppose that's out of the question now?" I bite my lower lip and he seems to read between the lines.

With a sigh, he takes a seat and motions for me to do the same. "I know what you're telling yourself, boyo, but me and Thomas...we weren't in love."

"But the letters...?"

"Let me finish. We weren't in *love.* We were two young boys who shared a secret. That is a connection that can be just as strong. When there's one single person who is available to you, rather than those *normal* boys who can chase any girl that strikes their fancy."

"What happened?"

"He wanted more." Doyle sighs. "But it wasn't enough for me to give up everything, it wasn't some faerie romance, like all of his poems. He had it in his head that we could be something other than what we were. He thought I was Oscar Wilde's faun." He tosses the Oscar Wilde book aside. "But I had to live in the real world."

"Yes, the letters say you found a woman."

"It, uh...it didn't work out." He averts his gaze.

Saying 'I'm sorry' feels silly considering the circumstances, and not knowing what to say leaves me saying nothing at all.

"So...how did he die?" I ask.

It is his turn to say nothing at all. His face goes white and, after one more silent moment between us, he leaves me in the dark, alone.

After talking with Matthew Doyle, my world seems covered by dark clouds. *Is this truly the life I have ahead of me? Unfulfilling relationships with women to save face in public while seeking out desperate ruttings with other men in the dark of night?*

I go drinking with Kinney, Colin, and the others more and more often. No matter how terrible they are to me, or how terrible I am to myself around them, it's still better than being alone in the shadows. All the while, Thomas continues to hover in the corner of my clouded sight.

We find ourselves in one of the town's seedier pubs, near blacked out from overindulgence and muttering gibberish into the stale air. God only knows what I've imbibed, anything and everything put in front of me.

A ray of sunshine breaks through the haze, the dusty pub lighting up like a summer meadow.

Then, strangest of all, a satyr of myth, a handsome swain, naked as the day he was born, with the horns and legs of a goat, dances into the bar. I laugh a drunken laugh, my eyes lighting up as it moves among the pub crawlers who take no notice.

"*Out of the mid-wood's twilight into the meadow's dawn, ivory limbed and brown-eyed, flashes my Faun!*" I belt out at the sight, Wilde's words flowing through me like a river.

"What are you on about, Guilfoil?" one of the other guys slurs, though I couldn't tell you which—they all blend together like watercolors.

But the faun's features become clearer, sharper. It looks exactly like Thomas.

I jolt to my feet, nearly knocking someone to the floor but not caring very much about it. I take Thomas-faun in my arms. A young Deirdre appears, just as she did in her locket image. She dances around us with long ribbons, as if we are a maypole.

Father Douglas is suddenly tending bar, turning pints into water. *Is he suggesting I slow down?* He'll be disappointed again.

"*He skips through the copses, singing, and his shadow dances along and I know not which I should follow, shadow or song...*" I sing as we dance, rather loudly as well.

I feel Kinney coming up right behind us. I turn to look and it's enough to induce a soupçon of sobriety.

My arms are empty, I'm dancing alone. The dark look on his face has chased the light right out of the bar and my satyr with it.

"*O Hunter, snare me his shadow! O nightingale, catch me his strain! Else moonstruck with music and madness, I track him in vain...*" I sing directly into Kinney's red face.

"Listen, Seaney." The angry young man hisses, "We've tried to be understanding, but we don't want none of this funny business, you hear me?"

The alcohol fuels my confidence and deadens my self-preservation instincts. "Why are you so concerned about it, eh Kinney?" I snap, jutting my chin.

"Excuse me?"

"You heard me. Why do you care about what may or may not be going on in my personal life so much?" I get uncomfortably close to him, pushing myself into his face and, when he fails to come up with a retort, I thrust forward and inelegantly smack my lips against his.

I'm pushed backwards and I barely have time to see his fist before my world goes black.

I'm not a heavy sleeper—usually the slightest breeze wakes me—even without a black eye or a body that's more bruised than not. To top it off, ever since I first encountered Thomas, it's gotten to the point where sleep is practically a foreign concept. Hell, I dream more when I'm awake. I lay here staring at the ceiling, listening to the grandfather clock tick away the hours.

The clock strikes three in the morning and I am no longer alone.

It is only his shadow at first, standing in a corner by my bedroom door, but it is unmistakably him. Soon his features come into focus, like a sketch being colored in.

"Thomas," I whisper.

He says nothing. He gestures for me to follow, just as he did in the cemetery. I throw off the sheets and jump up as his image vanishes through the doorway. As I stumble after him into the hall, I find a strange new delusion.

The light nearly blinds me; lamps are lit where none should be. *This isn't my hall and where is Thomas?* The pictures on the walls aren't of my family, they are of his. I see photos of a young Thomas smiling with family members, but as the other people age, he appears alongside them less and less.

I reach a staircase, one much larger than the one at home, and slowly make my way down as if following a fool's fire.

"Someone will hear." A muffled voice laughs as I reach the landing. There, in an unfamiliar living room, entangled and half-undressed, is Thomas and another young man. It only takes me a moment to recognize a young Matthew Doyle.

They lie on the couch, Thomas kissing and licking his way down Matthew's stomach. "I think I may be in love with you," Thomas whispers huskily between the smacking of lips and tongues on flesh. A spark of jealousy rises inside me.

"Why do you always have to ruin it with that shite?" Matthew sits bolt upright, a disgusted look on his face, pushing Thomas off.

"Matty..." he groans, closing his eyes in frustration.

"Thomas...I'm..." Matthew sighs, standing up. "I'm gonna go."

For a moment, he says nothing, sighing deeply himself, rubbing his face as Matthew dresses. "What is so wrong with that?" he mutters at last, glaring at Matthew.

"I've told you time and time again not to make this something it isn't."

"Why can't it be something else? Why does it have to be...*this?*"

"It's just the way it is," Matthew spits angrily before taking in his friend's hurt expression. "I'll talk to you later, okay?" He tries to mollify Thomas before leaving me alone with him.

Despite knowing he could not see me, every part of me wanted to reach out and comfort him. I take a step towards him—

A monstrous shadow looms over us.

"Father I..." Thomas squeaks. "I can explain."

His father responds in animalistic snarls and terrible vibrations, like a heart beating in violent fear.

"I am what I am," Thomas says, resigned, and the shadow becomes deafening in its silence. It swallows the whole room.

I find myself in my own unlit living room, standing stock-still, my skin like ice.

"Sean."

I focus my eyes and find my mother sitting in her chair, near where Thomas' father had been. She turns on the table lamp and it's clear she's been crying. She has the Bible in her lap.

"I heard what happened at the pub…"

"What don't you hear?" I laugh darkly. "Had any good talks with Father Douglas lately?"

Instead of a fiery retort, she seems sad more than anything else. It throws me off my game.

"Tell me how we can fix this?" she implores, clutching the Bible.

"I am what I am," I echo my Thomas' words.

"Then you need to go."

As I said, Father Douglas is not a wholly bad man. Even as he had fired Matthew Doyle, he now hired me as caretaker. This included a place to sleep in a small back room of the church.

I have very few possessions, even fewer since being kicked out. I had sold what I could for whatever money I could get. Now, I just have those books I took from the library, another sin; I truly didn't see myself returning them.

I'm reading one on botany since I now tend to the parish's flowerbeds. I hope it will teach me to cultivate a white rose bush with tenderness and love.

There is a gentle knock on my door and Father Douglas peeks in with a practiced smile. "May I come in?"

"Yes, of course." I put the book to the side.

"I met with your family today."

"Oh?" I'm indifferent; their mention brings no warmth nor sadness to my heart any longer. I'm done.

"They are…much unchanged in their thinking," he says diplomatically but I can read between the lines. "I want to help you find a path." He smiles.

"A path?"

"Would you ever be interested in taking holy orders?" The way he says it, it's clear he feels he's doing me a favor.

"Become a priest?"

"You could sustain yourself on faith, Sean, find a way to exist in this world."

"Life should be about more than just existing." I sigh, my eyes wandering to the *History of Samhain* beneath my pillow.

I am ready.

It is hard to believe it's been only a year since I first met Thomas and, at the same time, it seems like it's been decades. I carry a white rose and—believe it or not—a turnip. One part research, one part superstition, and pure recklessness to complete the triquetra.

I head straight for Thomas' unmarked grave, paying no mind to people around me, certainly not caring if they had anything to say about my presence; I don't care to spend any more time in this place.

I open my heart, my mind and, most importantly, my eyes, watching for any sign that he's returned. If he shows—and I know he will—I know what to do. To cross the veil with him, to leave this world behind. All the books said that the door goes both ways. That, yes, on this night, the dead may enter the world of the living but so, too, may we enter theirs.

People call my name. Maybe it's Kinney or Uncle Roy but I don't care. I think I see Deirdre in the distance. I almost hope she's here; I hope she sees someone accept Thomas unconditionally and, thus, have her questions answered.

As if answering my own question, I see Thomas in the distance. He stares at me wide-eyed from between twin trees just past his grave.

A doorway. A choice.

The choice is made already. I rush towards him, pushing past all between us. Without a thought, I jump like Jack Be Nimble over his grave-marker. A transition takes place; a transition that is completed as I break between the two trees and leap into his waiting arms.

His waiting arms. I can feel him, his weight, his warmth. He breathes a sigh of relief in my ear as we laugh giddily.

We kiss as if we never stopped. Every dream or visitation over the past year washes over me, over us; our dialogue never stopped, I know that now.

"Sean," he says simply, pure love in his voice.

"Thomas." I smile, caressing his cheek, his blush warming my cool hands.

"I can't believe this is happening," he whispers, taking the white rose I offer.

"I can." I nod confidently, before looking around. "This road, this Samhain Road lies between *real life* and what, exactly?"

He smiles back and looks into the distance, the sparkling fog winding around eldritch branches that surround us. "Everything else."

"Let's go then." I push forward, taking him by the hand but he stops short.

"You can't go back," he whispers in a more serious tone as he meets my eyes.

"Nothing to go back to. It's all ahead," I say without hesitation and his smile returns.

With his hand in mine, and the turnip-lantern in the other, we walk into the between to find something beautiful.

CHAPTER FIVE

HOSTAGES

Rebecca Jones-Howe

Snow fell outside the bistro window, the thick heavy flakes drifting carelessly toward the ground. Erin watched, hypnotized, unable to help herself from gripping the warmth of her coffee mug. Outside, cold tourists huddled together beneath patio heaters, hungry for the true experience of a mountain getaway. Erin preferred the indoors, and she was grateful not to feel like the only person not acclimated to her surroundings when a man entered the empty restaurant. A bell chimed above him, announcing his entry. He flinched before finding a booth beside the window, and ordered a plain coffee when the waitress came. He took no cream or sugar to mute the harshness of the brew. The bright snow contrasted against his black metal-rimmed glasses and his dark head of unkempt hair. Hunched over the table, he clasped at the hot ceramic of his mug, clinging like he needed the extra warmth, clinging just like her.

It didn't take long for him to notice Erin watching. His lips pursed. He gave her a double take and seized.

He remembered her.

Erin remembered that he'd smelt of gin, and that his throat bobbed heavily when an armed robber entered that liquor store they both happened to be in a year before. The man's voice was low and soft with a gentle rasp, and he'd told her to do whatever the robber asked. In the tension of the moment, he made Erin feel like her skin was vibrating.

Back then, Erin had a ring on her finger, which the robber took notice of.

She finally replaced her diamond with a cheap quartz ring from one of the many tourist shops in the mountainside village. The saleswoman had told her quartz was good for clearing the mind of negativity, but all that came to mind when Erin slid the new ring on her finger was the sound of the robber's voice screaming in her face, asking if she really wanted to die over a silly rock.

Across the room, the man took a sip from his cup, but the brew was still too hot. Coffee dribbled past his lip and down his chin. He wiped it off and drew a heavy breath that strained his shirt over his chest. Erin tensed, wanting to speak, wanting to move into the empty seat across from him, but the waitress approached his table with a slice of pie. The man jumped when she set the plate before him. She asked if he was okay and he nodded too quickly, too vigorously.

"I'm fine. I'm alright."

Erin knew those words all too well, had said them herself many times, despite not meaning them. Erin knew he was far from fine and far from alright.

The waitress left and the man's panicked expression turned into something cold and grave and dead. He fumbled with his wallet, swallowing hard as he retrieved the bills to pay for his meal. He picked his jacket off the back of his chair and hurriedly shoved his arms into the insulated sleeves, zipping it quickly before leaving.

Erin watched him through the window as he headed down the bistro's front steps and into the chill of the village. She made a fist and brought the quartz ring to her lips. Grating teeth over the texture, she could still hear his voice in the ridges of the purple stone.

She chose not to follow him. There had been times since the incident when Erin felt as though she was being followed herself. People treated her differently. Even her fiancé treated her differently, holding her hand extra tight whenever they shopped together, which only worsened her anxiety, eventually making it harder to breathe in situations that should have been normal. Erin's fiancé often said he wasn't sure what he could do to help her. He felt helpless, which wasn't normal, which made Erin feel abnormal. She'd been infected with something, a cold tension in her lungs.

And so, she stopped allowing herself to be around people.

Being alone felt easier. She moved out and got her own place, but then the sky above her felt too big and too encompassing. Her fiancé begged her to do anything to help her overcome her trauma. Erin chose to travel to a snow-covered mountainside, where the gray skies would feel like a proper ceiling.

The side of Whistler Mountain was lined with ski lifts and gondolas that took people into the clouds. She watched the red glass-bottom cabins venture beyond the haze and wondered what waited on the other side. All the people who plummeted back down into the village did so with a smile, their cheeks flushed with excitement. Most of the tourists carried skis or snowboards, leaving Erin to feel the blackness inside herself again. She wasn't here for the same reason everyone else was. She was different and wrong, and ill-prepared for the cold. So, she wandered the paved stroll between the restaurants and shops, purchasing scarves and hats, and little trinket souvenirs.

Before every shop entrance, there was a mass of chemical blue deicer. It was supposed to melt the snow but instead transformed it into a blue pile of sludge in the threshold, soaking into Erin's shoes, through her socks and up the cuffs of her jeans. She bought a pair of proper winter boots and returned to her hotel room, allowing her drenched denim to dry over the baseboard heater. She turned up the heat and stared at the void of her phone.

Beneath the blue screen, she searched for articles about the robbery, uncovering trauma she'd thought she'd buried. She remembered the robber's gun waving. She remembered her heart swelling in her throat, and the feeling of helplessness that came over her in the back corner of the store where the spirits were. She remembered the man with the glasses standing beside her in his gray suit.

He breathed heavily, already drunk and smelling of decay, despite the fact that he carried a briefcase and wore a collared shirt and tie. The robber made his way toward them and demanded their valuables. Erin's finger swelled over the band of her engagement ring. The robber grew impatient. He fired a shot at the ceiling. He fired a shot at the wall. Then the man with the glasses inserted himself between them. He held out his hand and tried to keep the robber calm.

"Nobody needs to die, alright?"

That soft rasp. That tingle in her throat. The ring slipped out of Erin's shaking grasp and the robber snatched it off the floor before firing one last shot directly into the man's chest. Erin remembered the smell of gin, the richness of blood, the chemical odor of bleach on the linoleum floor. She remembered the flashes of red and blue that burned her eyes as they loaded him into the ambulance. She scrolled the local news for days afterward, hoping to read news about whether or not he'd survived. Not knowing chilled her, made her teeth grind, made her fingers shake. She started imagining she still had her ring, her fingers swelling as she pretended to remove it over and over, hoping to do it faster, to bring the man back from the blackness in her head.

Erin woke to the sound of her phone ringing. It was her fiancé. She pushed the device beneath her pillow and rolled groggily from beneath the covers. She went to the heater to see if her jeans were dry, but ended up pulling on a pair of sweatpants instead, along with her parka and her toque. The ringing ceased and she hurried from the room before her fiancé could call again.

She hated it when he worried. She could go out and enjoy herself, even if she was alone. The only place she still couldn't go was the liquor store, so she found herself at the nearby pub instead, where she sipped her gin and tonic in the corner, her eyes on the curling game that played on the big screen. Red rocks replaced the yellow rocks and then the yellow rocks replaced the red rocks, all while the players yelled back and forth at each other in mid-sweep. It only made her think of the robber yelling.

"Everyone get down on the floor!"

The pub's floor was covered in melted snow, the muddy boot marks slick and slippery. A yellow sign was positioned over the worst of the slush, warning patrons of the hazard of melted snow. Erin watched the tourists wander in and out, walking carelessly and drunkenly past the silhouette of the man falling backward in a hopeless abyss. She finished her drink and brought the quartz ring to her teeth again.

She closed her eyes and thought of diluted blood, its metallic strength diluted by the juniper scent of the gin, twisting toward the nearest drain. On the screen, another yellow stone knocked yet another red stone out of play. The entire pub broke out into cries, cheers, wails. Erin couldn't make sense of the noise, and so she left a twenty atop the table and hurried her way back to the hotel, the crunch of the snow like teeth grinding. She tried to unclench her fists, but all it did was expose her hands to the cold. She'd forgotten her gloves, and she rubbed her palms together once she was in the elevator. She hurried down the hallway to her door, digging through her pockets, unable to get a decent hold of the plastic keycard that would let her into the privacy of her room.

Then the elevator doors chimed behind her. The doors opened and the man with the glasses walked out with a bag from the liquor store. He looked at her the same way he did in the bistro. His fist clenched around the paper bag.

"Did you buy gin?" she asked, feigning normalcy, but he looked down at her frostbitten fingers and swallowed, unable to hide his concern.

His suite overlooked the base of the mountain. The gondola lift sat motionless in the night, its cabins illuminated beneath the spotlights. Erin squinted, trying to see up into the clouds that overtook the mountain, but its peak stretched too high and too far into the dark.

The man poured two drinks. Ice clinked against the glasses as he brought them to the small table in the center of the room. He sat across from her, swallowing again. He had a habit of swallowing, maybe even before the robbery. Erin studied his reluctance. The vein in his neck twitched when he met her gaze. He shrugged out of his suit jacket, then turned to hang it up, returning it to its dry-cleaning bag in the closet.

"I never thanked you," she said.

"You don't need to. The guy still got your ring in the end." The rasp in his voice picked at her throat, moved between her lungs and settled there. He took his seat across from her, then emptied half the glass with the tilt of his head. "I see you've replaced it," he said, pointing to the quartz ring on her left hand.

"This is just tourist shit." She let go of her glass and slipped her hand beneath the table, out of his line of sight. "I'm just trying to do normal things and be a normal person. My fiancé worries."

A silence lingered. He glanced out the window, at the gondola it was clear neither of them planned on taking. "My wife sent me to a therapist," he said before finishing his glass. "It didn't do much, just made her more afraid for me. Afraid of me." He looked at her again, his expression hard, despite the glassy haze of his growing inebriation. He refilled his glass and tilted the bottle to top off hers. "I'm sure she was happy to see me leave."

"Why are you here?" Erin asked.

"For work."

"What do you do?"

"I work for a mining company. Gemstones. There's a conference here all week. People just drink and brag there. It's no place for me now."

"None of the articles ever said your name," she said.

"What articles?"

"The articles about the robbery."

He tightened his fingers around his glass, but glanced at the metal skeleton on the mountainside instead of taking a drink. "It's Edward."

"Erin." She reached across the table to touch his hand. The man accepted the handshake, but his flesh was chilled and cold from clutching his glass. His grasp held hers limply, lifelessly, taking what little warmth Erin had in the first place. She flinched, unable to hide the chill.

"I was never a warm person," he said. "That's why I drink, and why I usually do it alone."

He refilled both glasses, and their second drinks turned into third drinks, into fourths. Some of Edward's reserve gave way in his inebriation, and he told her of the worry that settled over his wife every time he'd come home from work with an open bottle. He spoke of the fear that grew every time he'd wake up screaming with his limbs shot full of adrenaline. He kept his gaze averted as he spoke, turned to the window and its view of the gondola lift and the red diamond-shaped cabins that hung motionless in the air.

"This whole time, I thought you were dead," Erin finally said.

Edward twisted the cap over the nearly drained bottle of gin and slouched in his chair. Then he touched the spot where the bullet entered him, just over the pocket on his button-front shirt. "I was halfway dead for a while. It wasn't bad, honestly. Comas are just dreams."

"Can I see it?" Erin asked.

Edward hesitated but she still found herself reaching. He pushed her hand away, the quartz ring thudding against the table. "You shouldn't touch me," he said, standing.

Erin remained in her seat. "I'm sorry. I just had to know you were okay."

"You know I'm not okay." He rubbed the gunshot wound, scratched at it like there was something inside that he couldn't get out. "You're not okay, either. You wouldn't be here if you were."

She stood, stumbling over her own feet as she walked toward him. He caught her and stumbled himself, his back hitting the closet door. It rattled against them, Edward's breath hitting her neck.

"Please. Please," he said. Begged.

Erin turned her face to kiss him, to taste the grit of him. At first he resisted, but she buried her tongue in his mouth. He still smelled of gin. His tongue burned of it and she savored the taste. His chest radiated heat beneath her palms. She pulled at the buttons of his shirt, but his warmth faded as he pushed her away from him. She stepped back, replacing his presence with what little relief she could get. Teeth to the quartz, she felt the vibrations. The tension. She swallowed, just like him.

"I have a meeting tomorrow morning. A presentation." His voice softened as he felt behind him, tugged at the suit in the bag. "I don't do so well with presentations. It takes a while to pretend, and I can't pretend if I spend any more time with you." The suit swung on the hanger, squeaking over the metal bar.

"I'm sorry," she said again.

"You're not sorry. You're worried."

She backed away and stood hopelessly in the center of the room, giving him a moment to steel himself. Instead, he picked her parka off the bed and pushed it into her arms. Then he went to the table and handed her the near-empty bottle of gin. "You'll be sorry if you come back here," he said, pushing the parka and bottle into her arms. "This will help you more than I can. Just drink. Forget."

The clear liquid sloshed inside of the bottle after he shut the door in her face.

Did you get there? You never messaged me. I'm worried.

Erin never answered her fiancé. She didn't apologize when she woke up the next morning either. She drank the rest of the gin, pulled her parka back on, and left her room, glancing down the hall. She pressed her ear to Edward's door, but he was no longer inside. She imagined him standing before a crowd of people in his pressed gray suit, imagined his voice shaking before them, in a sound unlike the one he used when he spoke to her, hard and authoritative and affirming.

It wasn't until she returned to the village stroll that she realized she'd forgotten her gloves again. Everyone around her wore thick insulated gloves, which they used to carry their skis casually over their shoulders. Erin lowered her head and wove between them to the nearest cafe. She took it in a paper cup this time, then clutched at the waxed paper as she lined up to ride the gondola. Thirty bucks admitted her inside one of the red cabins with a glass floor. The door sealed shut after she boarded. Then the lift started. The ground parted from her feet and the lift carried her above the mountain, high above all the people and the trees and the lakes that expanded below.

Halfway up, the doors rattled and a draft slipped its way through the gap that formed. Erin stared at the misaligned panels and took a sip of her coffee, hoping it would warm her, but all she felt was the grit of the grinds against her teeth. She set the cup on the floor and sat on the bench, staring at the peaks of the snow-covered cedars that drifted beneath her.

The cold quickly found her extremities, her fingers and her cheeks and her toes, which she curled tightly inside the confines of her leather boots. Tension worked through her. She hated the height and the way the cabin swayed in the wind. Her rib cage tightened around her lungs. She struggled to draw a breath, closing her eyes only to picture Edward lying on the glass floor, the view of the mountainside filling in with his alcohol-thinned blood.

A gust of wind rattled the doors and parted them wider.

She shivered as the cabin neared the mountain's peak. The sky turned black and endless, but the people gathered at the top of the mountain didn't seem to notice. They roasted marshmallows and put on snowshoes. Bonfire flames licked at their extended hands. The red cabin stopped at the peak's landing, but the broken doors refused to open.

Erin reached through the gap, only for her bare fingers to turn black against the dry mountaintop air. She shouted for help. Nobody turned. Nobody saw. Then the gondola started again. It carried her back down the mountain, where the sky brightened but didn't become clear, just remained in a perpetual state of gray. Trees poked their way out of the snow. Black dots turned into adjusted skiers who know how to stop at the bottom of the hill, their skis angled against the flat end of the slope to stop the momentum. Erin pounded the doors at the bottom. They opened for her and she scrambled out of the car, knocking over her cup of coffee. She left the spill behind and wandered back to the hotel as the sting of frostbite seeped into her unprotected fingers.

The elevator buttons felt like nothing. Every digit screamed, her fingers turning red and swelling. She reached inside her pocket to retrieve her room key but the flimsy plastic slipped through her useless grasp. Her cries echoed in the elevator, only to filter down the hall when the doors parted. The ache swelled through her entire hand, up her wrists and into her forearms. She fell to her knees and tried to retrieve the key.

The doors closed. She sobbed in isolation until the doors opened again, revealing Edward on the other side.

"Let me see." He grabbed her hands and gawked at the blackened swelling.

"I forgot my gloves in my room."

"Where did you go?" he asked.

"The gondola. I just wanted to be normal. I wanted to see."

He helped her to her feet and pulled her down the hall.

"They're going to have to amputate them, right?"

"No," he said, dragging her back to his room under his cold grasp. His hands weren't much warmer in front of the fireplace, but he massaged her palms, pressed his fingers between hers. Friction. Tension. He twisted the quartz ring off her left hand.

"My wife used to love this kind of shit."

"It doesn't work," she admitted.

"Of course it doesn't. It's a fucking rock." He set the ring on the nightstand and replaced it with his interlocked fingers. He turned the frostbite red, then white, then pink. The pain turned to pins and needles. The swelling disappeared. Sensation returned and gave way, finally, to his warmth. Erin curled her grasp into his and squeezed tightly.

She didn't kiss him this time, despite wanting to. They watched the flames dance behind the glass of the pretend fire. Erin laid her head against his shoulder. She felt him draw a tensed breath, but he surprised her by wrapping his arm around her waist and pulling her closer. This time, when she went to touch his beating heart, he lifted her chin and kissed her lips.

Piece by piece, they removed clothing, exposing flesh to the growing heat. Erin pushed him back and straddled him on the bed, and he lay beneath, staring at her. She worked herself over him, pressed her need to his erection until she found release. He held her, his breath steady and unchanged, so Erin continued after, hoping to do the same for him. She tried to please him, her back arched, her thighs aching. She writhed until she was exhausted and the tears rolled hot down her cheeks.

Edward reached up and wiped them away. "It's alright. Nobody can satisfy me anymore."

Night fell and the white lights in the trees lit the pathways again. Tourists traded in their skis for shots and debauchery. Their shouts rose up and reached through Edward's hotel window, waking Erin from her slumber beside him. The pretend flames twisted and contorted, illuminating the room with warm tones of amber and red and yellow. They flickered over Edward's bullet wound. It was just a circle of pale scar tissue over his heart. She touched it again. His heart beat steadily, but she barely felt it beneath her fingers. She pressed deeper, until his skin sagged over his ribs.

Then Edward's phone rang, the alarm shaking him awake. He gasped and flailed, grabbing for the device to turn off the sound.

"What is it?" Erin asked.

"It's cocktail hour at the conference." He placed the phone back on the nightstand. "I'm not going." He pulled her closer and took her hand in his. He tried to get a look at her fingertips, but she touched the scar tissue of his wound instead.

"How long did it take to heal?"

"It doesn't always look like that," he said. "It's never healed. Not entirely."

Erin tried to touch the wound again but he grabbed her hand. He opened her palm flat, then studied her fingertips, squeezing until the digits turned red.

"I should have died," he said.

"I'm glad you didn't."

He looked at her, releasing her hand so she could touch him. The scar tissue blackened beneath her fingers, the skin thinning as his heartbeat accelerated. She flinched, her fingers curling, scraping into the blackness that swelled up from beneath the surface of the wound. Her nails grazed ribs, scraped muscle, skimmed the edge of his heart. Edward groaned, but he clutched at Erin's wrist before she could pull away, the dead affirmation of his voice finally giving way to a moan. Her fingers burned but she buried them deeper, closing her eyes as she leaned over him. She kissed him. She tasted him, feeling the vibration of his cry in her lungs. His heart throbbed and she prodded at the life still inside him until he cried out.

"Please! Please!"

He touched her face, tugged at her hair. He looked like he did on the tiled floor of the liquor store. She kissed him, promising that everything would be okay as his moans vibrated hot against her neck. He kissed her, bit at her, until the wound turned cold under her hand. Erin pulled away as the black hole filled with ice. He gasped, flinching as it cracked, spilling blue sludge down his chest. It soaked into the sheets, but she curled herself beside him, caught in a threshold of melted snow.

She stayed the night and found the quartz ring gone in the morning. She went to turn on the little coffee pot in the corner of his room, but Edward sat up.

"We should go out instead."

They shared a plate of pancakes in front of the bistro window. He was still nervous in public. The metal fork slipped in his grasp and she nudged his foot beneath the table. He forced a smile, forced normalcy. Afterward, they clutched their gloved hands on the village stroll so all the people with their skis had to step aside to let them through. The sleeves of their parkas rustled as they walked the entirety of the stroll and back. The afternoon light came and went. They ate lunch and investigated the sights. They stood at the bottom of the mountain and watched people plummet to the bottom, their faces red and their smiles wide.

Edward's phone rang in his pocket. He pulled it out but quickly tucked it away. "Let's get some gin," he said, putting his arm through hers.

The lights on the trees came on and he led her through the darkening concrete paths to the liquor store.

Erin froze.

"It's fine," Edward said, tugging her through the melted snow at the doors. Her grasp tightened around his hand as he led her to the back where the spirits were. He selected a bottle of gin from the shelf. She looked in his eyes, but he was once again cold, rigid. He touched his chest through his jacket, his gaze hardening.

Erin tried to take his hand, but he moved quickly toward the till as if trying to outrace reality. She hurried to follow him, and watched him pay, his fingers still shaking. His phone alarm went off to prepare him for whatever conference event he needed to dress for. This time, he shut the phone off entirely before pocketing the device. He pulled her past the sliding doors, through the sludge, and back outside.

Despite the gloves, Erin felt her fingers grow cold again.

"Can we go back to your room?" she asked.

To her relief, he nodded and took her hand.

They shared the taste of juniper and pine as night fell over the village. Black seeped through the windows and they left the curtains open, creating warmth through friction. She wrapped her thighs around his hips and took the cold of him inside of her. Whatever heat they made would be temporary. She coiled her black fingers into his hair, breathed his name, her teeth grating.

The windows fogged over with release.

When it was over, she pressed her ear to his chest again, listening to the faint beat of his heart, telling herself that it was louder, maybe faster than before. He fell into sleep and she wrapped herself around his frame. She clung to him like he was a hostage she needed to keep alive, but his body turned rigid. The fog from the windows faded, exposing the mountainside, which was still lit bright with spotlights even though the gondola was closed. The skeletal frames of the ride climbed up the mountain like stitches and the little red cars swayed in the frigid northern breeze.

Erin looked back at Edward, his eyes closed, his chest still rising and falling. He looked somber, as though in a coma.

The bullet wound was different.

It was black in the middle and white at the edges. The skin of his entire chest had swelled and reddened. She hesitated before reaching, allowing her numb fingers to slip once again into the charred flesh. She pressed her entire fist inside, rooting for his heart. The beating had grown faint and nearly non-existent. She clutched at the trace warmth. Then, behind her, all the lights on the mountainside shattered.

She turned, gathering a breath, only for a pair of frozen hands to snatch her by the neck. Edward slammed her down against the mattress. She fought to loosen his grasp but his fingers only tightened and froze, trapping her scream in her lungs.

"Please! Please!" he screamed. He stared at her, begging like before, with terror in his dead eyes, a man fighting for life.

Erin couldn't beg. She fought and kicked, pressing her open palms against his chest as the room blackened. She wrestled her hand back into the wound, touching sinew and bone, but found nothing. Her eyes swelled. Her tongue protruded as the beating filled her ears.

"Please! Please!" His voice echoed, but then a knock vibrated.

The hands left her. The gondola spotlights flickered back on. Edward scrambled from the bed, clutching at his chest. He moved for the door and glanced through the peephole.

"Is everything okay in there, Edward?" a voice called. "You weren't at the conference today. I just came to check on you."

Erin gasped for breath, clutching her throat, trying to massage the warmth back into her. The fist pounded the door again and Edward pressed his forehead to the frame, clutching his chest as he looked at Erin with tears filling his eyes. She tried not to cough and held her breath in limbo.

"I'm sorry," Edward called through the door. "I'm sorry. I was hungover. I—I, it won't happen again."

"You were screaming—"

"I'm alright, but thank you," Edward gasped, shutting his eyes as though pained by the reality. "Thanks for your concern. I'll be there tomorrow, okay?"

Footsteps walked away and Erin turned her face into the cold sheets, using them to stifle the sound of her coughs. When she looked back, Edward was on the floor, trying to wring warmth back into his blackened hands.

"Now you know," he said. "This is why I push people away."

Erin hesitated. "Your wife—"

"I've done it more than once." He struggled to stand, pulling at the white robe that hung from a hanger in the open closet. The front of the terry cloth soaked quickly with the cold slush from his chest, but he went to the bathroom and filled a cup with water that he brought to her. "I'll do it again," he said. "I always do."

Erin sipped. The cold filled her throat, tightening her limbs, making her shiver. Her fingertips numbed over the plastic cup, creating condensation.

"Frostbite creates lasting damage," he said. "You don't feel things the way you once did. Eventually you won't feel anything at all."

She cleared her throat and drank, but the water seemed to freeze in her throat, prickling its way down. She looked outside at the gondola. All the lights flickered, and she blinked, wondering if she'd imagined it. She cleared her throat over the sore place where he'd held her.

"If you were smart, you'd leave," he said. "Your survivor's guilt isn't helping you. You're just reliving it all by coming here."

She winced at the truth. "I felt responsible. I thought you were dead—"

"You don't want to end up like me, Erin."

"I won't," she insisted. "I want to help. I don't want to be alone."

She reached for him, slipped her palm beneath the lapel of his robe. Tears brimmed in his eyes and he blinked them away, the cold slipping from his gaze.

"Do you really want me to go?" she asked.

"Please." His chin shook as he drew a breath. "Please stay."

In the morning, Erin woke to the coffee machine's rumble. Edward was already dressed. Not in a suit, as he'd promised his co-worker, but in his winter clothes. He slipped his glasses on and poured coffee into a paper cup. He brought it to her, the glare of the lenses reflecting the gray skies outside. "I'm not feeling the cafe today."

Erin cleared her throat, still feeling the pressure. She sipped the brew but it tasted of nothing.

"I'd like to go out. Just us. I'd like to take you for a walk, if I could." He adjusted his glasses, shifting the glare so she could see the gentleness in his eyes again.

"Where?"

"Lost Lake. It's a bit of a walk." He got up and gathered her parka, her boots, her gloves.

"I don't really hike."

"You can't spend all your time in the village," he said. "Nothing about it is real."

She finished her coffee, glancing again out the window where the red gondolas climbed the mountainside. He helped her into her winter garments, then wrapped a scarf around her neck to hide the bruising his hands had left. The coffee's warmth coiled in her stomach as they took the elevator down.

Their gloves protected their hands from the cold when they ventured out of the village and into the woods. Edward led her through the snow-covered paths. The pack was deep and difficult to walk through. Erin struggled to breathe, her throat still tight and pained. She followed his lead for what felt like forever, trying to step into the prints left behind by hikers who'd walked before. The woods seemed to darken around her, and she looked up, hoping to see the red veins of the gondola. The trees thickened as Edward pulled her onward, their limbs hanging down, the green needles looped together like nooses.

The footprints in the snow ceased, as if the woods had swallowed the tourists whole. The snow crunched beneath her feet, creating a grinding sensation in her throat. She let go of his hand and Edward turned.

"I want to go back. My hands are getting cold."

"We're almost there." He reached for her, took her, pulled her on as the trees towered above. The further they went, the more the cold spread. Wind slipped through the coils of her scarf. Snow crept into the tops of her boots. Her thighs started to numb, to itch. The lack of sensation tingled into a burn. Then she noticed the sign for the lake, a red sticker was pasted over it, reading CLOSED. Edward slowed. His glasses were fogged over when he turned.

"It's just the concession that's closed," he said. "Everything will be covered in snow. Untouched. It'll just be us."

"Edward, please. I'm hungry. I'm cold."

He huffed. "What was the point of coming here if you're not willing to see the sights?"

The path ahead loomed, dark and empty. The scarf tightened around her neck and she pulled at the layers. "There's nobody there."

"That's the whole point," he said. "Do you really want to be around other people?"

She tugged at the scarf, unable to catch a breath. "Please. I like being with you, but I don't want to be here. I don't like it here."

"It won't be like this at the end," he promised.

"I'm cold, Edward." Her breath fogged between them. Her voice broke. "I'm scared. I don't want to be alone. Please just come back and have a drink with me." She held out her hand, her gasps fogging the air between them until he finally reached to take it.

In the dark of the crowded bar, he once again became the man she saw on the first day. His shoulders tensed. The ice rattled inside the glass he shifted his grasp around. Beside him, the television blared another curling game.

"I never know what they're trying to do," he said, nodding at the screen.

"Neither do I," Erin said. "One day, maybe I'd like to understand the rules."

"Why?"

"So, I can feel normal again. My fiancé loves curling."

Edward finished his glass in one swig, drawing a breath and raising his gaze. The lenses of his glasses reflected the game on the television. One of the players threw a red rock. The two sweepers brushed furiously as the thrower yelled. The rock spiraled down the ice, granite hitting granite, knocking out all the yellow stones. The crowd roared around them, but Edward bowed his head and cowered.

Erin pulled them through the bar's interior in haste, their boots slipping in the slush. The wind whipped at them both when they emerged outside. The white lights glowed on the trees, leading the way to the liquor store. She felt less anxious of the space, for she was more worried about

Edward and the way his gaze would change once he selected the gin. In her worry, she snatched up a bottle before he could. She took it to the till, and paid for it. Instead of putting on her gloves, she twisted at the cap outside the store. Edward smiled, and they passed the bottle back and forth, a load lightened as they emptied its contents through the village walk.

The warmth filled them, made them laugh, made the cold less impacting. She dropped her gloves and her scarf and her hat, her face turning hot as she ran through the snow-covered cement, forcing him to follow. She laughed, running ahead, inhaling deep breaths of northern night air as Edward chased her toward the open pit of an empty water fountain. It wasn't running because it was winter, but its pool was filled with fresh snow that he pushed her into. Snow filled her boots. Snow touched her cheek and he wrestled her down, kissing her with juniper lips beneath the warm glow of the white lights.

"Aren't you cold?" he asked.

"No," she laughed, her head spinning. "Not at all."

He helped her up, but stumbled. It wasn't until she caught herself in the snow that she realized her hands were black, and the lights from the trees exposed the frostbite to everyone around to see. The people started to gawk and gather, but Edward took her hand. They drunkenly hurried back to his room, and he staggered again in the elevator.

"This is what it's like," he slurred. "This is how it feels every day."

Erin pulled his arm over her shoulder, struggling to maintain a proper grasp. She helped him into the room and onto the bed. She turned on the fireplace and hastily stripped his clothes, his frozen skin only chilling hers in return. She climbed over him and pressed her frost-bitten fingers into the hole that was slowly taking him away.

"How much longer are you staying?"

"Tomorrow's my last day," he said. "I don't want to go back. They're just going to worry."

"Who?"

"Them. My wife. My family."

"I was under the impression—"

"That I left them?" He winced but Erin pressed her fingers inside, finding a little bit of warmth where his heart was still beating. "They keep hoping I'll come back but I never do. Not all the way. They worry all the time, but they don't know how to help. I hate it when people worry."

Erin kissed him, then moved herself lower and pressed her lips to the wound. His icy flesh fused to hers, but she inched her tongue inside him, breathed her life into him. He gasped beneath her, reaching for her neck, trying to push her away, but he didn't beg.

"You're just a dream," he moaned. "You're a coma."

Her warmth wove his flesh, turned it pink, flushed, fused together. The glow of pretend fire made him look warm, real. He took her hands and warmed them in his. He grasped at her, held her close, like all he wanted in the moment was to keep her and make her stay with him forever in a dream.

She huddled against his body, doing herself lasting damage.

In the morning, Edward canceled his last conference meeting. Erin struggled to make coffee with the flimsy machine, her fingers still numb and stiff.

"We should see the top of the mountain," he said.

Erin used her teeth to tear open her pack of sugar, feeling the granules in the ridges. "You said that I shouldn't go there."

"It won't hurt as much this time," he promised, but then he put on his glasses and all Erin saw was the glare.

They held bare hands at the gondola lineup, paying the fare to climb into a red cabin together. The doors closed and the cabin ascended. Erin noticed the coffee stain on the glass floor, which blurred the view of the snow-dusted cedar trees that shrank beneath them.

"This is the same car," she said, pointing to the gap between the doors.

A breeze whispered from outside. Edward dropped her hand to investigate.

"No, don't."

He curled his fingers between the gap in the metal.

"Edward, please."

"I'm fine. I'm alright." He wrestled with the doors. They rattled as the car ascended, the locking mechanism finally giving way at his prodding. The doors slid open, slamming against the guard rails. Cold surged into the cabin, but Edward barely flinched when the gust tugged at his open jacket. He leaned against the edge of the opening, staring down at the trees and the lakes and the trails all buried beneath a fresh covering of white.

"Edward, get away from there."

He clutched at the door frame and leaned to glance at the void below. "I bet there's nobody down there."

The white mountainside blinded her. She reached for his arm but the puffy sleeve of his jacket gave no resistance. She tugged him backward, but he clung to the doorway with his opposite hand.

"I really wanted to take you there." He looked at her, his voice flat. Dead. "Imagine what it would feel like if people stopped worrying."

She reached out and touched his cheek, but her fingers only numbed. "Just wait until we get to the top, Edward. There's a fire there. A real fire. It'll be warm."

His glasses only reflected the tops of the trees below. "Nothing warms me anymore."

"Edward, please." Her eyes burned. Tears slipped, blistering her cheeks.

His limbs tensed when he finally looked at her. "You're worried, aren't you?" His tone settled in her mouth, grating against her teeth.

Erin shook her head, taking a step forward, closer to the open doors than she wanted to be. She tightened her grasp around his arm.

"Come with me. Just stop worrying and come with me." He reached, giving her no choice but to fight the desperate urge to cling to him and her need to let him go. He found her scarf and grasped it tight, the cable knit coiling around her throat. She gasped, trying to pry his fingers away. His boots skidded, slipping off the cabin floor. Erin grabbed for his arm in desperation—to help him, to save him—but he slipped his arm out of his jacket and its down-filled weight withered in her hold.

Beneath the foggy glass, a black dot disappeared into the mountain's white expanse.

The gondola stopped at the top of the mountain and Erin stumbled out, crying into the cold.

"Oh my God, your hands!"

"Why don't you have gloves?"

"What happened to you? Let me help."

A crowd of gawking witnesses crowded her, horrified by her swollen cheeks and her black fingers and her heaving sobs. They grabbed her by the elbows and brought her to the fire, covered her with a metallic blanket that crinkled around her frame. They all wanted to know what happened, and they stared with worried eyes as everything inside of her turned slushy and numb, just like he promised.

"Please," she begged, closing her eyes, hoping to dream. "Please."

CHAPTER SIX

BLOOD, APPLES, BLACKBERRY WINE

ASHLEY VAN ELSWYK

At the festival's close, as sunset stained the autumn sky red, the villagers poured out their last bottle of holy cider together with the freshly-spilled blood of the past year's Harvest Queen.

They raised their empty cups in thanks to the crackling bonfire of her bones, and their gods drank and drank heartily long into the night.

The newly-crowned Harvest Queen watched soberly from her applewood throne. Her hands trembled against the wood, and her predecessor's gasps dripped through her mind, drowning out the celebrations.

She let the bonfire burn her vision until she could no longer see any trace of red or gold.

When the first snows fell, they packed their queen into her winter home. Only one attendant remained with her: a tall, round-faced stranger—a newcomer lucky to have been chosen for this role.

Crates of carefully stored apples filled the cellar space under her feet, their cloying scent seeping up through the boards to choke the air. No windows: only candles lit the humble abode built in the center of the orchard, keeping her safe while the gods slept. Cold, still, perfectly preserved.

She ate nothing but the apples. Forced them into her mouth, too-sweet and crunchy, scraping her throat. The juices made her chin and fingers sticky, until her skin swallowed those last traces into her veins. And that was good, they'd told her, before abandoning her for the winter months. Good that she was taking in the gods' fruit so well.

She wanted to scream. Claw through the floorboards and crush every fruit, feel the waxy skins split white and crumble between her fingers. Break the locks and flee the orchard, cursing the gods who'd named her queen and waited, thirsting, for her blessed blood.

Instead, she sat achingly complacent while her new attendant unbraided her hair with gentle hands.

"It's a shame," said the attendant, "that we can't watch the snow fall. I've always enjoyed that part of winter. It makes the wait for spring more bearable."

The Harvest Queen contemplated the offer of conversation. "Then why volunteer to be locked in here?" she finally asked.

The attendant picked at a knot in the pale red strands. "For a change. That's the reason I do anything, honestly, ever since I left home. I haven't found much good company among these villagers though, so I offered my services to you," she said. "Besides, winter's the same every year. How often does one get the chance to attend a Harvest Queen?" Her tone was oddly sarcastic.

"Every year. The difference is she's never the same." The queen shuddered.

Her attendant stilled. "You didn't want this?"

"I accept what the gods decree." The queen's words filed out with a practiced ease. "They chose me as queen to embody their blessing, and it's an honor to give my life to ensure another bountiful harvest."

"A load of pretty words and none of them yours," the attendant remarked wryly. She combed her fingers through the loosened hair, and stepped back. "Would you like anything to eat?"

Anything but apples.

She sighed. "I am a bit hungry. Take a few for yourself too, or whatever else they've left for you. We can eat together."

The attendant soon returned from the cellar with a full basket. In her other hand, she held a bottle—filled not with the gold of cider, but a strange, dark liquid. The queen would've thought it black, if not for the rich flashes of red revealed by candlelight.

"What's that?" she asked.

The attendant blinked in surprise. Kneeling onto the floor, she replied, "Blackberry wine. A personal favorite. I suppose I shouldn't have brought it in here, but I've never much liked cider."

The queen nodded solemnly. "I won't say a word." She watched curiously as the attendant picked at an apple before abandoning it in favor of toying with the bottle.

"It's nice to taste something other than apples," she said. "One grows tired of them after a while. Don't you agree?"

"You didn't grow up here," the queen pointed out. "But then, I thought I was used to them, until the festival. Now apples are all I smell and taste, and—I can't stand it." She grimaced.

It felt oddly safe to confess. She'd never admit such a thing around the others, not unless she wanted to be reminded of the honor of her position, punished for edging close to blasphemy. This woman carried none of that fear or judgement. She simply hummed in agreement, and opened the bottle.

An intoxicating scent filled the air like a summer haze. The queen felt a vicious urge to grab the bottle and down every drop, to burn the residual taste of apple from her tongue. Her mind spun drunkenly as she spoke. "It scares me."

"What? The festival?"

She nodded.

The attendant's expression hardened. "It's a disgraceful ritual," she muttered. The queen was shocked at the sharpness of her words. "A mockery of ancient, more careful relationships between humans and nature. These gods have no grace."

The queen was almost ashamed to find that she didn't disagree in the slightest. At night, the bonfire flames imprinted red on the back of her eyelids, her last vision before she slipped into dreams of shapeless beings emerging from the smoke with tongues unravelling to slake their thirst with her blessed blood. She understood thirst. The wine gleamed tantalizingly in the attendant's hand.

"I want to…Can I try a sip?" She swallowed, nails digging into the mottled skin of her unbitten apple before she dropped it into her lap. "I've never had blackberry wine before. I'm supposed to drink only cider now, but…I want to taste something new, one last time."

Surprise bloomed across the attendant's face. Her gaze settled cautiously against the queen's own certain stare, and after a moment, she tilted her head. "If you'd like."

The tartness washed down her throat, cool as the glass, but raising warmth in her cheeks. Earthy, sharp, and far from the tooth-aching sickliness of apples. Her eyes prickled as she held the bottle to her lips and forgot to breathe in her bliss.

She only pulled away when the bottle was noticeably lighter. As her mind cleared, she flushed and reluctantly lowered it. The attendant's lips quirked in amusement.

"I don't think I caught your name," she mused.

"Does it matter?" The queen frowned. The apple shifted in her lap. "I'm the Harvest Queen. I'll never be who I was before the festival again, and dead in a year anyway. What's the use in dragging it up?"

"Why don't I give you a new name then?" asked the attendant. "A royal name, we'll say, just between us." She clicked her tongue in thought, then brightened. "Would Ide be agreeable?"

"Ide." The queen stretched out the initial ee, and cut it off with her tongue. A nice sound for a secret. "Alright."

She held the half-empty bottle out by the neck, letting it dangle in the air like overripe fruit. The attendant plucked it from her careless grip. Ide noticed the darkness of the wine matched the freckles on her sun-kissed arms.

"What's yours?" Ide asked, more out of curiosity than politeness.

"Does it matter?" the attendant replied, half-teasing. "Call me whatever you like, it's only fair."

She lifted the bottle to her lips—the same spot her own had touched, Ide noted with a peculiar flicker in her stomach—and drank and drank until the wine was gone.

Winter passed slowly while the gods slept, and Ide continued to choke down apple flesh as her own began to stiffen and ache.

Her attendant, renamed Ora, remained a heartening presence and confidant throughout the winter. But if she had any more blackberry wine hidden away, she never revealed it. The memory of their indiscretion clung to Ide's mind as stubborn as a stain.

With every sip of cider, every bite of apple, she imagined tasting blackberries.

Too soon, apple blossoms choked out the spring sky with white and pink storm clouds, and the doors reopened. Ide began spending most of her days in the orchard tending to the boughs, inspecting them for signs of growth or—gods forbid—rot.

She tried not to think of the consequences of rot.

"Ide?"

Ora emerged from a row of saplings with a sly smile and one arm folded behind her back. It had grown harder to spend time together during sunlit hours, but with most of the village away diligently pruning or spreading mulch in other sections of the orchard, they'd had most of this week for themselves.

"I expect we'll see quite a crop," Ide muttered, tracing her fingertips around the soft petals, itching to pluck them apart.

Their perfume was inescapable. Even the compost pits reeked of apple cores and skins, the corrupted sweetness burning her throat. Every night, Ide gagged into her pillow, trying to find peace in the fading memory of blackberry wine.

"That's good, isn't it?"

Ide's hand slipped down the scaly bark. "For the last queen. Presently, it only means I'm not a failure as a caretaker. If the gods are pleased, they'll reward me with a magnificent death, and the village with a grand harvest next year."

Ora grimaced, her hidden arm dropping a little. "You deserve more than just a rich death."

"If you're trying to make me feel better…" Ide trailed off, but offered a small smile to indicate her good humor.

"No, I understand," Ora said. "Ah—I have something for you that might help. I hope."

Ide perked up. Her mind wandered back to the wine and she wondered if Ora had brought another bottle to share. Her mouth watered at the thought.

Instead, Ora stretched her arm towards Ide and revealed a little sprig the length of her palm, covered with open blossoms.

Five-petal flowers on a gnarled twig. Ide gritted her teeth, her face hot and chest pounding.

"You think I haven't seen enough blossoms already?" she snapped, gesturing broadly around them. "I'm surrounded! Apples, nothing but apples in every wretched form. I don't need you bringing them to me— they've infected all aspects of my life, down to my dreams!"

She snatched the little sprig, threw it down, and crushed the flowers into the earth. A thrill raced up her spine at the brittle snap as it broke underfoot.

Ide's breath slowed to shallow pants. Ora bent down to pick up the broken gift, cradling it delicately in her palms.

"I should have given it to you another time," she sighed, her voice low and detached. "Or not at all. They do resemble apple blossoms rather strongly...I'm sorry."

Ide's heart sank as her attendant let the remains fall back to the ground, before disappearing between the rows. Stooping down to examine the broken sprig only made her feel so much worse because she'd been wrong.

These torn petals weren't pink, but a soft white, and unfamiliar down to the lingering scent. The leaves were wrong too, jagged and rough. With each difference, Ide found her mistake more unbelievable. Her stomach twisted remembering the hurt in Ora's voice.

By the time Ide finally found her sitting slouched against an older trunk on the far edge of the orchard, the sky was already swirling purple and orange.

"I'm sorry," she said, standing a few feet away. "They were blackberry flowers, weren't they?"

It was a guess, but Ora hummed affirmatively.

Ide shifted awkwardly. "I was rash. And thoughtless. You'd never offer me apples as a gift, you're more intuitive than that. I let a bad mood get the best of me, and it hurt you, and I'm sorry."

Ora looked intently up at her, dark eyes picking her apart.

"Apology accepted. And I'm sorry as well. It was childish to make you hunt for me all afternoon," Ora said, and shrugged at Ide's confusion. "I was watching you almost the whole time through the trees. My moods sometimes get the better of me too."

"Well, I can't blame you for that. I wish I'd had a better look at those flowers."

Ora rose with a small smile, and squeezed Ide's shoulder. "It's fine. Besides, I always know where to find more."

Apple tree shadows fell over Ora's head like a lace veil, the fading light turning her brown hair black. An idea wriggled into Ide's mind. She turned and broke a small sprig off the low branch beside them. The snap rang throughout the orchard like a warning cry. Ide froze.

Nothing happened. No gods or villagers came to strike her down for the desecration.

Ora remained her only witness.

She bit back a prayer to the gods for forgiveness. If they hadn't noticed, she didn't need to tell them. Raising the blossoming sprig to her lips, she gently kissed each flower, the petals soft as silk against her lips. With each kiss she left a silent blessing; an amend.

When the last flower was blessed, Ide lifted the sprig and fixed it into Ora's hair, just over her ear. Ora ran her free hand over the petals, her other gripping Ide's shoulder even tighter.

"Thank you," Ora said, quietly. "I'd like to return the favor someday."

"We can try your blackberry blossoms again," Ide said. "And roses are lovely too. I wouldn't mind the scratch of thorns." More satisfying than the agonizing smoothness of apples.

Ora laughed. "I quite agree."

They laid down, stretching across the cool grass together, and there, Ide began to think.

The wine, the dislike of cider, strange flowers. Ora had slipped sacrilege past men and gods, and now coaxed Ide effortlessly down that same path to desecration and unsanctioned blessings. Each day, the apples soured more in her mouth, and Ide realized she didn't mind at all. Instead, she wondered, almost hungrily, as she shifted closer to Ora's warmth.

How close could a Harvest Queen safely come to heresy?

Apple blossoms rained down, covering her like a shroud.

The hollow chittering of the waking gods' hunger-song drifted through Ide's dreams like the wind through trees, while the heavy scent of apples held her in place. They surrounded her with whispers and pleading teeth and starving tongues.

Not ripe.

Not yet.

She snapped awake with a mouth so dry it hurt, a painful contrast to the tears pouring down her cheeks. She cried out, waking Ora, who rushed over to keep Ide from hurtling herself out of bed.

Her comfort was immediate, Ora rubbing tender circles and soothing the itch under Ide's skin where the gods had carelessly scraped in their hurry to taste. Testing her.

One tear trailed down her cheek and into her mouth, and Ide nearly vomited at the sudden sharpness of cider on her tongue. She clenched her teeth before she could bite it off, and she shook, chest heaving, trying not to cry again, terrified that the tears would pour down her face and into her throat like poison.

Ora continued her delicate massaging through Ide's distress, and talked about nothing in particular. The draft she'd discovered in the eastern room, how she expected it would rain that afternoon, how she felt warm and hoped Ide did as well. With each word, Ide gradually eased down from her panic, nestling into the blankets.

"Did you know," Ora said, "in some places still, there are gods who walk among mortals? Not to consume them, but simply to enjoy their company, to observe, and experience what wonders such brief life can bring forth."

Ide couldn't imagine such a thing.

"It's one thing I miss about my home," Ora said. "Peace. You have so much fear here. I'd like to show you peace."

When Ora at last ran out of things to say, they quietly pressed against each other. Ide couldn't bring herself to disturb the calm to thank her.

Later, she promised, watching the pink lines of sunrise stretch across the ceiling.

Summer arrived humming with flies and activity. The apples grew rounder in the sun-soaked orchard, mottling gold and red, and the two women moved into a lighter hut between the orchard and the village.

The restless gods grew hungrier, and Ide weakened.

"I wonder," she mused, tracing the branching veins of her forearm, "if I took a knife and peeled away my skin, what would I find underneath?"

Ora pursed her lips as she poured the day's cider down a small hole she'd carved through the floorboards, into the earth. "Your own flesh. I won't dignify that with another answer. Now come eat before someone else shows up."

Stepping over to the table where Ide sat, she peeled the white cloth off a basket to reveal a wooden bowl of blackberries.

"What's this?" Ide asked, drinking in the clusters of tiny black bubbles.

Ora lifted a single berry to her mouth. "These apples are ripening so soon…You need to start eating something different. You've already stopped drinking the cider, and that's good, but it's not enough."

Enough for what? Ide cautiously plucked a berry from the pile. The skin shone beautifully in the light and she felt a peculiar urge to hide it, swallow it into shadow lest the gods strike it from her hand.

"Draining the cider is one thing, Ora, but refusing the apples entirely?"

Ide had never given herself entirely to the gods; if she had, she never would've touched the wine. But autumn's approach kept her increasingly on edge, and she wasn't foolish enough to pretend she wasn't terrified of them. What might happen, if one day they turned their attention upon her and Ora at exactly the wrong moment?

Not one sacrifice, but two. Not a blessing for the village, but a slighted, vindictive curse.

She was destined to be bled and burned, but she couldn't bear the thought of Ora meeting a similar fate, or worse.

The berry split, gushing between her fingers.

"No. I can't. This is too much, they'll find out—they'll know!" she babbled, scarcely comprehending the words as they spilled out. Imagining the gods catching her scent, the wrong scent. Their mouths ripping her apart, spitting her out in disgust.

She shoved the basket away, and Ora jerked forward to stop it tumbling over the edge. She pulled the bowl out of the basket, and left it sitting in plain view on the tabletop.

Ide clutched her arms and tried not to think of how unnaturally firmer they felt as her nails dug in, not at all the soft, squishy normal flesh they'd been before this nightmare started. The apples changed her with each bite that slithered down her throat. Their smell, their taste, an infection remaking her from the inside out. Wouldn't she be a perfect feast for the gods?

Everyone knew they thirsted for blood, but she'd never been told they'd take the liberty of sweetening it in such a terrible way first.

And she dared to taint it.

"What if they're with us now?" The gods didn't observe all the time—but certainly there'd never before been a Harvest Queen so lacking in devotion. "If they catch…If they think you've tempted me…"

"Am I tempting you?" Ora asked, tensing. "Tell me you don't want this, and I'll stop. You can take their cider and apples and wretched magic, until your throat is cut and they suck up every drop of you while those villagers dance around your pyre—I won't interfere. Tell me, if that's what you desire." Her voice wavered.

Desire. Ide had been mulling over this since that winter night when they'd first bonded over forbidden truths. Her gaze caught on the sprig of blossoms tucked over Ora's ear, unwilted even weeks later. Could she turn her back on her duty, her gods, for the sake of an unknown future? For the possibility of a life with Ora past autumn?

"They'll kill us…" she said weakly, but there was no heart in her protest.

She knew then, she'd never eat another apple again.

"I won't let them kill you," Ora whispered. Her eyes widened with a fevered gleam that sent shivers down Ide's spine. "We'll teach them what happens to those who stray down bloodthirsty paths to whet their greedy appetites. Who neglect the old ways and forget that others haven't."

"What are you saying?" Ide hissed, glancing nervously at the windows.

Ora gently brushed back Ide's sun-paled hair. "You'll understand soon, I promise. All I ask is for you to trust me." She nudged the bowl of blackberries towards Ide. "Please."

Her expression was so desperately entreating that even if she'd wanted, Ide couldn't resist. With each berry that passed her lips, each burst of sweet-sour juice between her teeth, Ora relaxed.

"I hope you know what you're doing," Ide said, when the bowl was empty.

Ora circled around the table to kneel again before her, fixing her with a burning stare that made Ide's head spin drunkenly and her cheeks flush. "Trust that all I do now is to keep you safe," she said. "Your gods have a thousand mouths, but no eyes, no ears, no earthly bodies—a price they pay for their hunger. This will be their downfall. They won't catch what we've done until it's too late."

She gently took Ide's wrists and drew them to her mouth, pressing delicate kisses along the lines of discolored veins, tracing them with her tongue. It didn't scare Ide like the gods' mouths did.

"I promise," Ora murmured between kisses as she moved up Ide's arm, her neck, her cheeks. "My queen. I promise."

When Ora reluctantly parted from her and crept away to dispose of their uneaten apples, Ide thought hard through a fading haze of pleasure about want.

She didn't want to be Harvest Queen, but she was. She didn't want to die, but couldn't fathom how to avoid it, despite Ora's promises. The peace they'd found lying together in the orchard seemed so unreachable, so long ago.

Ide licked her lips to catch the lingering traces of blackberries and something bitter, something wonderfully new. She trusted Ora. She only wished Ora would explain.

Staring down at her arms, another thought re-emerged like a worm after rain. What would she find, if she peeled away the skin? In seconds, a knife tip rested against her forearm and Ide nicked herself just enough to draw out a drop. A curdling wave of nausea gripped her stomach at the sight.

Her blood was as gold as cider.

The festival approached with all the danger of a starving beast: slow, but ceaseless. Autumn wallowed in its last peak of heat, while the ground swam in a mixture of steam, smoke, and falling leaves. Cider-brewing was fully underway, and the village filled with the smell of spices and apples being baked, stewed, or otherwise prepared for the winter preserves. What little peace Ide had carved out for herself in earlier seasons vanished as the villagers turned worshipful in the heady autumn glow.

Her days were laden with hours of walking, up and down the orchard rows to bless each tree with a touch, a prayer of continued health, and a single drop of blood upon the roots to feed them during the coming winter sleep. She didn't look at the blood.

Most frustratingly, it never took long for people to clamor around her and Ora on their way home. They praised Ide, clutching at her limbs, her hair; but this day was worse than suffocating.

Her head and legs ached with heat and exhaustion, so distracting that Ide didn't see the man reaching too close until a flash of pain tore through her shoulder. He had summoned the nerve to cut her himself.

Yanking her closer, he tried furiously to lick her wound, the sweet golden blood welling. His breath was hot against her skin, and Ide tried to scream but the sound caught in her throat. She looked wildly around for escape. There was no mercy in the villagers' faces; only rapturous hunger.

Queensblood, godsblood, cider sweet. The man's tongue slid across her broken skin like a slug, like the horrid children's rhyme in her head. She swore she heard the gods' crooning laughter. Why weren't they stopping him?

Ide's chest tightened with panic and she thrust her elbows out to fight him off, when suddenly she was pulled aside, and pressed against someone. She saw nothing but darkness. A choked yelp rang out, and her scream finally escaped her.

"It's me! You're safe, it's me!" Ora soothed, shaking as she held Ide against her chest. "All of you—back!" she snarled at the crowd.

Ide collapsed forward, weeping as Ora rushed them away from the mob, shielding her until they were safely home.

She asked Ora to stay in her bed that night. Ide relished being held in an embrace of soft arms and purple blankets, breathing in the scent of earth as Ora fed her blackberries and stroked her hair, humming a calming tune.

"From my old home," she explained, when Ide asked about the song. "You'd like it there. It's less suffocating. No orchards or bonfires, only the wild forest and the wild creatures within."

"Then take me. I'm sick of this place," Ide murmured. "I want to live."

She never saw the man again, but this did not comfort her. Worse, the gods' attentions only grew keener.

Ora began disguising the blackberries in apple skins. Ide wanted to recoil at the wrongness of their appearance, the wrongness of the berries inside such sacred forms, but not as greatly as she hungered for them. A delicate, pretty skin filled with the wrong fruit, turned out of shape, too stretched in places where blackberries strained to burst through the skin. It reminded Ide of herself.

She didn't ask how Ora kept them so perfectly, unnaturally intact, right down to the scent. Only peeled, chewed, and swallowed the evidence.

"We need to leave tonight."

Ide could barely sleep. The pop of burning bones, afterimages of the last Harvest Queen's gaping mouth, her throat—they haunted her every moment. And Ora avoided her gaze with a distractedness that only made Ide's trembling worse.

"Patience, my queen. We'll leave," Ora said, frowning at the windows facing the orchard. "But not yet."

"Not yet?" Ide gestured towards the village. "The bonfire is built. The festival is hours away, and you want to wait? Ora, they will kill me."

What happened to her promises? The rage that sparked at any mention of the gods' hunger for harvest blood?

"I can't do this without you—where would I go?" Ide begged. "Please, Ora, don't let them take me."

She could taste the apples now, even months after she'd given them up—crawling vengefully from her stomach, through her limbs, and into her mouth, saccharine bile. She wanted to rip the ghostly sensation out from her body. She wanted Ora to drive it away with bittersweet kisses.

Ora's sudden distance hurt worse than any thought of dying.

"I promised I wouldn't let you die, and you won't. You haven't eaten any apples, correct? But if the timing isn't right, they'll—"

"Is this a game to you?" Ide asked. She raked her nails through her hair. "Leading me from the gods to spite them? Was it always about them? You've ruined me, and now that the eve of my death has come, you're finished?"

Ora's eyes widened with pain. "Never. Never doubt that my feelings for you are true. Not once did I offer anything to harm you."

"Perhaps we should end things," Ide said, fighting to keep her voice steady. "There's no way out that the gods wouldn't discover. They'd hunt us down and punish us, wouldn't they? Maybe it's better you don't mourn a doomed love." She crumpled into her chair, utterly exhausted.

If Ora wanted to bury her emotions, to keep grief from killing her—how could she blame her?

"I should pray," Ide muttered. "I could still beg forgiveness for you, if not myself."

Their last skin of blackberries dropped in front of her with a deliberate thump.

"If you must pray, then do so. Take what comfort you can," Ora said. "But don't pray to those applewood gods."

She stood, rising before Ide with such a queer expression—not pleading, or angry, but something between, intense and commanding. Something more befitting a deity.

"Pray to me instead. And accept what I offer."

Her voice poured over Ide, and for a second, she felt the overwhelming urge to drop to her knees, dizzied with awe as Ora's eyes flashed black and she towered over her, seeming to fill the small room. For a second, Ide nearly succumbed.

Until she remembered who was queen, and who was attendant.

She didn't feel brave, or powerful. She wasn't ready to die, and hated that Ora might be prepared to watch her blood flow with the others. But she wouldn't cower. Ide drew herself up to match Ora's stance, and gripped the skin of blackberries.

"Then eat with me, if you'll offer no other comfort."

She split the skin, poured half of the berries out, and offered them to Ora. A shiver ran through her as Ora stepped forward with her hands cupped to accept her share.

"I'd prefer you ate them all, to keep your strength," Ora said, "But if it's what my queen desires, how could I refuse?"

Ide squeezed one berry enough to warp the soft flesh without breaking it. "Swear you won't drink a drop of cider or raise a cup to my death. No matter what, you won't celebrate. You owe me this, if you won't steal me away."

A strange expression crossed Ora's face, like she might argue. Then she bowed her head.

"For your sake," Ora said, gazing down at the blackberries glinting in the firelight, "I swear. But there's really no need."

Isn't there?

Ide nodded, not quite satisfied, but it was enough. She gave Ora one last kiss before falling asleep, hoping the bittersweetness might carry into her dreams, and her death.

Ide drifted through the festival in a haze: standing on the dead-leaf-strewn platform in the orchard to greet the sunrise, listening to the gleeful whoops as the villagers emptied the trees of their remaining fruit, the drinking and baking competitions. Children raced around with their cheeks painted red, waving candied apples on sticks. Their glaring giddiness made Ide sick.

Throughout it all, Ora was absent.

The sickening aroma of cider baths engulfed her lungs, and Ide fought to maintain her placid smile. Her ritual attendants stroked and cooed over her, whispering how they couldn't wait to watch her join the gods.

She pretended not to see the harvesters sharpening their knives as they laughed and thanked the gods for a good year.

The choosing of the next queen, unfortunately, could not be ignored. The girl shone in the golden afternoon light; saplings sprung from the earth at her feet, wrapping around her body to her head, enveloping it in a crown of apple blossoms Ide knew would rot before the night's end. She remembered seeing the girl at worship, gazing at Ide with bright, wet eyes. A true devotee. The gods would adore her.

Then night fell. Surrounded by smoky darkness and faces leaning towards her, glowing with feverish ecstasy and firelight, she could almost imagine it was a year ago when she performed her first ritual as Harvest Queen: ushering the death of her predecessor. Except she was now the predecessor. A new queen stood before her with a solemn face and fruit in hand, while harvesters waited steps away for her to fall. The world come full circle.

The girl offered Ide the final, most sacred apple, last of the last season, kept by the gods in holy preservation in the old queen's earth-brown blood. Three queens joined together in one brief moment: life, limbo, and death. Ide was so close to death she could almost feel the blades at her throat, taste it in the apple's sticky surface.

Except, the instant the apple touched Ide's lips, it blackened.

The whole fruit rotted in her hand before her teeth could break the bloody skin, melting strangely dark through her fingers and staining her white robes. Silence tumbled across the square. Even the bonfire faltered in its snap. She felt the remnants, wet around her mouth, and licked her lips. Blackberry?

The villagers reeled, and Ide felt their burgeoning horror as she let the pulpous fruit fall with a resounding splat at her feet. The flesh that spilled out wasn't crisp white, but a bubbling purple.

"What's happening?"

"Did the gods—?"

"Have they rejected her?"

"She's cursed!"

"She's ruined us all!"

Anger bloomed through the crowd with a crackling tension. A stench of spiced cider and apples that burned her nose and throat filled the air, as the gods' fury poured into her lungs.

Someone lunged, and the rest of the crowd surged with them, commanded by unseen forces. They would tear her apart to appease the gods, a desperate appeal for forgiveness for offering a spoiled queen.

Ide stumbled back, coughing and gasping as she searched for escape from the surrounding fury.

Save me, she pleaded to the sky, praying to anything but the gods whose hate bore down on her, phantom teeth at her neck. Hadn't Ora said to pray to her?

She wished she could see Ora before she died.

As she prayed, a tart, achingly familiar scent began drowning out the cider and applewood ash. The bonfire flared, and as if summoned by Ide's prayers, her attendant appeared.

She was much changed from the woman who'd held Ide so gently the night before.

Ora cut through the stricken crowd in a swirl of brambles and thorns, clothed in black—and to Ide's fascination, a deep reddish-purple stained her eyes and hands. The same liquid, Ide realized, dripping down her own skin and robes.

What is she?

"A goddess of a different sort," Ora answered, as if Ide had spoken aloud. She reached out with more joy than Ide had ever seen gracing her face. The air was choked with a fog of dizzyingly sharp scents, and the blackberry brambles broke through the platform, consuming the ground and forcing the villagers back towards the bonfire. One by one, the waiting barrels of cider rolled into the flames.

"You said you wouldn't let me die," Ide said, gazing in awe.

Ora laughed. "I promised, didn't I? So here I am," she said, with a low bow. "I will never abandon my queen."

With a twirl of her wrist, one of the brambles stretched towards Ide, weaving itself into a circlet of deep green leaves set with blossoms and clusters of blackberries like jewels. Ora shifted hesitantly, as if waiting for permission to approach. How could Ide refuse? She returned the smile, and immediately Ora stood so close that Ide felt her breath against her cheek.

"May I?" she asked aloud.

Ide nodded, fighting back a blush as Ora laid the circlet on her head. They kissed, soft and sweetly while the world fell to chaos around them. As they embraced, the red dripping down Ide's robes darkened to deep purple to match her lover's colors.

When Ide drew back, she relished in the last smear of red coating Ora's lips.

"Shall we go, my queen?" Ora asked.

"Gladly, my love," Ide replied, and followed the blackberry goddess off the platform and safely down a thorn-lined path.

The two departed hand-in-hand into the wilder world, as the village and the straight-rowed orchards and their shrieking, starving gods disappeared behind them, consumed by blackberry brambles.

CHAPTER SEVEN

A COLD ROOM
NEWTON

M eredith stood at the window, watching the late afternoon snow as it slowly collected along the fence line outside the hospital. It seemed the world had drained of all color. The black, wrought iron gate that read Witton Memorial, now rimmed with snow, perfectly matched the white cap, cuffs, and apron she wore over her dark gown. All of which precisely mirrored the plush white pillows and gray woolen blankets draped over Judge Taylor who lay unconscious in the bed behind her. The old man's breath came in ragged, wheezing huffs.

The honorable Judge Joseph Taylor had been something of a local celebrity for decades and, despite his advanced years, had continued to preside over his bench until three weeks ago when he'd been rushed to the hospital coughing up blood. The doctors had concluded it to be pneumonia. Being a man held in high regard within the community, along with his long-standing annual donations to the hospital, earned Judge Taylor his own private room, complete with a round-the-clock nurse. Unfortunately, his condition had failed to improve despite the added perks.

Meredith relished her shifts watching over the Judge. He required little actual care and slept often, which allowed her time to sit and read in peace, a luxury that shifts on the more hectic lower floors would never afford. She was fresh out of college, and still savored any opportunity to bury her nose in a book. At times she would even read to him aloud, although she was never really sure if he heard her or not. As he never complained nor endorsed the activity, she presumed it permissible.

She'd seen enough in her short time there to know Judge Taylor would not be leaving the hospital. Not upright anyway. She'd miss the quiet shifts, but watching this proud man deteriorate day after day had filled her with melancholy. She'd seen his friends and family come and go. They prayed for peace, they prayed for his suffering to come to an end, they thanked him for the life he had given them and for the life of service he had lived. Most often, they offered assurances in abundance that all would be well, and he was free to go to God.

And yet, he persisted. Occasionally, he would cough himself awake and beg for water, which he took like a man fresh from the desert and dying of thirst. Later he would roll over onto his side and piss the bed, the floor, and anything else within the vicinity. Other days he would lie awake for hours, just as lucid and articulate as at any time in his life, albeit struggling to breathe. Mostly, he just slept.

At six o'clock, Dr. Morris entered the room as he did every evening, loudly clearing his throat as if to announce his arrival. It was intended to prevent startling her from her reading, as he had done on two previous occasions. His grey beard and charcoal-colored suit expertly blended in with the monochromacy of the room. Meredith turned from the window and busied herself about the wash basin, as was her custom, wetting a rag should the doctor require one. Both doctor and nurse had familiarized themselves with each other's idiosyncrasies.

"And how is our patient today?" Dr. Morris inquired.

"For lack of a better word: unresponsive," Meredith replied somewhat drearily. "He hasn't eaten or asked for anything to drink to my knowledge. No bowel movements either."

"He's been given laudanum for the pain now," Dr. Morris said, looking down at the frail figure with the labored breath lying before him. He produced a small bottle of the reddish-brown liquid from his coat pocket and handed it to Meredith. "If he complains of pain or has another one of his coughing spells, just give him two teaspoons."

"Yes, sir," she said, depositing the vial into the pouch of her apron.

"I suspect the Judge won't be with us much longer," he said solemnly.

"Yes, sir," she said. "It's quite cold in this room, Doctor. Should it be so cold in here?"

"The cool air soothes the lungs. Helps with the congestion and the inflammation. I don't think he's in any discomfort at this point," Dr. Morris said, detecting the concern in her voice.

"I see," she said, "Thank you, sir."

"He's a good man, Meredith. The world will be a poorer place for his passing."

"Yes, Doctor," she said. "I quite agree."

"I've been told you read to him at times, is that correct?"

"Yes, sir," Meredith blushed. She was unaware anyone even knew. "I hope that's not against hospital regulations."

"No, I don't suppose there's any harm to it," the Doctor chuckled. "What are you reading today?"

"Romeo and Juliet."

"Ah, good. A love story," Dr. Morris said, "Let's try to avoid the tragedies."

"You *do* realize that Romeo and Juliet both die, don't you?" Meredith asked sheepishly. "Along with Mercutio, Tybalt, Paris and Lady Montague."

"Well, I never was much for Shakespeare," Dr. Morris admitted. "Ring me if anything changes. Have a pleasant evening, Meredith."

"Yes, Doctor," she said. "You do so as well."

"And a good evening to you, Judge Taylor, sir," the doctor called, waving goodbye as he exited the room.

Alone again at last, Meredith retrieved the book from her bag and drew a chair up to the side of the bed. She read silently at first, but the powerful prose soon found her quietly acting out scenes all on her own. A certain passage from the play struck her as peculiar, causing her to pause and read it out loud once more.

"*When he shall die, take him and cut him out in little stars, and he will make the face of heaven so fine that all the world will be in love with night and pay no worship to the garish sun,*" she recited the line from Juliet a second time.

"I can see him."

The words startled her so severely that she gasped and dropped the book. Judge Taylor had opened his eyes and was staring directly at her.

"Sir, are you all right? Can I get you anything?" she asked, still shaking.

"I can see him," he repeated.

"Who can you see, sir?"

"Death," he replied.

"Death?"

"Death," the Judge said. "He stands thus, just over your shoulder."

Cautiously, Meredith glanced back over her right shoulder, and then the left. The room was still cold, but it was also still empty, save for the two of them. Satisfied there was no one else in the room, she turned her attention back to the Judge.

"You say you can see Death, sir?"

"Death lies on her like an untimely frost, upon the sweetest flower of all the field," he said.

Meredith recognized another line from Romeo and Juliet, the scene where Capulet spoke of Juliet being deceased. Her one-woman recital had apparently stirred the Judge from his stupor. She hastily thumbed through the book and found the corresponding passage.

"O lamentable day! Oh, woeful time," she read, continuing the play.

"Death, that hath taken her hence to make me wail, ties up my tongue and will not let me speak," Judge Taylor recited the next verse.

"Come, is the bride ready to go to church?" Meredith continued.

"Ready to go, but never to return," the Judge said, recounting the play perfectly. *"O son! The night before thy wedding day hath death lain with thy wife. There she lies, flower as she was, deflowered by him."*

"Very impressive, sir," she exclaimed. "I had no idea you were such a fan of the theater. You certainly know your Shakespeare."

"I can see him," the Judge again said solemnly.

"Shakespeare?" she asked curiously.

"Death," he replied.

"You can still see Death?"

He nodded.

"And what does Death look like?" she inquired.

"There are stars…no," the Judge began, "there are…constellations within his wings. He is beautiful."

As soon as he had spoken, a fresh coughing fit overcame him, causing his body to spasm. The bed shook violently beneath him, blood and spittle spattering the blanket. A horrible rattle arose within his throat. The Judge collapsed back into his pillow, exhaled one long, last wheezing breath, and died.

Meredith sat in the chair, silently transfixed by the surreal scene that had just played out between them. How long she sat there, she would never quite know. When she finally rose, she crossed over to the Judge, took a white, cotton handkerchief from her apron pocket, and gently dabbed the blood from his lips and chin. Holding the cloth up to the light, the crimson stain stood out in stark contrast to the rest of the dull, uncolored room. She cradled the handkerchief in her hand like a delicate flower, a bright red rose somehow in bloom amidst a snowdrift.

Dr. Morris sat with Meredith while the orderlies removed Judge Taylor's body, cleaned the room, and changed the linens. The speed and efficiency with which they worked astonished her, until the grim reality that the reason they were so good was because they had to do it so often settled over her like a pall. Within a matter of minutes, the room had been emptied, swept, sterilized, and prepped for its next occupant.

"Did he have any last words?" Dr. Morris inquired as they sat.

"He quoted some Shakespeare," she said.

"Did he now?"

"I was reading aloud from Romeo and Juliet, and he recited a few lines from the play."

"Fascinating," Dr. Morris said. "Did he say anything with any legal ramifications? Any deathbed confessions or last-minute changes to will and testament? Anything of that sort?"

"No," she replied, then added, "He said he could see Death."

"Come again?"

"He said he could see Death," she repeated. "Said it was standing there in the room with us. Right behind me."

"My, that must have been frightful," the Doctor exclaimed.

"Not really," she admitted. "He said it was beautiful. Actually, he said, '*He* is beautiful.' Meaning Death, that is. Those were his last words exactly."

"Positively chilling," Dr. Morris shuddered.

"There was no malice in it," she said. "He seemed almost...happy."

"Happy to see the specter of Death looming over him?" Dr. Morris asked pointedly. "I hardly think the poor man would be happy to see Death, Meredith. Let's keep that little nugget of information just between you and I, shall we? I mean, what would his family think if we told them that he was happy to see beautiful Death in his final moments?"

"Yes, sir, I understand," Meredith conceded, then, "May I ask you a somewhat personal question, Dr. Morris?"

"Of course, dear."

"Is Death really so terrible? Is Death not simply part of being alive?"

"This is a hospital, Meredith. What do you think we do here?" Dr. Morris chided her. "Our mission is to heal, to battle back and conquer death. Death is the enemy we wage war against every day."

"I understand the purpose of a hospital," she said plainly, "but what about those who have no hope of recovery, those who cannot be saved? Why must they be made to suffer? Is Death not a mercy for them?"

"Ah, I see," Dr. Morris said. He reached into his coat pocket and offered her a butterscotch candy, a peace offering, which she reluctantly accepted. "In our profession there will be countless occasions when a merciful death may appear to be the most humane option. The only option, at times even. I've seen patients beg for death, pray for it even.

"But we do not trade in merciful death. It is not for us to take away that which God, and only God, has given. Thou shalt not kill, right? So, we clean and dress, and we stitch and sew, and we rail against the dying of the light, even at times when we know, beyond any shadow of a doubt, that all of our time and efforts will ultimately prove futile. This is what it means to be a doctor. Or a nurse, for that matter. It is our curse when we fail, and our blessing when we succeed."

"You speak very eloquently, Doctor," Meredith admitted. "You would do Shakespeare proud."

"Thank you, you're too kind. The only theatre I've ever performed in is an operating room," Dr. Morris said, "And those truly were all tragedies."

"Thank you, Doctor. I appreciate your insights."

"Think nothing of it," he replied. He reached again into his coat pocket and produced a small, timeworn Bible, which he presented to her. "Please, take this. It has provided me answers in times of uncertainty."

Again, she reluctantly accepted.

"I could arrange for you to take a few days off, if you feel you require some time away. I'm sure it would be no trouble at all," he offered.

"No, thank you," she said. "I'm fine. Truly I am. Honestly, I would rather be here than anywhere else."

"Are you sure?" he asked.

"Yes, sir," she affirmed, "As you said, this is both our curse and our blessing."

"It is, indeed," he smiled.

The next few days passed quickly for Meredith. The unusual encounter with Judge Taylor, and the subsequent conversation with Doctor Morris afterwards, replayed in her mind over and over again. They somehow seemed to be the two most meaningful exchanges of her adult life, both centering around life and death, both citing centuries-old texts. She read Romeo and Juliet again from cover to cover, then spent hours poring over the Bible that Dr. Morris had given her, notating any verses that referenced death or dying. One line in particular stuck with her. A passage that stirred something within her, even if she did not fully understand what it meant: *"For we do not wrestle against flesh and blood, but against the rulers, against the authorities, against the cosmic powers over this present darkness, against the spiritual forces of evil in the heavenly places." – Ephesians 6:12*

She found herself spending more and more time at the hospital. She would linger before and after her shifts, idly chatting with assorted hospital staff and even patients at times. Especially elderly patients or anyone the nurses had rumored to be terminal. Anyone articulate enough or reasonably comfortable with discussing the various philosophical aspects of mortality had her full attention.

The small bottle of laudanum that Dr. Morris had given her for Judge Taylor had also earned her attention. No one had mentioned it during the flurry of activity that followed the Judge's passing, so she simply kept it. She knew it was regularly prescribed for headaches, which she suffered often, and thought it only practical that she utilized it. Judge Taylor was certainly no longer in need of it. She found the medication, although terribly bitter to the taste, worked wonders for her headaches, as well as generally improving her mood overall.

Her mood was exceptionally elevated as she reported for her evening shift, exactly one week after the Judge's passing. She had traded shifts with another girl who needed the night off to attend a wedding. Meredith had been happy to oblige, as the night shifts were generally quieter, with less busy work to be done. She had a slight migraine in the morning and decided to self-medicate with the laudanum. Though tempered, the headache persisted into the afternoon, so she opted to take another slightly larger dose before her shift started. As it was, she began work that evening feeling delightfully light-headed.

The hospital proved to be uncharacteristically dull that afternoon as dusk faded into twilight, which swiftly deepened into night. Meredith went about her labors with peaceful proficiency, happily filling out paperwork, checking supplies, and following up on the few slumbering patients in her care. She had just sat down to read for a bit when the head nurse, a woman named Agnes, called her name.

"Meredith," Agnes called from behind her desk at the end of the hall. "Do you have a moment, please?"

"Yes, ma'am," she called, stuffing the book back into her apron and heading to the desk.

"Could you be a dear and help out the orderlies up on Six?" she asked. "Seems they're dreadfully short-handed this evening. Something about a big wedding happening tonight down at the Cape. I'm guessing you and I were the only ones *not* invited. Besides, there's nothing happening down here tonight, praise God. First slow night in weeks."

"Yes, ma'am," she said. "Right away."

The sixth floor was practically deserted. Two grumpy orderlies and one very tired-looking nurse were doing their best to restock the closets, empty the trash bins, and handle all the other basic necessities of maintaining a hospital ward. Meredith was hastily handed a stack of clean linens and ordered to empty any trash or bedpans and change the sheets of any room in need, starting at the end of the hall and working her way back up.

She walked down the corridor to the corner apartment, which she knew all too well. It was the private suite Judge Taylor had occupied up until a week ago. It was still bereft of color, but the room itself was now in complete disarray. The two small chairs had been set against the far wall at odd angles, used tissues littered the nightstand, the bed was unmade, the pillows rumpled and askew. One of the gray woolen blankets lay on the floor in a heap. Meredith frowned at the shameless desecration of this space that, to her, had become almost sacred.

Instantly determined to put right that which had been wronged, she attacked the mess with vigor. The trash was collected and placed in the bin, the furniture wiped down and returned to its rightful positions, the bed stripped, straightened, and remade. She even cleaned the windows and the floor. When she finished, the suite was spotless, and every aspect of the room had been arranged to exactly mirror the way she remembered it. It was then that Death walked through the door.

A solitary figure, tall and lean, stood in the doorway wearing a floor-length, midnight blue dressing gown. His face was pallid and gaunt with high cheekbones that framed dark, deep-set eyes, and a sullen expression. A thick mane of coal black hair curled down about his temples and rested upon his slender shoulders.

He is beautiful, Judge Taylor's words rang out in the back of her mind.

Meredith stood frozen, unsure of what to do or say. After a brief moment, she finally managed to blurt out, "I...I cleaned the room."

Death silently shrugged his shoulders and spread his wings. They filled the space, their long, blue-black feathers, the shape of sabers. Deep within their folds, an entire cosmos of stars slowly rotated.

There are...constellations, came the Judge's words.

Mesmerized, Meredith stood in awe of the figure before her. She trembled, not with fear, but wonder. Her face was flushed. She felt warm. She had asked a dying man what Death looked like. She had asked a doctor if Death was truly an enemy. She had purposely loitered in the company of those close to Death, as if she might somehow catch a glimpse or hear a step. She had invited this presence, and now here he stood before her.

"I...I..." she stammered, unable to formulate any cohesive thought.

Death approached her. With pale fingers he unfurled his robe and allowed it to slip from his shoulders and fall to the floor. His body was a sculpted marble statue, the anatomy perfect and hairless, colored in mottled gray and white, the muscles hard as chiseled stone. His lips were red, the only drop of color inhabiting the entire room. He opened his arms in welcome, his sex erect.

Meredith unpinned the white nurse's cap from her hair and let it fall to the floor. She unknotted the apron from about her waist, slipped it over her head, and allowed it to join the cap at her feet. Unable to take her eyes off the visage of Death, she fumbled with the clasps on her frock. In frustration, she yanked the garment apart, popping several buttons and tearing the collar in the process. Awkwardly, she kicked off her shoes, shed her slip, and eagerly joined with Death in naked embrace. Together they fell onto the bed, their passion ablaze.

Wrapping her legs around him, she pressed her hot mouth to his and drank deeply. The room fell away into nothingness, the hospital with it. They made love by starlight in the deepest recesses of the night sky. The

Moon hid its face, shamed by their state of undress, while comets sped past in trailing tails of sparks that lit their bodies aglow. Meredith felt as if the waves of the ocean were breaking upon her, cascading over her again and again and again. She gazed upon the cool, sweet face of Death and knew she would never feel more alive than she felt right now, tightly entwined in his alabaster arms.

The ebb and flow of their desire gently waned. The stars in her eyes proceeded to spin, but their pace gradually slowed. She had laid herself bare and Death had taken her, until there was nothing left. Her entire being was wholly spent. She closed her eyes as he released her from his grip, and she collapsed backwards into the black.

Meredith awoke, shivering and alone, upon the bed of the sixth-floor hospital suite. The room was still as bitter cold as it had been a week prior, a fact made all the more severe by her being nude. She rolled off the bed to the floor and frantically scrambled about for her clothing, which seemed to be strewn everywhere. She dressed herself as quickly as possible, fear welling up inside her. Her dark blue frock was ripped and missing buttons. Her plain, white cap had brown smudges on it from where it appeared to have been stepped on.

The mirror above the washbasin was less than kind. Face red with embarrassment, hair unkempt and out of order, clothing soiled and wrinkled, the best she'd be able to manage at this point would be a slightly disheveled mess. She splashed some cold water on her cheeks and took several deep breaths. Steeling her resolve, she peeked her head out the door and peered down the dim corridor, fully expecting to see the tired nurse and angry orderlies staring back at her in obvious disgust.

But they were not. The hallway was completely deserted. No one had seen her. She wheeled back around to face the cold and empty room. No more Angel of Death. No more blood red lips. No more starlit Milky Way in which to swim. She was once more alone and, apparently, forgotten.

"Am I dead?" she quietly asked no one in particular.

A loud clatter from somewhere down the hall came as her only response. Nervously, she stuck her head back out the doorway once more. At the end of the hall, one of the orderlies had dropped an empty trash bin, one of several he attempted to carry all at once. He noticed Meredith looking at him from the far end of the corridor.

"Hey," he called to her, looking annoyed. "Are you going to spend all night working on that one room? I need a hand down here."

"Just finishing up," she called back. "Be right there."

She hurriedly smoothed out the blankets on the bed, then double-checked her face in the mirror.

"Why? Why am I still here?" she asked her reflection, fighting back tears, "Where did you go?"

Denied a response, she straightened her cap and apron, exited the suite, and headed back down the hall.

The next few days passed slowly for Meredith. The intensity of her encounter with Death, and her subsequent abandonment, had left her mind reeling. To her credit, she managed to keep up appearances. She ate, she slept, she spoke, and she showed up for every shift, never letting on that anything out of the ordinary had ever happened at all. But it had.

Any and every chance she got, she would find an excuse, or even fabricate some reason, to venture up to the sixth floor. She would quickly slink down to the corner suite and peer inside, hoping her gaze would be met by the deep, dark eyes of her lover, Death. But each time, she was met with cold, empty disappointment. She sought no comfort from either Shakespeare or Scripture. Her headaches became more frequent, and more severe.

A full week after the incident, she managed to trade with another nurse in order to procure a shift on the sixth floor. She bristled with anticipation at the prospect of having multiple opportunities to stand within her chosen sanctuary. She stowed her coat, checked in with the head nurse, and raced upstairs. As she bounded up the steps two at a time, she rounded a corner and nearly collided with Dr. Morris.

"Whoa there," he bellowed. "What seems to be the rush?"

"I'm so sorry, doctor," she apologized breathlessly. "Just didn't want to be late for my shift."

"Punctuality is an admirable characteristic," the Doctor replied. "But not when it comes at the expense of safety."

"Yes, sir. So sorry."

"Meredith, I hate to even ask, but have you seen anything or anyone… suspicious-looking hereabouts lately?"

She froze. Would a naked man with dark-as-night angel wings qualify as suspicious?

"What do you mean?" she asked.

"I was just speaking with Agnes, and she said there have been a number of thefts reported recently," he said. "I know you're here quite a bit and I know how observant you are. I was wondering if you'd seen or heard anything."

"Is that so?" Meredith replied, "No, I hadn't heard. What did she say has gone missing?"

"Well, nothing too valuable," Dr. Morris began. "One of the other nurses apparently had some clothing stolen from her locker. And one of the stewards reported a few vials of laudanum gone missing."

"Come to think of it," she said, "I was on Six about a week ago and one of the orderlies did strike me as a bit…off. I didn't see him steal anything, but he was very rude. He also dropped a trash can which made a terrible noise while patients were trying to sleep."

"Thank you, I'll mention it to Agnes," Dr. Morris said. "There's no place for rude and clumsy here at Witton Memorial. Now you'd best be along. I'd hate to be the reason for your tardiness after praising your punctuality."

"Yes, sir," Meredith smiled. "Have a good day."

"And a good day to you." The Doctor waved as he plodded off down the steps.

Meredith checked in on Six and promptly set about her work. Once her usual tasks were completed and nothing more was immediately required of her, she slipped away towards the end of the hall. Holding her breath, she said a silent prayer, and once more stepped into the suite.

A woman lay sleeping in the bed.

The bed where Meredith, just seven days prior, had lain with Death itself and tasted the infinite, was now occupied by a blonde woman of no more than twenty years old. A green glass vase filled with blue and yellow flowers adorned the nightstand. A pink dressing gown had been lazily thrown over one of the chairs. The young lady slept fitfully, tossing and turning about. Sweat beaded at her brow. She was clearly suffering from a fever. Meredith wondered if the girl was dreaming and, if so, of what? Or whom?

Without warning, the girl's eyes fluttered open. She sat up with a start at the sight of Meredith standing over her. A vicious coughing fit instantly followed, nearly choking the girl. Meredith fetched a glass of water from the table and held the girl's hair until the fit subsided enough for her to get a drink.

"I'm very sorry," the young woman said as she regained her voice. "You frightened me."

"No apologies necessary. My name is Meredith."

"I'm Rebecca," the girl offered. "You're a nurse here, yes?"

"I am," Meredith replied.

"Could you please have them turn the heat up?" Rebecca asked as she laid back in bed. "It's so cold in this room."

"The cool air soothes the lungs," Meredith informed her. "It's good for congestion and inflammation. I could get you another blanket, if you'd like?"

"Yes, please. Is there anything you can give me for this damned cough?" she asked. "It's making my lungs hurt so bad."

"Are you in a great deal of pain?" Meredith asked.

"Yes. I've been coughing for three days straight. My chest feels like it's on fire. Meanwhile the rest of me is freezing."

"I do have something that may help," Meredith told her.

She produced a small amber colored bottle and a spoon from her apron pocket, and moved to the bedside. She measured out a teaspoon of the reddish-brown liquid and held it up to Rebecca's lips. The girl sat up, sipped at the medicine, then made a sour face.

"That tastes horrible," she said.

"It's very bitter, I know. But I promise it will help your cough and help you sleep." Meredith poured the girl another spoonful. Rebecca winced as she downed it but did not object. Meredith then administered a third spoonful. And a fourth.

"What is it?" Rebecca asked.

"It's a love potion," Meredith said as she held the bottle up to her own lips and took a long, healthy swig. "You'll see."

"A love potion? What's that supposed to mean?"

"Are you familiar with Romeo and Juliet?"

"The play?" Rebecca asked.

"Death lies on her like an untimely frost, upon the sweetest flower of all the field," Meredith said as she took another pull from the amber-hued bottle.

"I feel dizzy." Rebecca laid her head back onto the pillows.

"Can you see him?" Meredith asked.

"What? Can I see what?" Rebecca asked. Her words were slurred.

"Can you see Death?"

"Death…" Rebecca said. Her eyelids drooped.

"I can see him." Meredith smiled as she drank from the bottle once more, this time draining its contents altogether. "He is beautiful.

CHAPTER EIGHT

BARED BONES

Maddie Bowen-Smyth

The train deposits her on the fringes of a dusty main street. Darkness yawns beyond a dim oil lantern that marks the short path from station to saloon. A group of men cluster outside the establishment; one of them, fingers hooked around a grimy flagon, calls out, "Where are you headed at this hour, darlin'?"

Marlene clutches the telegram in one hand and her weather-beaten trunk in the other. "I'm looking for—" Her spectacles slip down her nose while she squints. She's read it several times over, so she's not sure why she needs to check. "Ashdown Manor."

A collective shiver ripples through them. One man takes a long drag from a cigarette. "What business takes you up that way, miss?"

Sweat beads along her back despite the cool evening air. "Employment," Marlene replies.

"Horse and buggy goes to Crookston in the morning," the first man offers, gesturing in a vaguely westward direction. "It'd take you near enough. It's a couple hours' walk, otherwise."

"Thank you." Replacing the telegram in the folds of her skirt, Marlene adjusts her hat and walks past the men. Flummoxed, they leave her in peace.

The path out of Valentine leads to gloomy shadows stretched wide. Marlene picks her way through them, the silence settling around her shoulders. It's comforting, really; any time spent in silence is time valued. The quiet is punctuated, every now and then, by murmurs and whispers—sounds trailing after her footfalls, curling spidery tendrils around her ankles.

Marlene ignores them. She's getting better at that.

The Ashdown Manor, in the end, is not particularly prepossessing. The house bulges inwards as if holding on tight to a badly-guarded secret. The front doors swell with age; time's careful attention warps the windows; the sign crumbles into the pathway. Vines creep towards the rafters, illuminated by lanterns scattered around the house's edge. The gate seems to be held shut by the sheer force of its disrepair.

She bumps the gate until it scrapes open with weary reluctance, then slips into the main courtyard where the manor looms large above her. Perhaps, in a fit of optimism and opportunity, it was meant to mark the beginning of a legacy.

But not all legacies are good ones.

Marlene raps at the door, gray dust smearing across her gloves. There's a series of odd noises: a shout, shuffling, jangling, muffled cursing.

The door creaks inwards. A shock of black hair appears around a very winsome face; the lady of the manor, Marlene assumes, from her proud bearing and affronted expression. She dons a bicycle jacket hastily buttoned over a men's union suit. Her partially laced boots are more soil than leather.

Marlene clears her throat. "Mrs. Ashdown, is it? I—"

"Who the bloody hell are you?" The woman runs a hand through her hair, dislodging it into even more of a curled freefall. "Whatever it is, I'm not interested."

She pauses for a beat. "I'm Marlene Schüttmann. You—sent a telegram."

There's a startled silence. "Oh, *you*. I wasn't expecting you for days. I thought you were coming from New York."

"You *did* say it was urgent," Marlene observes.

"I suppose I did." With a sharp, breathy laugh, the woman steps aside. "Fine. You'd better come in, then."

Marlene crosses the threshold. Whispers rise up on either side, leaving a sticky, dragging nausea in their wake. They aren't always so bad, not now that she's used to them. Euphoria, satisfaction, hopefulness—*those* are heady, bolstering, almost intoxicating. Sadness, anger, regret; those pull at the threads inside oneself, unravelling what they find there. But this—

It isn't quite either. It lurks; it envelops; it drips like hot candle wax.

"So, Mrs. Ashdown—" Marlene glances down a darkened hallway. "Did you inherit this house?"

"Call me Lola." She forges ahead into what might generously be called a parlor, though most of its furniture is either covered in begrimed sheets or in a state of disassembly. "And yes, through marriage. Then my husband went and died on me, so here we are. It wasn't *as* awful until all this started."

"Ah." Marlene follows after her. "I'm very sorry."

"No need for that." Lola heads straight for a drinks trolley in the corner, which is somehow the most spotless item in the room. *Moderately alarming*, Marlene thinks.

Mrs. Ashdown throws a knowing look over her shoulder. "A spot of gin? You get used to the tug, eventually, but liquor certainly helps."

"I don't drink on the job," Marlene demurs politely. "What do you mean by 'the tug?'"

"It's worse nearer to the cellar." Lola pours herself a healthy glass. "Now, I'm sure you're well-versed in fucked up family tradition in your line of work, excusing my language. But have you ever heard of something as ludicrous as transporting a *crypt* across the Atlantic? Well, its contents, that is. They were told the stonework was too heavy."

Marlene sets her trunk down on the least offensive patch of rug. A beetle skitters into a crack between floorboards. She notices a wedge of dirt swelling underneath it. "That does sound somewhat…ghoulish."

"And *how*." Lola drains half the glass in one swig. "The bones of ancestral Ashdowns, from Europe to the Nebraskan Sandhills. Not to shit on my late husband's ancestors, but something about it isn't right. Or their crypt, for that matter, given the house is now collapsing on top of it."

Marlene kneels down next to the swelling dirt, tracing a finger along it. "Displacement can have long-reaching effects. It's only natural. Resting places don't take kindly to being disturbed."

"You advertised that you assist," Lola says, "in banishing restless spirits, or whatever it is that's getting itself in a tizzy."

"Not spirits, precisely," Marlene replies softly. The whispers frazzle under her fingertips. "Bones."

Lola waves an airy hand. "Honestly, I don't care what your methods are." She frowns. "Sorry, was it Martha? Anyway, as long as you do *something*. I feel I've been thrust into the position of sentinel of this moldering midden, so I just…need a solution."

She nods. "I believe I can help. It's…" Amidst the murmurs, the nausea persists. Marlene adjusts her spectacles. "The best term I have for it is 'bone song.'"

Midway through pouring another glass of gin, Lola guffaws. She settles into a dirt-stained chair and kicks her feet up on a decaying table. "What on earth is a '*bone* song?'" She wiggles her eyebrows. "It sounds a little suggestive, doesn't it?"

Marlene reddens. "No matter your stance on spirits or ghosts or, well, the immortal soul—it's often thought that something is left behind in people's bones. An imprint. A shadow. It doesn't have much of them left, so it's uncontrolled. And if it's disturbed, well…" She glances around. "There's enough there that it can come alive, so to speak."

This time, Lola's reaction is cautious. "Alive?"

Marlene removes one of her gloves. "When it's agitated like this, it reverberates."

She presses a hand down on the exposed soil. A great rumbling lurches beneath, thrumming in time with Marlene's pulse. Fissures of dirt begin pushing up from neighboring floorboards, until one cracks entirely from the force of it.

The whispers grow louder and louder. They don't have a form, a real language, at least not one that Marlene has ever been able to discern. Perhaps it's projection, but when they're this loud, she can almost feel the words they'd have, if they had any to give. *No,* comes the whisper. *It isn't fair. It's never fair. Please, let us—*

The words stutter to a stop as Lola threads her fingers through Marlene's and gently prizes her hand away. "I think…I get the idea."

Her cheeks are pink from the gin, her breath sour, her hair rumpled from disturbed sleep. But she *is* very beautiful, in a way that gravitates, and it's distracting. Underneath all that, there's a pallor to her, a tremble to her hand.

Marlene stops, swallowing. "I apologize for cracking your floorboard."

"No apology necessary." Lola pulls Marlene to her feet. "I can't promise particularly nice lodgings, but you'll have a roof over your head while you solve this mess. And, of course, due recompense. Do we have a deal?"

"Naturally," Marlene says. "Or I wouldn't have spent several days on a train to get here." Dubious, she surveys the parlor. "It…isn't all like this, is it?"

Lola tuts with distaste. "Most of the ground floor is. But that's the benefit of a manor, darling. Plenty of space." Retrieving the half empty gin bottle, Lola swings Marlene's trunk over her shoulder and sets off towards the stairs. "Onwards and upwards!"

The second floor is much less dirt-ridden. The floor still bulges and creaks, the windows buckle open from creeping vines outside, and the candlestick flickers and sputters in a phantom breeze. Lola brings her to a chamber a little way down the hall, throwing open the door with a flourish. "I hope it's to your liking, Martha."

Marlene peers inside. "Thank you." It's oddly desolate, for a house so big. "It's just you here?"

"Who'd want to work in this shithole? Those days are long gone." Lola dumps the trunk at the foot of a blessedly clean four poster bed. "I'll be just down the hall. The kitchen is downstairs, but it's awful at night, so I keep some things up in the drawing room. Please do help yourself." The tremor, mostly hidden, returns for a flittering moment. "If it's all the same to you, I'll withdraw for now. I was having such a pleasant dream until *somebody* knocked on my door."

"Good night, Mrs. Ashdown," Marlene mumbles, eyeing her carefully. "They can't hurt you up here. Further from the ground, there's less reach."

"We'll see." Her smile is strained. "And it's Lola." With that, she sweeps away, disappearing into the swirl of darkness.

The whispers are still here, but quieter. Marlene kicks off her muddied clothes, collapsing into the bed with a faint sigh. It's certainly more comfortable than a cramped train car with her trunk squashed into one corner.

And yes, all right, she's in a collapsing manor with a drunken widow who calls her Martha, but there have been worse jobs. There have definitely been ruder, less attractive clients.

Marlene doesn't typically dream; there's too much that grasps at her in the waking world for that, and that suits her just fine. Still, dreamless or not, her sleep isn't always restful. Sometimes the thrum of the song creeps in, driving its burrs in deep. Sometimes she wakes in a cold sweat, an unexplained ache trailing along her spine.

Sometimes, less often—though not *that* rarely—she's woken by wailing.

Mrs. Ashdown's chamber isn't far down the hallway, obscured by inky shadows. Moonlight slants in through a small gap in her drapes.

Lola seems caught in her own somnolent terror. Her body jerks away from unseen threats; her breath is labored between the wails.

Marlene's job description isn't really meant to extend to the living, but—well, the living are usually rather invested in the bones she deals with, and bones incite all manner of complication. Skeletons rattling in closets are the least of her concerns.

So, Marlene settles into a wingback chair next to Mrs. Ashdown's bed. She hums a mostly forgotten tune, a vestige of something long-buried. It isn't good for much, but it blocks out the whispers. *The tug*, Lola had called it.

The crease smooths from Mrs. Ashdown's brow. She stills; her breath evens.

It isn't much, but small victories can be hard to come by, so it's wise to count them.

The whispers are softer in the morning light. Even the dirt has more of a rustic charm when paired with the yellowy glow filtering through the vines.

After returning to her own chamber, Marlene doesn't sleep much. Neither does Mrs. Ashdown, apparently, given that she saunters downstairs at roughly half past eleven, a tumbler in one hand and a cigarette in the other.

"Oh," Lola stares at her. "You're still here, Martha."

Marlene pulls on a pair of tattered gloves, pushing aside the biscuits she'd foraged. "This all does appear quite dire, so I thought I'd get to it. Shall I access the cellar?"

Mrs. Ashdown slumps against the kitchen counter. Her tight curls fall from their hastily erected chignon. She's exchanged the bicycle jacket for a three-piece lounge suit; given its fit, Marlene assumes it belongs to the late Mr. Ashdown. "Goodness, first thing in the morning?"

"The cellar?" Marlene presses.

Lola waves a hand. "Past the pantry." She peers at Marlene closely, her expression fuzzy from lack of sleep—and, more likely, the gin. "Are you certain you know what you're doing?"

"Of course." Marlene takes one last fortifying sip of tea, then gathers her things. "You did choose to hire me."

"It's just that you dress like a governess," Lola points out. "Not like somebody who solves hauntings. I've heard there's a lot of con artistry amongst Spiritualists."

"I'm not a Spiritualist. And it isn't a haunting," Marlene says. "You'd be able to tell the difference. More doors slamming and windows rattling, less dirt consuming the house."

The cellar door is held shut with a rusting farmer's rake; the original padlock, badly snapped, lies on the floor nearby. Marlene disentangles the rake and cautiously pushes open the necrosing door. The darkness sinks in its claws, despite the glow filtering into the rest of the house. Mud and moisture spread past her shoes.

"Disgusting," Lola remarks. "Should've burned this place down when I had the chance."

"Cremation *is* regarded as a worthy burial rite in many cultures," Marlene replies.

She hikes up her skirts, puts away her spectacles, and descends into the cellar's depths. Marlene doesn't bother with a lantern; like moth to flame, the song tends to track movement and light. She pins her skirts into a quick bustle, letting her footfalls grow silent. Trailing a gloved hand along the rotting wood of the cellar, she feels the hum. The thrill of the vibration. Tense and waiting.

Many believe that people's souls can inhabit the bones they leave behind—Marlene doesn't know if that's true, but there's certainly *something*, and whatever it is, it normally doesn't go gentle into the good night.

Behind her, there's a crash. "Bloody stairs."

Marlene clears her throat. "Mrs. Ashdown, you're very welcome to stay above ground."

"It's Lola," she answers. "And I'm quite looking forward to seeing your creepy bone shit, actually. It's going to be the highlight of my year, sad as that sounds."

"As you wish," Marlene says, and tries not to laugh as Lola's clanging continues. There's no room for immoderacy whilst on the job.

The cellar apparently once housed the Ashdown family's wine and liquor collection. Now, broken bottles litter the ground; the floor is sticky between all the mud. Marlene picks her way through the detritus. Everything smells saccharine, like fruit splitting open from rot.

"They moved the bones, you said?" Another set of stairs descends further into the dark. "From Europe?"

"*All* of them." Lola punctuates her derision with an edge of something unidentifiable. "My husband and his parents have only added to the collection since then. 'Too important to leave behind,' they said, but considering *this* is what came of it…"

Marlene stops. She wouldn't consider herself to be a particularly superstitious woman—bones and hauntings notwithstanding—but there's prudence in details. "If I may ask…"

"You may not." Lola steps around her. "They were all in coffins, you know, not just loose bags of bones. The cellar became their new crypt, once the house was built. But then…"

There's a crunch underfoot. Rotting wood peels away from Marlene's shoe. "Perhaps the coffins couldn't hold."

The lower area of the cellar is clammy; stale, powdery air presses in on all sides. From her pockets, Marlene retrieves her bag of tools. Lola lingers behind her, silent now. The whispers fill the gaps, as they're wont to do, and she can almost feel the shape of them—*alone, abandoned, so dark, no light. Where? Where?*

"I never knew what the point was," Lola wonders in the stillness. "Bones crumble to nothing in the end."

"We've always had a preoccupation with them," Marlene murmurs. She's had occasion to read treatises on the subject, over the years. "Some say winter's severity can be determined through a goose's breast bone. Some think wishbones hung above doorways will draw in a worthy suitor." She traces the shapes in the dark until she comes to what must be a coffin's lid. "Some believe that bones and incantations can control the weather. Some insist the word bonfire came from 'bone-fire;' a midsummer's sacrifice." Gingerly, she lifts the lid. "And, of course, there's a long-held legend that if you take a bone from its gravesite, it will torment you until it's returned."

Mrs. Ashdown is quiet for a long moment. "Are you saying I have to take these bones to fucking Europe?"

The broken coffin lid screeches with effort. The bones inside are desiccated, strangely sun-bleached, mercifully stripped of all flesh. These are old, by the looks, centuries old. It's dark, near impossible to see, but it's not the sense she needs. A quick scan indicates they might be the oldest bones here; it's always useful to go about things chronologically.

Marlene's heart quakes. It's a visceral discomfort, as ancient as mortality itself. The whispers rage in her ears, seek purchase in her ribcage, bloom outwards down her arms and legs. She can feel herself shivering, distantly, as if it's happening to some other woman foolishly poking around in a room full of dead things.

Bracing, she removes her glove. She hears Lola's sharp intake of breath; some part of her, primal and afraid, notices Lola's fingers clasping the back of her shirt. An anchor, maybe, or else a chain.

When Marlene touches the sun-bleached bones—the smooth planes of a femur—the room upends. Everything falls sideways. The bones *shudder*, jolting against the moldering lining of the coffin.

The whispers become screams.

She might call it 'bone song,' but it has neither rhythm nor tune. It's flashes of pain, hunger, and envy, of arrogance and timidity, of pleasure and kindness. Whole lives imprinted in ossified splinters, buried and eventually forgotten. *Alone. Abandoned. So dark. No light. Need more— need more—*

NEED.

MORE.

The cellar explodes in shards of wood, fabric, and dirt. It bears down on them as coffins twist and break to pieces, as slurry submerges them up to their knees, as bugs skitter and a damp, wet putrefaction seizes the senses. Marlene holds on to the femur grimly, her fingers wound tightly around it—hard enough to hurt. Lola doesn't move, either.

Sometimes bones fight like this. Usually their struggle is quiet, unobtrusive, coiled around everything like a snake in brumation. They don't have consciousness, a mind to reason with, logic to appeal to. But somehow, Marlene sings to them.

The words are nonsense; decided when she was a child and never quite changed. A smattering of German, of English, of other phrases she's stumbled across in academia that sound or seem magical. Its rhythm is jerky, its tune off-kilter, but she sings while the bones rage.

Carpals grab at her skirt and hair, dragging it from its careful governess bun. Lola stiffens, letting out another string of curses; her fingers are pulled roughly from the back of Marlene's shirt. Skulls rise up, their socketless eyes staring in mindless accusation. Ribs, sternums, clavicles, fibulas; they swell from the mounds of wood-strewn dirt, pushing and bulging. The stench is almost unbearable. It isn't dust, dirt, or rot. Something else, something deeper.

The smell of death.

The dirt pushes higher, higher, higher—until, suddenly, it fills her mouth and nostrils. Marlene is pulled under, squeezed tightly by grasping hands, held close to ravenous bones. Lola's scream cuts off; the earth shifts; she's been dragged further into the piling dirt. They're angrier than Marlene's seen in a while, years of torment held at bay by a family's reverence, broken now that no blood ties remain. Marlene quickens her song with what little air she has left.

It's not enough. She can't see, she can't *breathe*, and sharp fragments scrape at her cheeks and arms. Her eyes sting, blinded by the pulsing muck. This is new; interesting, academically speaking, and it would be novel if it weren't so terrifying. Her hand brushes something warm, something very much not a skeleton, still encased in muscle and skin—

Then Mrs. Ashdown hauls her from the grime, blood streaming down her face. Her lounge suit is in tatters and she's wildly clear-eyed. "Is this your strategy, Martha?"

"I did tell you," Marlene spits out a mouthful of dirt, "to wait in the kitchen."

She has some netting and a braid of rope, some nails and a hammer. One of the coffins is largely intact, not yet split apart by the festering heap. With the femur still held tightly, Marlene keeps singing to the bones. She makes her way to the coffin. *You're free,* she wants to say. *You aren't caged, not anymore.*

Need more. It reverberates through her body. *Not fair. Never fair. So cold.* Like moths to flame, the bone song follows her movements. Fissures of dirt make a line for her. Lola hangs back.

Some of the bones are newer, some have collapsed to dust. Regardless, they follow with an electric hum. With her ungloved hand, Marlene presses feather-light touches to calm them. She begins to secure the netting around the coffin; with touch and song, they begin to settle. Caged, wary, restless. Calmed.

"That one was my husband's coffin." At this, Lola sounds less gin-tinged and, instead, emptied.

"It's newer," Marlene offers. "It will be sturdy enough."

"You clearly aren't successful based on your bedside manner," Lola grumbles. She still keeps a cautious distance.

"I'm afraid we don't have much choice," Marlene says. "You'll have to forgive me."

So cold, the bones whisper. *Please, let us.*

The dirt pools around their ankles now, slivers of shattered bones and burrowing bugs.

"Will this solve it?" Lola asks.

"For now," Marlene replies. "It's the first step."

Her own song peters out once the bones are interred inside their makeshift resting place. Marlene shuts the lid with a heavy thud. Wordlessly, Lola holds out her hand for the hammer.

"Your arms are matchsticks," she says, all tact and grace. There's a bite to her tone, the only way to let out whatever else is underneath. "Let me do it."

Marlene doesn't argue the point. The dull thundering of nails hammered into wood replaces the starved whispers.

Between the thunder, Marlene still hears the steady, quiet hum. It's there, underneath the wood. *Need. More. Need. More.*

They sit in the parlor, afterwards. Marlene says no to gin, no to gin-laced tea, and no to the scant bottles of wine Mrs. Ashdown rescued from the cellar before it collapsed.

"What fun are you?" Lola complains, but she fills her tumbler nonetheless. Meanwhile, Marlene stirs her unsweetened tea.

"How is 'the tug?'" Marlene asks her, once Lola's tremor has dampened from alcohol and several deep, gulping breaths.

She frowns. "Still there. Muffled, perhaps."

The netted coffin sits in lieu of the coffee table. Lola hasn't torn her eyes from it since they struggled upstairs with it.

Need more, Marlene hears.

"There were less than I thought." Lola swirls her drink. "For centuries of bones."

"Some must have crumbled," Marlene says. "How long they last depends on conditions."

Lola mulls that over for a moment. "So now what, Martha?"

"We've exhumed them." Marlene stares into the eddying steam of her tea. "Now we'll need to give a proper burial, with rites and grave goods. Something of yours, or any Ashdown heirlooms you have to spare."

"I'm veritably drowning in them," Mrs. Ashdown drawls. "They can have the lot, as far as I'm concerned."

"Tomorrow." The exhaustion settles into her own bones. It's draining, somehow, in a way she doesn't fully understand. She supposes bone-singing isn't *normal*, whatever it might truly be—a primordial practice, maybe, garbled through time and culture—and so its levy on the body isn't normal, either. "In daylight hours. For now, this should hold them."

"Forgive me if I find that difficult to believe." Lola sniffs. "They tried to bury us alive several hours ago."

Marlene removes her gloves again, sinking to the mold-mottled rug and resting one hand against the coffin's side. "Trust me."

"Hm." Lola finishes her drink and sets it down with a decisive clack.

Marlene shuts her eyes. There's a rustle from Mrs. Ashdown's direction, and then warmth; Lola sits down next to her, her hand hesitantly finding Marlene's. Lola's is calloused, rough, scarred. Its heat flowers across her palm.

"That's why you always wear gloves," Lola notes. "I would too, naturally, if my touch caused spooky bone shit to happen."

A laugh echoes in the miserable parlor. With a start, Marlene realizes it's hers. All right, a little immoderacy is affordable. "When bones are at rest, my...abilities, such as they are, appear to disturb them. Once disturbed, they have the opposite effect." Her breath fogs her spectacles. "I've learned to be selective."

"Well." Lola's hair tickles her cheek. "To me, your hands are just very cold. You must have terrible circulation."

"I suppose." Marlene's veins stand out, blue and luminous, against her pale skin. Lola absently traces them with her thumb.

"Thank you." The sincerity lasts for a long, lingering moment before it bleeds into needling. "Though I'm dubious about the gratitude. You did make a complete wreckage of the cellar, and now I have to spend the night next to my husband's coffin."

"It seems it's more company than usual." Marlene furrows her brow, remembering her journey here. "The people in Valentine keep their distance, I assume?"

"Wouldn't you? This place does look cursed," Lola snorts. "That, and the fact I married into the Ashdowns in the first place. It raised a few eyebrows; I'm not what they expected, apparently, and surely my complexion isn't suited to riches. Then the Ashdowns all died, that raised more eyebrows, and now I'm here in the ruins of their wealth. As if my plan all along was to be the languishing widow of this dustheap. Very cunning, I'm sure."

"What's tying you here?" Marlene traces Lola's hand in turn. The russet brown betrays only warmth, at odds with the rest of the manor.

It mustn't do any good to stay; Marlene suspects the gin bottle and sleeplessness are casualties of that loyalty. It's an unbecoming speculation, far too familiar, but the proximity makes it somehow feel earned. Wanted, even.

"I've considered leaving," says Lola. "Perhaps, after all this, there won't be cause to look back."

Marlene nods. "There usually isn't much cause to look back."

It's an uneasy kind of camaraderie, forged in dross and dust, but it lasts through the night. Marlene likes to cleave to propriety; getting involved is typically—if not ill-advised—depressing and futile. People must master their own grief. It's an arduous mastery.

But regardless of rules, etiquette or decorum, she falls asleep with Mrs. Ashdown's hand clasped in hers, with their bodies curved towards each other, with skin brushing skin. Her other hand braces the coffin, dampening the whispers of the bones inside, and, beside her, she feels Lola finally succumb to sleep, too.

There's a juniper tree in the courtyard. It's alive, albeit ill-tended, and while it all seems a bit on the nose, it's going to have to do.

Lola leans on a shovel. She eyes the patchwork grass around the base of the tree with deep skepticism. "We're going to just…dig a hole and bury the coffin in it?"

Today, Mrs. Ashdown sports a Charvet shirtwaist with a chemisette and bloomers. She's also rustled up a hat with several large feathers tucked in its brim; the ensemble looks less suited for grave-digging and more suited for cycling to a garden party, but to each their own. Marlene's own wardrobe is modest, bordering on monastic, and so she wears the same dirt-stained clothes as yesterday. Her skirts have torn at the hems. She'll need to mend that later.

"Yes, that's the general idea." Marlene raises her own shovel. "Bones should be given proper rites. What that means is up for debate, but what's important is intention."

"Might as well carve them into jewelry or cups or something," Lola grumbles. "Then at least their hanging about would be useful."

"You're quite welcome to," Marlene says. "If you could get them to behave long enough for the carving. Surely nobody wants a necklace that might try to choke you."

"Was that a joke?" Lola narrows her eyes suspiciously. "Why, Martha, you're an odd duck."

They dig the hole. Marlene convinces Lola to leave her gin bottle inside the manor, replaced with a carafe of water while they toil. It takes hours; skin rubbed raw by the shovel's rough handle, dirt crusted under fingernails, sweat-swathed and bug-bitten. The sun slides like butter across the skyline. The bones' whispers pick up to a cacophony, swirling in the wind.

Finally, Marlene is satisfied. "Do you have the grave goods?"

Lola indicates first to a glass bottle with an indeterminate liquid inside, then a hideous gem-encrusted brooch that's shades of lime green. "My father-in-law was always talking up his vintages. And my mother-in-law adored this ghastly thing; it was only by my husband's decree that she wasn't already buried with it." Here, she removes her wedding band, adding it to the other items. "Supposedly this was his great-grandmother's. There was a *huge* kerfuffle when I nearly dropped it down the bathtub drain this one time—" Her story stutters to a stop as Marlene bundles up the items and neatly ties a cloth around them. Lola doesn't finish it.

The coffin is easy enough to push into the grave. They don't have the finesse of an undertaker, the solemnity of pallbearers, or the endorsement of an epitaph. But they have four hands between them and it makes for light work. Lighter than the gravedigging, at the very least. Marlene places the bundle of items carefully atop the coffin, murmuring the nonsense-words; the song, stilted but steady.

The whispers try with final, grasping terror to claim them. *Please, let us. Need more. Not fair. So cold.* Sorrow chases her cuffs, guilt caresses her collar, and Lola's silence drags at her ankles. Still, Marlene fills in the hole until the whispers are muffled by six feet of packed dirt. She continues the song, says the words, performs the rites in the best way she knows how. Sort of pulled together in a mess of traditions, like scraps of fabric sewn into patchwork.

Lola shakes her head when Marlene asks if she'd like to say anything. "I said my goodbyes." Her words cut close. "Ideally, that would've been the end of it, and yet here we are."

It's quiet now in the darkening courtyard. Behind them, Ashdown Manor gasps as if exhaling a breath held for a second too long; creaks and groans rattle the windows, and the doors burst open in the breeze. They judder to stillness after a few moments.

The house settles. Then it, too, is quiet.

"How is the tug?" Marlene asks.

Blessedly, this time Lola just says, "Gone."

Marlene manages something close to a smile. "Thank you for hiring me, Mrs. Ashdown. It...wasn't an easy fix, but I hope it's one that will bring you some small comfort."

"Lola." The correction's automatic. She folds her arms. "I suppose now you'll return from whence you came?"

"Well," Marlene says. "Only once you cut me a check."

There's an edge to Mrs. Ashdown's own smile, an undercurrent; a new kind of tug, fleeting but inviting. With her sleeves rolled up and bloomers tragically muddied, she looks like the heroine of a dime novel, like she's one step away from adventuring to a distant land in search of treasure and peril. She gets the impression Lola's the sort of woman to tumble right into danger, either by dire accident or flimsy deliberation, and she's not sure what to make of that.

Marlene thinks there wouldn't be much to find in the adventure; nothing but desolate places and troublesome bones, tucked in the gaps where brightness doesn't reach, far beneath the dirt. There wouldn't be very much to offer, perhaps, and yet—

"Say, Marlene." Mrs. Ashdown is a mite too nonchalant. "Are you in need of an assistant?"

The smile is more manageable, this time. "I've been wondering," Marlene replies, "if it might be a prudent investment, Lola, given that your house attempted to bury me alive yesterday."

"In that case..." Lola winks. "I am rather good with a hammer."

CHAPTER NINE

CAULSTON

PERRY WOLFECASTLE

CAULSTON MONASTERY, 1472

A sharp breeze whistled about the old rock. A dampness crept upon them, staining the once-sandy stone black, the only color left was the browning moss clinging to the moisture.

"Is it ready, my love?" The words dripped like honey from her ruby lips.

The fifth candle sputtered to life, the tallow stained with red fingerprints. "Soon." He stepped over the body of a nun and headed for the eastern pedestal.

"No. Please. Oh, Lord. Please have mercy." The final nun shuffled back, pressing herself hard into the wall, as though the brick would absorb her, save her. Her habit was ripped and tattered after this brute had dragged her—like her sisters—from bed and down the stone steps to the monastery's depths. "Please." Tear-stained eyes met her assailant's. She knew pleading would be futile; he'd butchered five of her sisters. The holy father lay prostrate on the floor, the body greeting them all as they were thrown into the dark—one death she hadn't been forced to witness.

A blood-soaked hand reached down and wiped a tear from her cheek, leaving a red streak across her face. "Please, don't cry. This is a happy day."

His eyes were full of sorrow, the grip on his knife full of determination. He clutched her by the chin, lifting her head. She gagged as blood—the blood of her found family—touched her lips.

"Hurry, my love. Free me." The man turned to gaze at his desire, stood at the center of his carnage. A smile crossed his face, a single tear ran down his cheek, dropping onto his once-white shirt, stained red and brown.

"Hush now, sister. Don't move. I'll make this quick." His victim followed his gaze to the middle of the circle. Blood flowed in small carved troughs to pool at its center. She watched the madman nod. "You shall soon be free."

A light mist gathered. *Was he talking to the mist?* She couldn't understand. Squinting, the sister thought she saw a glimpse of something, someone, in the swirling void.

His dagger found her throat, and she had time to wonder no more.

With care, he lay the nun on her side, aligning the slit in her neck with the grooves he'd carved before. He positioned her right hand palm up, and took a matchbook from his pocket, fumbling to strike one not coated in blood. Lighting the last candle, he dripped wax into the palm, then used it as a base. He placed the candle and walked to the middle of his dark work.

"Come to me."

He did as he was bade, and knelt in the pool of blood.

"Do you love me?"

"More than anything."

A pale hand reached for him, a porcelain face tipping forward from the mist, a pouting red mouth. "Then kiss me."

Finally, after all this time, his lips touched hers.

Black fog surrounded them.

CAULSTON-ON-WYE, 1723

Rain battered the manor house's windows as Giselle pressed herself against the cold glass. The panes misted over as she counted under her breath.

Rumble.

Four, she thought to herself. *The storm is four miles away.*

She screamed as an unexpected bolt of lightning struck the ancient monastery on the hill not half a mile away, setting fire to the roof.

"Come away from there, come away at once." Mrs. Harkins grabbed her arm and tugged hard, like she had when Giselle was a child left in her care. "Really, all this daydreaming simply must—"

"The monastery is aflame, oh, Mrs. Harkins, should we not tell someone?"

"Never you mind that, old place could do with a good fire if you ask me, anyhow. Now put this on." She shoved a blue linen dress at her young charge, dark blue ribbons adorned the lighter fabric. "Do that and then I'll sort that nest you call hair." Giselle touched her bushy black locks, but didn't dare to meet the challenge in the dowdy housekeeper's graying eyes. "Come on now, girl. We haven't got all day. *The* Lord Butterton wants you downstairs and presentable—at the very least, I'll have you there." She looked Giselle up and down, tutting.

"My father, but why?"

A nasty grin creased the maid's haggard face. "His Lordship's business is none of ours, girl. Are you going to change or do I have to do it for you?"

"I shall do it."

"See that you do."

"Ah, here she is, here she is."

Giselle walked down the stairs, careful not to put weight on the broken step, and was scooped up by the arm of her father.

Lord Butterton was wearing his Sunday finest, which had seen better days. "Best behavior, girl," he said to her through gritted teeth, his gray beard wiggling with his multiple chins. She noticed the good tapestries adorning the walls, hiding chipped plaster and worse. *Whoever was visiting, they were important.*

"Mr. and Mrs. Clayton, allow me to introduce my daughter, Giselle."

The pair were standing in front of the fireplace, he in a suit of the finest tailoring money could buy. Black hair slicked back, graying at the temples. Mrs. Clayton swooped forward, her blood-red silk mantua flapping around her. Taking hold of her eyeglasses, which hung from a chain of pearls about her neck, she did not hide her appraising looks.

"Sir, Madam. How do you do?" Giselle put on her best smile, took the sides of her dress in her hands, and curtsied low.

"So, this is her, is it?" began Mrs. Clayton, ignoring the young girl. "Not as dire as we feared, not a bad-looking filly, is she, George?"

"N-no, not at all, darling."

"We worried, my husband and I," she addressed Lord Butterton. "You've kept her hidden away so long, people were wont to think something was wrong with her. But no, no. She'll do."

"I'll do for what?"

"Do for what? Is she a touch slow then, Butterton? Well, never mind that, got good hips—"

"Arabella, do come away and give the girl some space." Mr. Clayton took his wife by the arm and led her a little deeper into the drawing room. The Buttertons followed.

"The girl doesn't know yet," said Butterton, sucking in his stomach as Mrs. Clayton passed him to collect her fox fur. "Didn't want to get her hopes up, you see. Not until you'd had your look at her."

Mrs. Clayton gave her husband a nod, which he took as his cue. "You shall have your deal. We'll set the date for two months from now, on the 5th. I assume you'll be able to make arrangements with the chaplain?"

"That shouldn't be a problem, and the dowry?"

"Paid in full after the 'I dos.' We must be on our way. These mills don't run themselves." With a hearty handshake and a hastily spoken goodbye, the Claytons left the manor house.

The second the door closed, and Lord Butterton dropped his daughter's arm almost as quickly as the smile plastered on his face.

"Dowry? Father, what is—"

"Silence. Your seventeen years of living at my expense ends now. It's high time you were of use to me. You shall marry the Clayton's son, Ernest. Back to your room."

Knowing better than to argue, she did as told.

"I hear we are to be rid of you at last," sneered Mrs. Harkins as she slid into Giselle's bed chambers. The young girl turned from the window, where she had been watching the storm turn to a light drizzle, smoke pouring from the monastery. "About bloody time if you ask me."

"Nobody asked you."

"Don't you talk to me like that, ungrateful girl. Be glad to see the back of you."

"No, Mrs. Harkins, it is I who shall be glad to see the back of you and my father. Neither of you have ever cared for me."

"Care for you? *Care?* I bathed you, dressed you, and that was enough. The poor Lady Butterton, murdered in her child-bed as you clawed your way out of her—that's what caring for you—"

A slap across the face cut the old crone off. "You will leave my chambers at once or I shall throw myself from the top of the stairs. What would you and Father say to the Claytons then? You can't claim a dowry for the dead."

"You impertinent—"

Giselle raised her hand again, and Mrs. Harkins left without another word.

Giselle flung herself on her bed, grabbed her pillow, and hugged it tight. "Mrs. Ernest Clayton." It wasn't much, but it couldn't be any worse than this. She smiled to herself as the clouds cleared.

"What? You popped the question and didn't tell me? Who is it, you old rogue? Not Beth from the tavern." James Chichester weaved his way backwards about the hedgerows, not wanting to break eye contact with his companion.

"If you would be quiet for a second, I'll—watch out now!" An arm shot out to grab James. It slipped through the crook of his arm and grabbed at his waist, pulling him close moments before he could trip over the half-hidden gravestone.

"Thanks, Ernest." He let himself be pressed up against the other man's chest, feigning another stumble to shift his head into the crook of Ernest's neck, who, pretending not to know what his friend was doing, allowed him to stay for a moment.

"You okay now?" He patted James between the shoulders and moved his other hand from the small of his back.

James took a deep breath, savoring his friend's earthy scent, and, placing both his hands on Ernest's broad chest, pushed himself free. "Thank you. I'm uncertain what came over me."

"Just be careful it doesn't come over you again in other company."

"I'm quite sure I don't know what you mean." James returned to his backwards skipping. "Now, what's this marriage business?" The smile was genuine enough, but nothing could hide the betrayal in his eyes.

"Don't give me that look, you realize I—"

"I do," he cut him off and focused on the spot between those hazel eyes. "But I, as your best friend, should have been informed ahead of time."

"You'd think, as the groom, I would have been afforded that courtesy too." He halted to sit on a low wall, hand sweeping through his sandy hair. James stopped, but remained standing. "But alas, I found out today."

"I'm not sure I follow you."

"Arranged. I am to wed the daughter of Lord Butterton."

"She's real then?"

"Real enough to marry. Mother and Father met her yesterday. I have yet to be blessed with that pleasure." He scowled at the ground, imagining the moment when his future was sold.

"But why?"

"Blood," Ernest spat the word.

If James had been daring enough to wear his pearls outside of his room, he would clutch them. "Blood?"

"She has it, I don't. Blue blood, noble. My parents, rich as they are, are as common as this dirt beneath us. A grandchild with the blood and title of the Buttertons is the only logical rung on the social ladder. My nuptials are a business deal, nothing more."

"George and Arabella Clayton, the Mr. and Mrs. Medici of the Yorkshire Dales. Who'd have thought it?"

Ernest gave a grim smile. "Hark, who indeed."

"And you've never seen the girl?"

"Has anyone?"

"Point well made. Say..." A sly grin crept over his face. "We're not that far from the manor, we could always—"

Ernest stood and clapped his friend's shoulder. "Want to check your competition for my affections, do you?"

James abruptly stepped back to check their surroundings. "Will you be—"

"Calm, my friend. Nobody shall harm you, not when I'm around."

"I'm more worried about the chains."

"Lead the way."

"To the prison house? Oh, how I've longed to hear you say—don't give me that look, heavens, I know better than most that you're not so inclined," he added, noting Ernest's raised brow. "I know what you meant. It's this way. Off to Butterton Manor we go!"

"Hold a moment, James. What's that?" Ernest stopped at the broken gates of the monastery, the room blackened and still smoking.

"Oh, didn't you see it last night? The old place caught a strike of lightning."

"Lightning hitting a church? Who'd have thought—" A loud crack cut his words off. Instinctively, James grabbed his arm as Ernest stepped in front of his oldest friend. A large stone gargoyle broke away from the guttering and slammed to the ground, smashing into a multitude of pieces. The head rolled to a stop before the pair.

"Good God. I thought it was going to squash us." James tugged at Ernest's arm. "Let's make haste toward your lady love."

"Hold a moment. What's that?"

"What's what?"

The impact of the gargoyle had cracked open a large stone slab, revealing a stairwell. "I wonder where—"

"No, you don't. You're not taking me on one of your misadventures. I still have the scars from when we broke into the mill because you were certain there was treasure in there." James pulled up his brushed velvet sleeve to expose a long scar.

"And did I not kiss it better for you?" said Ernest, enjoying the blush it caused his friend.

"Now, I didn't say there wasn't a treasure there. Pity you didn't enjoy it more."

Ernest barked laughter. "I don't need to like it to pay my debts. Who knows what treasure you could earn down those steps?" He gave a wink.

"You, Ernest Clayton, are a menace. I never should have told you my secret. But, no. You're to be a bridegroom after all." He took a seat on a tree stump and crossed his legs. "Go if you must, I shall wait here."

The damp, moss-covered walls added a staleness to the air. Ernest had to stoop low as the steps turned into a shaft. He supposed he was under the monastery proper. At the very moment he gave thought to turning back, the tunnel opened into a large, high-walled room. There was light, but he could not tell where it was from. A chill passed up his spine. His skin prickled to goose-flesh. *This feels wrong,* he thought. Yet, as he turned to leave, he noticed a mass of black rags. Despite his misgivings, he moved toward it.

He jumped back as his prying foot was met with an assortment of bones. "What in the world is this?" he said aloud as he probed again. The ragged cloth slipped.

The hollow eye sockets of a human skull stared at him.

Terror took him for only a second before he made his retreat, yet, in that second, a fog seemed to form in the room, swirling toward the center.

"Do...yo...l...e..."

"What was that? Who's there?" Ernest spun around, checking each corner of the chamber.

The mist had thickened.

He squinted.

There stood a figure, taller and broader than himself.

"Lo... me..." An ethereal male tone, swirling about the chamber, as thin as the mist. This time, Ernest ran and did not look back.

"Here now, what's got you in such a fright?" James jumped up from the tree stump.

"I—bones—and—" In the bright of day, it was hard for Ernest to voice what he had experienced. *Surely nothing more than a trick of the light and the confines of the space.*

"You broke into a crypt, didn't you?"

"I—yes. I must have."

"We can report it to the chaplain on Sunday. Are you sure you're well?"

"Yes. Yes, of course." Ernest drew himself up, yet felt fatigued as the adrenaline left his body.

"Then…" James checked their surroundings and, confident they were alone, looped his arm through Ernest's. "Shall we see if we can spy the future Mrs. Clayton?"

"Yes, let's."

Neither unhooked their arm until they reached the main path, much to James' surprise and silent delight.

Do you love me?

It sounded in Ernest's mind. In the corner of his eye, a large man shifted through the trees, following them, yet when he looked directly at the point or instructed James to do the same, they saw nothing.

Do you love me, Ernest?

Four days had passed since Ernest had stumbled down the monastery steps. He hadn't slept a wink since that moment.

He lulled at the dining table, soup dribbling back into the bowl from his spoon, lost in a dreamlike void that seemed to lack meaning.

"Are you listening to me? Ernest. Ernest!"

His mother's voice jolted him away from his half-life dreaming. *What had he been seeing? In the depths, he knew, but in the depths,* he *shall remain.* "Yes, Mother?"

"What has gotten into you?"

"Now, now 'Bella. It's normal for a gentleman to have nerves and second thoughts before his big day. Well, I remember back before you and I—"

"You had doubts?" The daggers in her eyes clarified no answer was required. "Ernest, I expect you to be at your best tomorrow night. Do you understand me?"

"Yes, of course. What's tomorrow?"

"Wha-what's tomorrow? You haven't been listening to a word, have you?" Arabella Clayton slammed her butter knife down onto a small bread plate, causing the fine china to crack. Standing, she paced the length of the old mahogany dining table back and forth. "Tomorrow, we are to dine as a family at Butterton Manor. Tomorrow, you shall meet your future wife. Tomorrow, we will be one step closer to securing this family's legacy well into the future."

"Quite right, dear. Quite right."

"Sup, and then to bed with you, Ernest. I don't like the look of you lately. Sickly," she said, without a hint of Mother in her voice. "Your father and I went to that run down manor to check the girl wasn't malformed. I shall not be embarrassed by turning up with a son who looks half a foot in the grave."

"I understand, Mother."

"All in your best interests, son. You'll see," added George as his wife took her seat once more, waving the maid over to replace her bread plate. "Not a bad-looking girl, either. I think you'll be pleasantly surprised indeed."

They supped without another word.

Love me.

Come.

Come to…

Ernest bolted upright in his bed. The full moon hung high in the sky and poured into his chambers. The embers of a fire still smoldered in the fireplace. Before he knew it, he had swung his feet out of bed and had put on his boots. His white underclothes clung to his frame as the cold sweat seeped into them. Pulling on a large overcoat, he crept quietly around the landing—avoiding eye contact with the giant portrait of his parents at the top of the stairs—and made his way to the drawing room. The maid had left a knife out, and it was this he slid into the drawers of the chesterfield to break the lock. He safely tucked both away in his overcoat.

What am I doing? he thought to himself. Before an answer could form, he was through the gate and out into the night.

Ernest took the steep steps two at a time. In his rush, he stumbled, but steadied himself against the tight stone walls and used the momentum to propel him quicker down the passage.

All at once, he found himself in the chamber. His breath was heavy and clung about in the cold. In a haste, he made his way to the center of the room, the mist already forming, shapes shifting, falling in and out of focus until a solid foot stepped out. The work boot hit the floor as a man emerged. A leather overcoat covered a broad frame and, although taller than Ernest, the shadow caused by a wide-brimmed hat hid many of his features. Yet bright red lips shone from the depths.

"Wh-who are you?" Ernest found his voice—maybe himself—once more. He wiped his sweaty palms on his overcoat and, for the first time, felt a chill through his thin underclothes.

"You came to me." The mysterious man's voice flowed like a warm stream of honey, yet his lips barely moved.

Ernest shuffled on the spot. "I did, but I don't know why."

"For love."

"Love? I don't know you and you're a man, I don't love—"

The stranger's hand cupped Ernest's cheek, and he cut off at once. He nuzzled into the rough, calloused palm, like a cat being pampered. "For love."

"For love," purred Ernest.

"'Ere now. What you doing down 'ere at this hour?" The chaplain's assistant had been summoned by the light of a torch that Ernest couldn't remember lighting. "It's not safe down here. Come away at once."

"Will you prove your love for me, Ernest?"

"I will."

"Good to hear it," said the aide, unable to hear the stranger's voice.

"Then show it."

Ernest reached into the pocket of his overcoat and gripped the handle of his stolen knife. He turned, with reluctance, from his love, and stalked toward the assistant.

"Aye, that's a decent lad now. What on Earth were you thinking?" He turned to lead the way up the steps. "Guess the notion to explore is a strong—"

Blood gurgled from his mouth as the blade crossed his throat. Ernest dropped his weapon and dragged the body deeper into the chamber. But the stranger, along with the mists, had vanished.

Staring in disbelief at the horror he had wrought, Ernest ran home on shaking legs, only stopping to empty the contents of his stomach on the way.

The Clayton's carriage pulled up outside of Butterton Manor at 6:58p.m. sharp. Two minutes to decamp George, Arabella, and a reluctant Ernest, and a short walk to the door. George let the knocker fall from his hand at precisely 7p.m. He snapped his pocket watch shut and tucked it back into his waistcoat with a satisfied grin.

"How impertinent to not have anyone here to greet us." Arabella wrinkled her nose at the door frame, its wood showing signs of rot.

"Now, now Arabella, if it wasn't for his Lordship's lack of funds, this union would never have been possible."

"I shall send my regards to the bookmaker. Ernest, dear, do try to look like you want to be here. After all, soon all of this shall be yours."

"It shall?" Ernest stepped back to look at the manor house.

"Why of course, you'll be the next Lord Butterton."

"Lord Butterton," Ernest repeated. A colossal figure loomed in his periphery but he ignored it. He had tried not to think of the stranger again after that night. Tried and failed. Every thought, every feeling, was dominated. He knew he should feel guilt for the poor man lying dead in the chamber, he tried to force the feeling upon himself sometimes, yet—it was all for love.

The door creaked open, and an old hunchbacked woman with a large gray bun and a small split in her lip bade them enter. "Please, go into the lounge." She pointed to a room hung with heavy tapestries. "I shall fetch his Lordship at once." She bowed out of the room.

"Ernest, remind me to look for new help when you inherit. What a ghastly old thing." Arabella had taken to holding her handkerchief before her nose.

"Ah, Mr. and Mrs. Clayton, how wonderful it is to see you again." Lord Butterton bounded into the room, red-faced and wheezing, his rotund figure decked out in a suit two seasons too old to be fashionable. "This must be my future son-in-law." He took Ernest's hand into a limp handshake.

"A pleasure to meet you, my Lord."

The Lord turned his back as though he hadn't heard. "Allow me to introduce you to my daughter, Giselle." He, along with the Claytons, looked expectantly at the open doorway. After a few seconds, his Lordship spoke again, "My daughter, Giselle."

Nothing.

"My daughter, Giselle," he repeated, louder, enunciating each word.

At last, she appeared in the doorway, wearing the same blue dress as before—something that did not pass the notice of Arabella Clayton. "Good day to you all." The girl gave a polite curtsy and a smile. She entered the room, her smile only faltering as her father took her arm.

"Now, to the most important introduction of all. Young master Clayton, may I present to you my only daughter, Giselle." The Lord offered her hand to the young man, but Ernest did not take it.

His eyes were transfixed on a point just past Giselle's ear, for in the doorway, all mist and swirls, was the stranger.

A sharp pain in the side—inflicted by his mother's bony elbow—returned his attention to the moment. He took the offered hand and, as his father had instructed earlier in the day, bowed and kissed it. "Delighted to make your acquaintance at last," came the well-rehearsed words.

He looked into his future wife's deep brown eyes, then his gaze traveled to her soft skin and plump lips, and he gave her his first genuine smile of the day. His father had not lied, Giselle was beautiful. He felt her appraising him as he had. She returned his smile with a squeeze of the hand.

"Well, that's quite enough of that," said Arabella, breaking the moment along with their grip. "Butterton, shall we get down to business."

"Arabella, dear, I shall be the one to discuss business with his Lordship. Is the church booked, old boy?"

"Indeed, it is. Poor chaplain was beside himself though, his assistant has run off."

"Run off?"

Ernest shuffled back and forth on the spot, eyes on the floor, yet he could feel his future wife's on him still.

"Yes, the fellow—"

A gong sounded from the doorway.

"Dinner is served," croaked the housekeeper. One by one, they moved to the dining room.

"Good Lord, what was that meat? I've never had to chew so much in my life." The carriage wobbled on the cobbled stone tracks as the Claytons rode back to town.

"And really, dear, I do fear I'll be tasting that gravy again for a week," said George between hiccups.

"May I walk the rest of the way home, Mother?"

"What, Ernest, dear?"

"If this carriage moves about anymore, I worry you may see that sinewy stew again."

"Hold the carriage," Arabella yelled, banging on the roof. It came to a halt at once. "Yes, best you walk. We've only just had this reupholstered. Don't dawdle home," she said, slamming the door shut behind him.

Ernest watched the carriage round the corner before making for the woodlands, and the swirling mist that drew him closer.

A rustling of leaves below her open window took Giselle away from her daydreaming. She had pictured her future husband, far more handsome than she had expected, as her prince charming riding to the manor to save her. "Only I can save myself," she mused, allowing thoughts of Ernest—her dream Ernest—to fall away. A second rustle of leaves drew her eye. She could see a figure and a torch.

Skipping the creaking stair in only her nightdress and a thick shawl, she padded barefoot out into the courtyard. "Ernest? Ernest, is that you?" She rushed toward the figure with his back to her, torch held high.

"For love. For love I must," muttered Ernest. He wrapped a handkerchief around his fist and smashed a small pane of glass. He stopped as Giselle's hand grasped his shoulder. "What—What am I—"

"D-did you come for me?"

"Oh, sweet Giselle, I do not know. I fear I am losing my mind." He looked about furtively, but they were alone in the night.

"What a couple we shall be, I, a shut-in denied the world and you, a half-mad sleepwalker. You know…" She moved her hands to hold his, picking glass from the handkerchief. "We are to be one, you can tell me what you were doing."

"Some force compelled me—oh, Giselle—to burn the manor."

The young woman gasped but did not loosen her grasp upon her fiancé's hand. "With me and my father inside?"

"Aye, my sweet."

"You wish me harm, Ernest?" Doe-eyes filled with tears. "I know our union would not be ideal, but yet—"

"No." His voice was firm. Taking his hand from hers, he cupped her cheek. "My heart skipped a beat when I met you today. I am certain once I found my right mind, I would have run into this building to save you."

"My sweet fiancé." She kissed his hand. "Your flame would save me from more than you know."

"Giselle?"

"My father—no, the *Lord*, for he has no right to the title Father— has never once shown me affection, quite the opposite. The maid is a vile witch. This house has never been a home for me. It is a prison. They, my jailers, locked me away from the world. My only crime: being born. I must confess, I do not know or want to know what possessed you to come here with torch aflame. But knowing that you would save me, you have saved me, for you are my escape from here."

"Then we shall go at once." He wrapped his free arm about her waist and lowered the torch; his hand shook as a thin mist formed at the gate.

"Do you still feel a compulsion, Ernest?"

"Giselle, I already cannot lie to you. I do."

"Kiss me." Their lips pressed, foreheads meeting as Ernest planted soft kisses about his future wife's face. The lovers breathed as one. Giselle took hold of the torch. "Allow me to save us both, my love."

She threw the flame into the dining room. The old, dry tapestries went up in an instant, firing the whole manor. The soon-to-be orphan kissed her lover with a passion she had never felt, the flames dancing in her eyes.

Freedom, she thought, as the oil lamp in her father's chamber exploded.

"A fortune. It will cost a bloody fortune to fix."

"Arabella, please. Don't you understand the opportunity?"

"George, a Lord must have a manor and Butterton Manor is—"

"And now that decrepit shell is out of the way, with it the history of the Buttertons. We can rebuild it. Records will forever know it as Clayton's manor. Don't you see?"

"Brilliant."

"Have you heard from Giselle?" Ernest placed his knife and fork down on his plate next to the bacon and eggs he'd left untouched.

"The Butterton girl? She'll be ready for the wedding. Thank God you'd seen the fire and went to investigate, or all this would have been for naught. Eat your breakfast," Arabella replied, waving a hand at his meal.

"I bet it was that horrid old maid—Lord's mercy to her soul," added George, with no real meaning. "Left the candles lit and those tatty tapestries, well, a recipe for disaster if you ask me."

"Saves us airing out the moth-bitten things."

"Every cloud, dear."

"I'm going for a walk," said Ernest, standing without waiting to be dismissed.

"You're not the Lord of the manor yet, boy, you'll wait for your father to—"

"Oh, let him go, Bella, I dare say we'll have a busy day here anyway now the organizing of the wedding has fallen to us."

"Did that fat oaf—rest him—do anything?"

"Not really—"

Ernest didn't hear the rest as he fled the dining room.

The assistant chaplain's body had become bloated with gas.

Careful not to touch it, Ernest slowed and laid a cup of ash in a neat pile before moving clockwise and placing a second.

"You have done well, but I need more." The mist pulsed and out stepped the stranger.

Ernest ran to him at once, kicking the arm from the corpse in his haste. It clattered against the far wall as he sunk his head into the figure's chest. "I couldn't give you her. I'm sorry—I—"

"Do you love me?"

"Yes."

"I thought I saw you. You been avoiding me? And what are you doing down here again? Oh, it's even more wretched than I imagined." James' voice echoed around the chamber. "That awful smell. Ernest, why are you crouching there? Come away, come here."

"Do you love me?" The mist-man asked once more.

Ernest looked up into his coal-black eyes, "Yes."

"Yes? Well, move over here then," said James.

A knife formed in Ernest's hand. "Give him to me." The mist stroked his face.

"Yes." Concealing the blade in his sleeve, the lover walked toward his only friend in the world. "After you." He swept an arm to show the passageway.

"So, avoid me, have me follow to this place, and then deny me a good view on the way back? You really are a monster, you know?" James shifted to leave. Ernest got in close, ready to make his move. His victim stopped. "Lord in heaven. What is that? A body?" James turned as the knife slashed down. It grazed his cheek. "What are you doing?! Ernest. Ernest?"

Another swing, another dodge. James fell to a knee. Feeling around behind him, he grasped the first thing he could find and swung it with all his might. The corpse's arm hit Ernest in the jaw, staggering him. James tried to run, but he was too slow.

Ernest grabbed his leg and dragged him back into the room. Getting to his feet, he stopped James as the man tried once again to escape.

A backhand across the face sent James to his knees, bottom lip split open. "Ver-very well. I shall not run, nor will I shame myself by dying on my back." James stood and adjusted his velvet jacket. "You are not Ernest, of that I am sure. Grant me one last request?" He looked into Ernest's eyes, but there was no answer or recognition behind them.

A hand grabbed James by the lapels and dragged him in close. Ernest placed the dagger beneath his friend's chin.

"Pay your debts," said James before pressing his bloodied lips against Ernest's. For seconds, there was no movement.

Iron. Rust. Blood.

Ernest lowered the blade and stared into his friend's eyes, tears stinging his own. He pulled away from the kiss and let go of the lapels. "James, I'm sorry."

His would-be victim was already backing up.

Behind him, Ernest could see the mist throbbing. "No!" He charged and grabbed James once more. This time, he flung him toward the exit. "Quit this place. Leave me and never come back. If you don't, I shall kill you, and then myself."

James struggled to his feet and bolted up the passageway.

"Do you not love me? You love me, don't you, Ernest?" The mist-man stepped out once more, arms outstretched, offering an embrace.

Ernest took a step forward, then another. Suddenly, he stopped. "Begone."

"Love me."

"Begone, foul daemon! Begone and torture me no more, for I felt love. The man you would have me kill gave it in spades, and this is not it."

"You will realize my love."

"Begone!" Ernest threw the knife, but it sailed through the figure. "I hold no affection for you." He ran from the chambers.

"I now pronounce you man and wife. You may kiss the bride." The chaplain clasped his hands together and Ernest planted a soft peck on Giselle's lips. He brushed a strand of her hair behind her ear, careful not to knock her veil. He pulled back, and they shared a smile.

The herald sounded at the rear of the church, "Ladies and gentlemen, may I introduce to you, Mr. and Mrs. Ernest Clayton, the new Lord and Lady Butterton."

Hand-in-hand, they walked down the aisle, people neither had ever met whooping from the mahogany pews. Well-wishers threw dried rice as they exited the chapel. Arabella Clayton took her son's arm, as George held that of his new daughter, and the family toured the grounds toward the awaiting carriage.

A smaller taxi pulled by two horses crossed their path, a bulk of cases tied to the top. From the window, James tipped his cap to the couple before slamming the blind shut.

Moments later, the Claytons were galloping home.

Ernest awoke, feeling a draft upon his back. It was their first night in the newly rebuilt manor house. He felt for his bride, yet the bed was empty. *No matter,* he thought to himself, *Giselle had never been a sound sleeper, and now with the baby on the way.* He rose, dragged on his trousers, and walked to the windowsill, where he spied a figure all in white crossing the gardens. Boots pulled on, he threw his cloak about him, and followed what had surely been his wife in her nightdress.

A dread terror settled upon him as he entered the grounds of the old monastery. A torchlight flickering on the damp walls confirmed his suspicions as he prepared to enter the chamber once more.

"Do you love me?" The words snaked and soothed about the walls. Ernest saw Giselle stood before the mist, an arm stretching out for her from it. "Giselle, do you love me?"

Ernest bounded into the room. "It is I whom she loves, daemon. Begone." His words were strong, only to be betrayed by a quiver in his tone.

"Oh, Ernest." His wife coaxed him over and they held their hands to her belly. "Take us away from this vile place. I don't know what I have done... What I would have done. Did I already..." She looked to the hem of her white nightclothes, a red stain crept upwards. "Take me away."

"I shall, I—"

"Do you love me?" The mist pulsated as the daemon emerged.

"Yes," man and wife said in unison, their eyes glazing over.

"Prove your love."

Ernest and Giselle faced each other as they had on their wedding day. He stooped so that their faces were level. They shared a lingering kiss. Ernest pulled away, shaking his head trying to remove the fog from his mind. "Wife, we must—we must leave..." he trailed off as a cloud swirled about him.

"It's alright, my love," said Giselle as she ran a hand over his cheek. The mist flowing into her nostrils.

The mist-man grabbed them by their chins. They smiled at each other, and then at him as he turned them to face him. Mist swirled in their palms, forming into daggers as each clasped a handle. "Give me your love."

Lord and Lady Butterton put a knife to each other's throat. Still smiling, they sliced in unison. Blood cascaded down their fronts, mixing on the floor.

"Kiss me," said the daemon. He leaned forward and his lips first met Ernest's, then Giselle's. He guided them to kiss each other as their life drained out of their body.

In their last moments, they locked their mouths with the daemon's in a trinity of ecstasy.

The mist turned black as Ernest and Giselle's bodies hit the floor. It rolled over them, absorbed them. In a flash, they were gone.

In their place lay a man, the mist-man, naked as the day he was born, sobbing on the hard stone. "I'm so sorry," he whimpered. Yet, as a white cloud formed about him, he sprung to his feet and ran.

Caulston Monastery Ruins, 1845

"Come on, Bette, in here!"

"Arnie, no, not there. It's haunted."

"Haunted? You're having a laugh, ain't ya? Only thing that'll be bloody haunting about here is us if your hubby gets wind of this. Or maybe you've gone off me."

"Never," spoke the adulterous woman, grasping her lover's groin. "But here, in a church?"

"What better place to do a bit more sinning?" Arnie winked and pulled the lace of her bodice, causing it to fall open.

"Get off, oh, alright, quick over there, nobody will see there."

"Nobody but the Lord and Lady."

"Don't say that."

"I didn't think a big girl like you"—he cupped one of her breasts—"would still believe in old tales such as that." He licked her nipple.

Bette pushed him away and lay on a grave marker next to a boarded-up hole leading to the basement. "We'll have less of that, if you want some of this." She lifted her skirts.

"Too bloody right. They say you can hear the baby crying—"

"Arnie!"

"I'm only teasing, pet."

"Speaking of babies, don't you dare—"

"I know, I know. On the belly—what was that?"

"What was what? Don't be playing silly buggers."

A bang on the wood next to them paused their activities. Arnie pulled up his breeches to investigate. "Probably just a trapped stray. I'll let him out. That'll be my good deed before we get down to the bad one."

As he parted the timber, Bette joined him.

"'Ere, what's down there?"

"That is paradise."

"Paradise?"

"Aye, neither your hubby nor his spies would look down here, would they?"

They walked down the worn steps, hunched slightly as the damp walls closed in, before entering the large chamber.

"Our little love nest," said Arnie, surveying the area, leading Bette deeper by the hand.

"Be a bit of alright once we get some things in here, don't you agree?"

"Only thing I need in here right now is you up against that pillar."

They headed to the center, where a fog swirled.

From it, two figures emerged. One, a tall and broad-shouldered man, the other, delicate and airy, a bundle of clothes clutched to her chest. Holding hands, they stepped from the cloud to greet the unfaithful pair, he before Bette, she in front of Arnie.

"Do you love me?" They spoke as one, their lips as red as rubies.

CHAPTER TEN

FAIM

MEGAN BONTRAGER

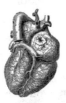

We always knew that Niklaus would be driven to madness. We knew it as soon as we'd heard of the man he'd beaten to a pulp for deflowering a dancer in Niklaus's usual balcony suite at the Moulin Rouge. There was never any question why he'd done it, nor did anyone blame him for it. His mother, once a principal dancer at the Moulin, sat him in the third box from the orchestra and told him to be good, to watch and wait, even as she disappeared into the wings to smoke and be vulgar with her patron saint of gold-digging. And when a bullet split her head in two outside Pâtisserie Chez Maître Jean, they raised a plaque above the box in her name.

We'd always known that he would descend into madness because of the way he watched the dancers, as if looking for Marguerite's split skull amongst their headdresses. He was hungry, and always looked at them like he might a bloody steak. Hungry, mad, and motherless; who could blame him for losing it? Only a madman chooses to open a mortician's practice in the same pied-à-terre where his mother had once conducted an illicit affair. He called the place "rotbeest," for he'd always believed its owner to be the man who killed her, and had, in turn, filled the place with death—death, prettied up and painted like a chorus girl.

Paris, the loveliest of all hallucinations, glimpsed in fragments between the dark creases of night and the honey of imbibed day; it was no place for a girl who made poetry out of ghosts. They sang louder than the troupe at the Moulin, rising to linger in the heady opium smoke above the booth reserved for Niklaus. From where I sat, sewing beads and pressing silks behind the curtain, I wondered if he could hear them, too. I could sew them back together again, present them to Niklaus in ribbons. Perhaps then he would return from the precipice of madness, where he seemed determined to remain.

So often, when he peered down to memorize the painted faces of the chorus girls, I imagined him looking right past them, through the billows of their beaded headdresses to where I sat hunched over a spool of fabric with needles for fingers. I was to be a part of the scenery, something unseen and unremembered. It was what I prettied up and thrust beneath the lights that he'd remember.

But, of course, Niklaus knew all about forgotten things.

During the curtain call on the last night of *Formidable,* I dared to stand. I left my silks and threads abandoned beneath the flickering light of my single lantern, and edged closer to the curtain. Specters buffeted me as I went, though none other could see their hands at the small of my back, nor the feathers in their caps brushing the tip of my nose. Even the spirits seemed not to notice as I slid between their meticulous rows, still maintained as if the crowd would leap to their feet and raise the Moulin's shingles in applause once more.

Cast in the shadow of the towering Hippolytas, I felt deftly to the edge of the velvet dark, salivating for the feeling of the warm stage lights upon my face. I, in tatters and hand-me-downs; I, with plum-bruised fingertips and harrowed eyes; what would I become in the light? What would Niklaus see? Could he paint me, too, to be beautiful, and perfect, and far from dead?

I dangled at the leash of my own need. It had grown teeth, gnawing me through. No darkness had ever been deep enough to extinguish my personal knowledge of love, and I saw traces of it everywhere. The ghosts were made of it. Why else would they stay?

Behind me, as I reached the tassels that fluttered at the end of the velvet curtain, my worktable rattled as if shaken from beneath. I paused, whirling; for a moment, I'd thought that the stagehands had found my post abandoned and sought to tear my work to shreds as punishment. But the table was empty, forgotten as ever in its corner beneath the rigging. Even the specters that danced through walls and half into the wooden floor-planks left it untouched. And yet as I stood with neck craned and eyes wide, back hunched like an animal caught in a beam of light, I saw it rattle again, shaking so fiercely that a spool of silver thread toppled to the floor. A harried passerby kicked it away, and I watched as a single silver string stretched, and stretched, and stretched, until it came to a stop at the toe of my boot.

I could hear the chorus beginning their final bows. My chest tightened. This would be my last chance to catch a glimpse of Niklaus, to meet his eye as he searched the chorus line. It would be my last and only chance, for I doubted I'd be brave enough again, to step into the light.

How I would *love* to be painted, and cared for, and as utterly mad as he.

I stooped to take up the spool of thread, spilling silver over my calloused and bruised fingertips. The music gave a tremendous swell, and my breath hitched high in my chest; like the moment of breathlessness after a fall, I felt it bloom and billow within me, numbing the tender feeling of thread looping taut around my ring finger.

I swayed on the spot, and for a moment the curtain shifted. The dazzling lights cast heat upon the stage-side of my face. No one in the audience seemed to notice that, for only a moment, I had inched halfway into the sun. I could see the men working the lights on the scaffolding overhead; even they did not notice my eyes, wide with shock, nor my tattered garments, which stood in such ugly contrast to the beauty I'd created. I often heard them whispering about what lay beneath the sweeping silks and dazzling beads that I crafted for each dancer. They wondered at the slope of their waists, what nestled between their thighs. I wanted to sew their mouths shut, like a rip in burlap tied to a neat seam.

My eyes shot up to the box reserved solely for Niklaus. The music swelled again, and a breeze from the movement onstage shifted the curtain, obscuring me once more. I had been given only a moment. But the moment had been enough.

His eyes held mine as I shrank back into the shadows, spooling the loose silver thread in tight loops around my fingertip. I pulled it tight, the flesh swelling and purpling like a failing organ. He watched as I stepped back from the curtain, gaze following me long past when he could have still seen me.

Did he imagine me? Did I haunt him, all at once, as he haunted me?

I felt his gaze inside me, a strange spark of creation in the pit of my belly. Transfixed as I was, I wondered if I might wander back onto the stage and find him leaning over the gilded railing, his hand outstretched. I'd toss the silver spool up into the air, and he would catch it deftly. Like a maiden in a children's fable, I would wrap it about my waist and he would pull me up, and up, and up, over the golden rail.

I pocketed the thread. The ghosts sighed.

The theatre emptied as it always did, leaving echoes of laughter and verve to accompany me. They scattered to their various corners, to the bar across the street or to the director's maisonette to drink and be merry. I was happy to be left, relishing the quiet afforded by their absence. Liminal space this was; somewhere suspended between impassioned applause and heady adoration, and the quiet cold of an empty theatre.

Onstage, the ghost light—the single bulb that burned bright to keep the spirits at bay—flickered once, twice, and then extinguished. Only the glow of the oil lamp kept the pitiless dark at bay; the pool of light around my table, my chair, and the folds of fabric beneath my work-weary fingers nestled safely within its halo.

"Hello?" I called. The sharp end of my needle pressed hard into the flesh of my forefinger. The ghost light never extinguished on its own; perhaps a stagehand had wandered back to the theatre with a dancer in tow, eager to do vulgar things to one another onstage, where it was most forbidden. "There's someone here!" Perhaps my presence would deter them; no one wished to linger in the dark with *me*.

A single body inhabited the stage, standing beyond the proscenium with his back to me. He faced out, gaze upon the darkened theatre. Only the weak light of my oil lamp, reaching sleepily across the stage-right wing, lit the broad plane of his shoulder, the rugged arch of his jaw, the sunken dark of his cheeks. I knew him at once. I would know him in the dark. I would know him blind.

"Why are you alone?" I asked, my voice no greater than a church-mouse. It was one that very much did not belong on a stage; it warbled, fizzled, and died before it reached the darkened ghost light.

He stirred, as if roused from sleep. His head turned, but only just. "Am I alone?" he mused. "Truly?" I felt his voice like an ache, gripping me by the throat, the hip bone, the hand. I slipped along the curtain, not daring to draw nearer. His eyes, exquisite in their melancholy, remained trained upon the empty seats beyond the stage.

My eyes fell to his hands. I imagined, this close, I'd see them covered in blood, stained crimson and dripping viscera. I imagined that I might smell the madness on him, like a creature of prey hails its predator. He was dressed impeccably, opera glasses dangling from a chain on his pocket. Even from the far end of the stage, he smelled of wine and cardamom and blood. It was an intoxicating familiarity that I could not shake.

He turned to me then, as if I'd spoken aloud. It was the first time I'd seen his face with such startling clarity. I was suddenly all too aware of my own body, my sullen and sodden appearance. My finger continued to bleed against my palm. I wiped it across the front of my skirts. Niklaus watched as I left red behind, the telltale heart of my solitary work.

"The others have long since gone," I said. I searched his face for the disappointment that so often accompanied my appearance. I was a shadow, meant to be forgotten. He'd gone astray from a party, surely. He'd wandered away for a smoke, only to find himself here. No one came looking for the dark after the light had gone.

He shook his head. "I know." My stomach lurched. I reached into my pocket and felt for the silver thread, which had twisted and knotted in my pocket. "I saw you," he said. "During the curtain call. A glimpse of you; between the folds of the curtain, behind the towering mass of beaded headdresses, between the fluttering skirts of the can-can dancers…there you were."

I flushed, crimson creeping from my neck and up to the tips of my ears. "I was not meant to be seen."

"And what a shame that is."

He held out a hand, palm facing the darkness above. I felt the multitudes that lived in my periphery pause, as if holding their breath all at once.

I took a bold step forward, slipping fully from the curtain and onto the stage. The air was warmer here, awash with the memory of light, of activity. But nothing was brighter, more vibrant, more real than his gaze transfixed upon mine. Never had I felt more solid, more real; realer than I'd ever felt before.

"My name is—"

"*Celine,*" he finished. Like a prayer. Like a wish. "I know who you are."

Of course, he did. Why would he not?

My hand hovered over his, the tip of my finger still dripping crimson, like the beads from an unraveling headdress. *I daren't touch him.* But he bridged the gap that I seemed so unable to, reaching up to take my hand in his and hold it tight. And then, with the utmost care, he turned my palm upward, leaned down, and pressed his lips against the bloody bloom. His eyes never left mine. My blood swept across his lips like rouge. He was disquieting; seducing and disturbing, magnetic and frightening. I took another step.

"Will you come with me?" he asked, his voice a low murmur as his lips ghosted to my palm. I could feel eyes over my shoulder, watching the crimson smear he left behind.

I did not know where he meant, and I cared little to ask. I feared that if I did so, I would blink and find him gone, and myself alone on a quiet stage. "Yes," I said, nodding fervently. "Yes, I will."

To my surprise, the ghosts at my shoulder trembled. Niklaus paused, as if he, too, could feel their disquietude. And then, as if to defy the stars, he gripped my hand tighter.

The ghosts grew far louder on the doorstep of Niklaus's *rotbeest.* I didn't know what I expected when I stepped inside, led along like a spot of soot on the sole of his shoe; I did not belong here, and the ghosts that curled lecherous fingers over the ridge of my orbital bone, my collar bone, my rib, seemed to agree.

The curled edge of a chaise caught my hip, the leg of a long table clipped my toe; even the grandiose maisonette seemed to know that I did not belong. The mortician's practice occupied the underground floor, while the second and third belonged solely to Niklaus. I wondered what he felt, sleeping so close to the dead. Did they invade his dreams as the dead did to mine?

As I followed Niklaus, I heard the moans and cries of the dead from beyond. It was impossible to make out what they said, for their muddled voices clamored over one another like rats in the sewer below. I wanted nothing more than to clap my hands over my ears.

But then, as Niklaus retreated across the room to attend the wine rack—*built into the wall itself, how wildly decadent*—a single voice rose above the rest. Hers—for they were all women in my mind—sang like a mezzo soprano from the crook of my neck to hook like fishing wire between my eyes. I startled, knocking my hips against the marble island at the center of the kitchen. A vase of oleander flowers sat at its center. The water within trembled, the petals quivering at my intrusion.

Listen. The voice was as immediate, as close, as if the woman stood on my toes. *You must listen.*

I always listened. I listened, and listened, and mourned that which I could not answer. But not tonight. "I will not," I hissed, swiping a hand across my brow.

"You will not what?" Niklaus turned, his expression placid. He held two glasses of Shiraz, the deep crimson sloshing along the sides. He looked as if I'd caught him mid-thought; I'd hardly realized that I'd spoken.

"I—" I blanched, my face blazing with heat again. "I simply—I cannot believe that this is where you *live*. My flatmate has four legs and a pink tail." My dreary corner, the single room I rented for near the entirety of my pay, existed in another universe entirely, so wildly removed from this one.

He laughed, and I sagged with the relief of his easy acceptance. It was a delirious sound. I felt dizzy, overcome. I imagined myself on the last evening of *Formidable*, losing control and leaping onto the stage amidst the dancers and mezzos with purpled fingers, tattered apron, and secondhand stockings, my hands thrust high as I declared my strange love for a man who barely knew my name. Even now, standing in the glow of his unwavering gaze, I could barely fathom why he had invited me here.

I took the wine offered, hands trembling as I brought the fine crystal to my lips. The smell alone was better than the swill I picked up in paper bags at the corner store.

The taste was beyond compare, as silken and opulent as the velvet curtains that shielded the apartment from the moon. A single sip, and I felt myself spinning, light as a breeze and just as changeable. I felt expensive, grandiose; I wondered if I might float up and into a far corner after a full glass, like an overfull balloon.

Niklaus took a bold step forward, closing the gap between us, bringing with him a warmth that did not belong in such a mausoleum of a place. His hand rose to rest upon the ridge of my jutting cheekbone. His knuckles were feather-soft upon my skin. A shiver danced along my spine.

I wondered idly if he could smell the virginal inexperience on me, like an oversaturation of perfume. None of the Moulin's workers knew how many women he'd brought to his maisonette, but we could certainly speculate. I was not the only soul to intrude upon this velvet cocoon of Niklaus's creation. I was, perhaps, the most out of place. Like a plastic knife in a drawer glutted with silver spoons.

"You're beautiful," he said. Plainly, shortly, as if it were a fact of life. Irrefutable.

An ugly snort escaped me. For the second time, I felt my neck, my face, my ears deepen with hot crimson. "I am—" I shook my head, the skin of my cheek hot against his rough fingers. "I'm only a seamstress."

"A beautiful seamstress," he said. "A creator. The Norns, the Fates, Neith, Leto of the Golden Spindle." Niklaus set his wine aside, instead taking my slender fingers in his. I felt dismantled, counted for parts; under such scrutiny, I should have felt unsettled. But as he marked me—a gentle touch drifting over the callouses and scars that riddled my hands like constellations—I knew all at once that this was the most wonderfully *seen* I had ever been. To be known, to be loved; they felt, suddenly, the very same.

"I don't feel beautiful. I don't feel like much of anything at all." The words slipped from me before I could tame them. For years, I'd felt a scream perched beneath the ridge of my jaw, just waiting for an opportune moment to fly. I felt it now, though all at once it felt less like anguish, and more like relief.

He tightened his grip upon my fingers. His gaze burned, intent and ferocious, as if he looked right through my skin, past my skull, and into the catacomb of my mind. I wondered if he could hear the ghosts within, if he could see the multitudes as they shifted and washed like a tide through sand over my open visage.

I wondered if he could feel their disquietude; so much more than my own. They loomed like shadows over my shoulders, craning to peer up at Niklaus with open skepticism. I wished to bat them away. A ghost was nothing more than a wish, a dream unfulfilled. I would not allow them, no matter how loudly they lingered, to squander mine.

"Come," he murmured, voice conspiratorial. "Follow me." My wine glass teetered and spun as I slid it onto the marble countertop, given no time for one last taste. He pulled me out into the corridor, past a darkened study, and through a pair of solid mahogany doors at the far end. Niklaus did not release my hand as he hastened about the room, lighting deep crimson candles that smelled of autumn, a dresser, a bedside table.

The darkness of the room gave way, opening like rose petals around an enormous bed at the very center. Bookshelves laden with leather-bound tomes, statuettes, faded portraits and photographs, and jewelry in glass cases occupied the walls, giving the impression that Niklaus had wanted a library more than he'd wanted a place to sleep. The necessities were an afterthought; the armoire sat crammed between two sets of shelves containing various copies of Shakespeare's works and Bibles translated into languages I'd never heard spoken aloud, the dresser slid beneath a circular window that overlooked the Seine. The four-poster bed, laden with various dark silks and scattered pillows, stretched far enough to nearly occupy every corner.

A sacrificial altar, it seemed. I would gladly present myself upon it.

I shivered. Niklaus paused; he'd felt it.

He sat me upon the bed, arranging me like a doll to be presented to a child. He held up a finger as he worked, smoothing my hair over my shoulders and touching my elbows, wrists, hands with the utmost gentility. I allowed myself to be moved, pliable beneath his hand. My feet hung lamely over the side of the bed, my hands folded in my lap as I resisted the urge to pick at a loose thread in the hem of my dress. This close, I could smell his cologne.

Niklaus was just as I had imagined. I wanted nothing more than to nestle my face in the crook of his neck. I wanted him to touch me, to make me feel as real as I'd imagined he could.

"I would like to show you something," he said. At once, I imagined myself flung back upon the bed, his expressive lips writing soliloquies across the pale ridges of my protruding ribs, my angular hips. Niklaus had always seemed to gravitate toward the dancers, the mezzo sopranos with voluptuous curves and supple frames. I was no more than a skeleton, a ghost improperly buried.

And yet he looked at me like a man seeing God for the first time. He knelt beside the bed, and, for a moment, I envisioned him at the Sacré-Cœur, rosary in hand. Niklaus watched my eyes as I marked him, watched my expression flicker and change as he reached beneath the bed to produce a leather-bound suitcase. My brows quirked; I was unable to contain my confusion, my uncertainty.

One of the chorus girls had once spread a rumor that Niklaus kept floggers and gags in a box beneath his bed, and that he collected trophies from each of his conquests. I knew better. Even though I had never met him, I knew him implicitly. Niklaus was not that sort of man.

A puff of rebuking dust rose from the surface of the case. It sagged onto the mattress beside me. With a click and a creak of leather on leather, he lifted the lid, allowing the dusty top to fall heavily onto the duvet. Within lived a collection of jewels, beads, silk scarves. No cheap fabric or torn threads, like that which inhabited my own measly collection; these bits and baubles had never seen the inside of a secondhand store, as all my clothing had.

From within, Niklaus carefully lifted a necklace bedecked with rubies and gold, the weight sagging against his fingertips. He met my eye and gave a short nod as he held the jewels up to my slender neck. I obeyed the silent command, brushing the hair from my shoulders and tugging at the frayed neck of my dress. Niklaus shifted, still on his knees, and pressed his weight against mine. With the utmost patience, he waited for me to part before slipping between my thighs. He reached up and around, laying the necklace flat against my collarbone. The metal was cold, but his breath was hot, immediate, and flush against my neck as he leaned closer. His fingers worked the clasp at the nape of my neck.

As if of their own volition, my hands fluttered to rest upon his shoulders. A low hum vibrated deep within my chest; nerves, or thrill, or arousal—I couldn't decide which.

Next, Niklaus tied my hair with a wisp of silk the color of the sky. A wisp of silk in a forest of dark wool and faded linen; he collected my hair in a braid, pressing more firmly between my thighs so he could work more easily, his fingers ghosting along the slope of my neck and shoulder.

Over Niklaus's shoulder, the tallest of all the lit candles flickered wildly, the flame whipped in the stagnant air as if it had been set before an open window. The light was distracting, casting strange shadows upon the wall and over the bookshelves. The smoke twisted and refracted in the air, taking shape before my very eyes. I froze beneath Niklaus's working touch, but he seemed not to notice as he plucked an errant hair from between the chains of the necklace.

The smoke curved around the sharp angle of a chin, a jaw, a downturned lip. A head turned from within, looking from the window to me—directly to me—and then disappeared just as quickly. The candle snuffed out, casting the wall behind Niklaus into a bleeding, swallowing darkness.

He searched my face earnestly. At once, I missed his warmth, the cool air of the room abrasive in the absence of his body. "Are you comfortable?"

I pulled my gaze from the empty blackness behind his head. "Yes." I nodded. "I am sorry. I—this is too much." I pressed a single bruised finger to the jewels at my neck. They were heavy on bones that only knew the weight of work. "I feel like a child," I said, my lips twitching at the corners. "Playing dress-up in someone else's things."

Niklaus waved a hand in the empty air between us. "Nonsense," he said. "It is my greatest joy to reveal beauty where it does not wish to be seen." He rose, extending a hand. "You believe yourself unworthy of it. Incapable."

"I—"

"Of beauty and love both."

I blanched. Before I could act, he reached for my hand, where it had fallen into my lap. He pulled me to my feet. I felt as if I'd tip over, that I was top-heavy. If I was pushed into the Seine at this very moment, I'd sink to the bottom.

Niklaus steered me across the room, abandoning the suitcase full of secret finery, to the mahogany armoire and the mirror atop it. "Sit," he commanded. I did as I was told. "Look."

This, however, was not as easy.

With great trepidation, I met my own gaze in the mirror. The candle on the armoire reflected light from the gold of the necklace and onto my face, so unfettered by my wild curls. I watched in the reflection as Niklaus moved from one shoulder to the other, producing a pearlescent compact and horsehair brush from within the drawer. It tickled my cheek, leaving behind a vibrant swath of color that no human could surely ever produce naturally. I thought of the chorus girls, rouging their cheeks, their necks, and their cleavage before taking to the stage.

I want to look like I've just been ravaged, they'd say. *I want them all to feel like voyeurs. I want them to imagine me naked.*

But I didn't look sex-flushed, as they so seemed to desire. I didn't look like a doll, or a portrait, or a dancer. I looked—

"Alive," Niklaus said, as if he'd known my thoughts all along. "It is my greatest joy to make even the most timid of ghosts feel alive." His eyes gleamed. He followed the brush in the mirror as it dipped along the slope of my neck, coloring my pale skin with the heat and verve of life.

"But—" I blurted. "How are you to make the dead feel alive?" I snapped my jaw shut. "I mean to say…why take such care for the dead?

Surely they do not know the difference." I imagined that I knew why. I had always imagined it. I had dreamt him, dreamt his answer, until I knew it in my bones. He and I were the same. There was beauty in the shadows, in the forgotten. I just wanted him to say it.

Niklaus set the brush aside, his hands instead rising to my shoulders. His fingers played at the frayed neck of my dress, the cool metal of the necklace. *Alive and dead.* "Even the dead deserve beauty," he said. "And what is dead is not forgotten. Dead is not gone; dead is merely someplace else."

I wondered what he might think if I spilled my secrets to him, if I admitted aloud for the first time that the dead followed me, that they inhabited my dreams, that they presented themselves to me like the bottomless dark of a wishing well.

They watched me even now, standing at Niklaus's shoulder with open, pleading faces. All women, I noted. Some wore silks like that which tied my hair between my shoulder blades, while others were bedecked in jewels and glitter. Some wore nothing at all, stark naked in my periphery.

Even as I shifted back in the upholstered chair, daring to press myself against Niklaus, I felt terribly observed. I was never granted a moment's peace. Voyeurs to my every waking and dreaming moment, they would not allow me to melt into the embrace I had so craved without a watchful eye.

One of the women at his shoulder turned slowly, translucent feet moving, dragging, without touching the ground. My eyes followed— though I schooled my head and shoulders into stillness—as she moved toward the dark stretch across the adjacent wall. She disappeared into the still-rising tendril of smoke atop the extinguished candle and disappeared. The others all turned to watch, their silks and jewels and beads shifting lazily with the movement of their bodies.

And then, from somewhere below, a great crash broke the silence.

Niklaus's face changed, a shadow falling over his stark features like a phasing moon. He startled as I did, eyes darting to the stretch of unlit wall and bookshelf. His hands stilled upon my shoulder, the tips of his fingers playing absently at the unblemished skin of my neck.

"What was that?" I muttered, my voice no more than a timid squeak. "Is there someone else here?" Another trio of thumping sounds, like feet on the hardwood below, filled the hall; this time, the sound came from below.

He shook his head. "No," he said. "We are alone." There was something in his voice, in his face, in the hard draw of his lips that demanded to be said. But I couldn't put a name to it.

A crash came from below, the tinkling of China on marble. Before I could speak again, Niklaus withdrew his hands from my shoulders. As if desperate to avoid his touch, the women in the mirror dispersed, making way for him as he turned to the bedroom door. He crossed the room in long strides, his fingers clenching and unclenching at his sides. I felt horribly small and terribly cold without his presence at my back and his hands on my neck. I wondered how I'd managed this long without it at all.

Niklaus paused at the door, turning to glance at me only once. "Stay here," he said. A command. "I will return." A promise. My imagination fluttered at the edges of my bravery. But something was wrong. I could feel it like an ache somewhere in the hollow of my chest.

He slipped from the bedroom, shutting the door with a click. At once, a flurry of sound and movement filled my senses; phantom hands tugged at my sleeves, my hair; hot breath spoke harried words against the base of my skull and the flesh beneath my ear; another candle by the window snuffed out, the full figure of a woman appearing and disappearing just as quickly.

Get up, the voices said. *Get up. Get up.*

I rose and crossed to the dark stretch of wall opposite the bed, where the ghostly woman had disappeared just moments before. I felt my arms guided, my hands prompted; I felt around in the dark, counting the spines of books with my fingertips.

"What do you want me to see?" I hissed, my voice alone in the dark. "What do you want me to look for?" I wondered what Niklaus might think if he came back to find me blindly feeling his collection of first editions.

My hand stilled atop a thick leather spine. I felt pressure from all directions, hands gripping my wrist, guiding my fingers, holding my elbow aloft. Had I gone entirely limp, I imagined I'd be held up by the axis of my wrist. Curious, I gave the book a tug, only to find it partially affixed to the bookshelf. It slid halfway out at an angle, clicking at some sort of mechanism within the bookshelf. Before I could replace the book, the entire shelf began to shift, swinging outward across the rug like a heavy door.

Within, a single spiral staircase descended into the dark. I cursed. This, I knew at once, I was not meant to have seen.

But a voice—a multitude of voices—spurred me on. I spun on my heel, reaching for the candle on the armoire. I gripped the bronze votive like a dagger, relishing the warmth against my palm. I cast one cursory glance at the bedroom door before returning to the half-ajar bookshelf and slipping inside.

I was not alone as I descended the spiral stair. The iron railing was warm, as if a hand other than my own had gripped it not so long before. At the base of the staircase, the small landing gave way to a single door. It was simple compared to the rest of the apartment, as if installed as an afterthought.

It swung open silently. The candle bathed me in a shallow ring of warm light, past which I could see nothing. I felt along the wall until I found a long handle, protruding like a headman's axe.

Two rows of bulbs flickered to life, along the length of the room, the sound of burdened electricity groaning through the quiet space. I shielded my eyes, my grip tightening on the candle despite the heat.

And then, with a gasp that was swallowed whole by the ghosts on my tongue, the candle slipped from my hand and onto the stone floor.

The room looked as if it once had been a part of the mortician's practice; sterile tables in rows, racks of embalming tools and hooked surgical gear on the wall, coolers in neat rows against the far wall. Each instrument had been pushed to the side, the sterile normality of a mortician's tools giving way to a mismatched collection of chairs, a chaise longue, a rattan chest. A mirror sat propped between two armchairs, both thick with dust.

And in each chair, upon the chaise, and propped like a marionette before the mirror, was a body. On each table, from beneath the crisp white sheets, peeked women's feet, all in mismatched character heels and low heels. A hand hung from beneath the nearest sheet. The fingers were painted a vibrant red, filed to points at the end.

Each body that I could see had been dressed in faded dresses and shoes that often did not fit on their bloated feet. From where I stood, I could see their eyes pinned shut, their lips sewn. Some wore silks like head-scarves, others dripped beads and diamonds from drooping earlobes and bulging fingers. Fine jewels and gold chains hung from their necks. Their skin, rubber in texture and dull gray in color, had been smeared with vibrant rouge of various shades, as if their caretaker simply could not decide which color would suit.

And on the wall above them all, looking down with a disdainful gaze, was a portrait of Niklaus, with Marguerite at his shoulder. She was an austere woman, with rubies and gold at her neck, and a silk tie in her hair.

I gagged, skittering across the room to find my reflection in one of the many latched freezer doors. I already knew, with certainty, what lay within. My breath ragged, I pawed at my face, wiping the rouge from my cheeks and onto the front of my dress. I tore the silk from my hair, ignoring the knots and tangles that ripped from my scalp along with it. As if struck, I tossed it onto the ground, Marguerite's reflection burning in the unblemished steel.

Behind me, the door slammed closed. "The distance between love and harm," Niklaus's voice filled the room, "is more ambiguous that you could ever understand."

I whirled, and at once he was upon me. I expected to be struck, to find his hands around my throat, my skull—but instead, he embraced me. He pulled me close, cradling my too-narrow shoulders against his chest and my head against the hollow of his throat. Niklaus pet my hair, stepping away from the autopsy tables and cadaver freezers and into the center of the room, shushing me as if I'd merely been frightened by a bad dream. I felt tears, hot and unbidden, on my cheeks before I even realized I'd begun to cry.

I wriggled in his grasp, my cheek flush against his collarbone. "What did you do?" I cried, my weak voice muffled. "Niklaus, what have you done?"

"They didn't understand," he murmured. He shook his head, his chin rubbing against the top of my head. "None of them. Not like you do, and not like I. What it is to be lonely, to be lost, to be unwanted. Wanted in a way that *matters*. Lauded with applause and false adorations, like idols—" he sighed, as if somehow what he said would ring conspiratorial and true. "I cannot make them what they are *not.*"

My legs sagged, knees buckling. Niklaus held me up, like a doll that he refused to let touch the ground. I recognized some of the women the longer I looked at them. Dancers from the Moulin who we'd all thought had simply run away with a wealthy benefactor. An artist who'd come to paint the mezzo sopranos. A can-can dancer who'd broken a heel mid-performance.

Women came and went from the heady underbelly of Paris like migrating birds. They came and went, and no one asked questions. We all knew better than to ask questions, those of us who were grounded here, rooted and unwilling to budge. We wondered, speculated, traded theories like bets. I always liked to imagine that the women who disappeared from the illusionary vignette of Paris had found their way someplace warm, someplace sunny.

This was where they had all gone. Just like me—seduced, mystified, and left here to rot.

"*Please.*" Tears bubbled over my lips and down my chin. "Why have you done this?" This did not belong with the perfect Niklaus that had lived in my imagination. He was meant to fix broken things, to shepherd death into the beauty of the afterlife, into the infinite. He was meant to understand lost things, to give meaning to death and decay, to violence and injustice. He was meant to heal wounds, to make violence into virtue.

His voice was soft against the top of my head, like a secret. "Marguerite…" he sighed. "I thought you, of all souls, would understand."

Marguerite?

All at once, the room was overfull with sound, with bodies, with movement. I was thrown back from Niklaus, ripped from his grip and flung against the far wall. I battered through the cluttered rows of autopsy tables, my wheeling hands finding a too-soft leg, a sheet-covered breast. I landed with a thud, the back of my head smacking against the cool metal of the refrigerator doors. The spool of silver thread slipped from my pocket and rolled across the stone, casting a single silver arrow to the door.

The women who inhabited the mausoleum of my skull flew around him like furies, a translucent cloud of flying hair and ripping hands. They tore at him, loosing screeching battle cries into the still air. I could see them now more clearly than I ever had. The can-can dancer, the socialite, the *mezzo soprano*. I could see the blood beneath their hair, the sickly caving of their skulls. I saw the bruises on their necks, hidden beneath jewels and vintage scarves. They matched their lifeless bodies perfectly, where they lay motionless across the room. I could only wonder how long they had waited for me to find them.

Niklaus's eyes wheeled, his hands flung to cover his face. I could tell from the unfocused quality of his gaze that he could not see them—but I could.

I scrambled to my feet and lunged for the door. Niklaus swung wildly, reaching for me as I fled, but was pulled by the lapels, the sleeves, the waist, by the women that only I could see.

"Come back!" he cried. "You cannot leave me again!"

I barreled through the door, slipping on the spiral stair and falling onto my hands and knees. I crawled, stepping on the hem of my skirt. With a cry, I grappled at my throat, ripping the jewels away and tossing them aside. The golden brocade shattered on the stone, sending rubies like blood scattering across the floor.

Out into the empty bedroom I fell, the sounds of Niklaus's struggle at my back. I sprinted from the room, feeling hands pushing, urging, pressing at the small of my back. Down the corridor, past the kitchen; the street lights outside shone through the stained glass that hung over the door to Niklaus's pied-à-terre. *Pompes Funèbres,* in bloody lettering.

I inhaled deeply, filling my chest in preparation for a scream. I'd call for help, tear along the avenue, and hide in the nearest corner shop. I didn't know this neighborhood; it was too expensive for my blood. On my usual block, the shopkeepers would have come to me in an instant. But not here; this was a foreign place, a hostile sliver of opulence and decay, romanticized to the point of rot.

As I reached for the doorknob, a hand clasped hard upon the nape of my neck. It pulled me back, spinning me around. Niklaus threw me to the floor, watching with a mad gleam as I bounced off the long table in the hall, shattering a framed photograph of Marguerite, and scrambled across the runner. He looked harried, mussed, as if a hundred hands had tried to hold him below.

He took me by the ankle, sinking to the floor and holding me firm. I screamed, and from somewhere beneath the floor, the voices of the other women echoed my fear. Niklaus straddled my hips, his rough grip pulling my wrists over my head.

"You can't!" he boomed. "You cannot leave me. Who will love you if you go?"

The words wounded more deeply than the fresh bloom of blood prickling beneath my hair. My mind spun. "Niklaus, *stop!*" I cried. "It's me! It's—I am your Marguerite! Look at me!"

His eyes swam. I watched with horror, a sob choked in my throat, as his expression changed, falling like the Moulin's curtains. "*Maman?*" His voice was small, like a child's. "Do not be mad, Maman." He crumpled, his weight knocking the air from my chest. His hands fell, his cheek pressed against my breast. He gave a great sigh, and was still, his fingers petting absently at the bare flesh of my arm.

My eyes wheeled wildly, at last finding the broken glass that had fallen from Marguerite's portrait. Her visage had faded, and what once had been a youthful smile had fallen and decayed, faded with the photograph's ink. A long shard of glass glimmered in the colorful light from above.

In one movement, I threw my hand sidelong and wrapped my fingers around the jagged edge. As Niklaus stirred against my collarbone, I arced the glass through the air and plunged it into the soft flesh at the base of his skull.

The sound that he made did not belong to the Niklaus of my imagination. It was small, a wet pop and a gurgle, followed by a high whimper. It was that of a child—not a man. His blood bloomed over my hand, wetting the makeshift blade and mingling with my own. With a cry, I gave the glass a twist and Niklaus bucked atop me.

The light above the door flickered and extinguished. The half-dressed bodies of countless women gathered at my feet, watching as he struggled. Their faces remained impassive, only flickering with recognition when I rolled Niklaus onto the floor, skittering from beneath him as he crumpled on the wood, spluttering and clawing at the back of his neck. He pulled the glass from his flesh and cast it aside—but I knew with certainty that he would not rise again.

The sounds of unquiet dying followed me as I stumbled back into Niklaus's bedroom. The air had gone still, though the doors and windows were crowded with the watchful eyes of his victims. I knew what needed to be done. The breath ragged in my throat, I limped from candle to candle, tipping each onto the rug, the bed, the tasseled curtains.

The flame caught quickly. I turned once to my ghostly companions. They nodded, a single movement from the furthest reaches of my periphery.

By the time I returned to the foyer—Niklaus's bedroom too hot to stand any longer—he had gone still. Smoke filled my nose, my throat. Even the very tips of my ears burned. I pulled the tattered neck of my dress over my nose and mouth, stooping to press Niklaus's eyes closed.

I glanced up once more at the flames that crawled and licked from the open bedroom doorway. The women within, one by one, began to fade, blinking into the smoke and ash like embers. On the floor beside Niklaus, Marguerite's photograph had been entirely swallowed, drowned in the blood of her offspring. I hoped, wherever she was, that she was alone.

As if called, she appeared within the smoke. For only a moment, a glimpse of silk in a forest of dark wool, she showed herself. And then, with a nod, she was gone.

The leash of my need had gone slack, the gnawing of longing absent from the spaces between my ribs. I would be alone, yes. But I would be free. And I would be only as mad as would keep me alive in the wild.

CHAPTER ELEVEN

THE WITCH'S HOUSE

ALEXANDRIA BAKER

There are many words for what I am: witch, hermit, whore, harlot. But I think my personal favorite is "eccentric." I live alone, and I am content. No man dirties my polished wooden floors with his boots, and every night my bed embraces me with a comfort that no lover's arms could match.

I am content to be alone, and that frightens them.

Though, I am not entirely solitary. The forest provides plenty of company, if one knows where to look. Every day, I spend hours tending my garden on the edge of the forest, pressing my fingers into soft soil and nourishing the ground to bear my fruit. Under the hedges, small eyes stalk me. I always leave out milk and bread for wayward spirits who find my cottage.

My longest companion was a mad March hare, who dashed out of the woods and sprang over my rickety fence, overturning a basket of carrots. Though he was frantic and twitched if I stared too long, he wouldn't return to the woods, even when I propped open the garden gate.

I am not sure what he was running from, but my home is generous, and I had plenty to share. He made his place under a bush beneath my windowsill, and every night, I left root vegetables and leafy greens for him, only to find them devoured the next morning.

We passed the days in companionable silence and, over time, he stopped jumping in fright when I neared. I never named him, because wild things have no need for names. While I enjoyed his company in the winding and overgrown rows of my garden, he never came inside. Though, I never invited him in.

Our homes are the truest reflection of our souls, of what we love and cherish, the blemishes and messes we tolerate, and those we do not. We must be careful who we let inside.

The lack of company has never bothered me. Though I live alone, I am far from celibate. I find my pleasure in the comforting recesses of my cottage, in homespun bedsheets and soothing baths drawn at midnight. What those in the village do not understand is that my cottage is as much a living thing as the hare in my garden. When I exhale in ecstasy, the ancient rafters and soft beams of my bed creak with me. And on rare occasions, when the moon is full or that primal urge rises from deep within, my home provides a little extra magic in a well-formed broom handle or a certain vegetable from my garden.

For some, my existence is an abomination—something to be eradicated, lest other women go seeking liberation for themselves. For others, I am a tragedy—a lone woman perennially without a male companion, doomed to spend eternity alone. Despite my apparent damnation, I answer to no one, heed no whims but my own, and if damnation is the cost of freedom, it is a price I am more than willing to pay.

I should have known, however, that this was not an answer the village would accept.

The first time I saw the woodsman, it was an overcast midafternoon. The pines loomed in the treeline, and the air was pregnant with the promise of rain. I stood at my vegetable patch, wiping the dirt from my hands onto my worn apron, when the hare in my garden stiffened in the breeze.

He froze instinctually, sensing a change in the environment that I had yet to detect. I scanned the woods, expecting a fox—or perhaps a bear—but I, too, froze when my eyes fell upon the man among the trees.

He was handsome, by all accounts. A rugged type, with a full, dark beard and shoulders shaped by years spent swinging the ax that hung on his belt. He wore a cotton tunic beneath a vest of fur, and when his icy blue eyes landed on me, I felt a jolt run up my spine.

It was not fear I felt, not exactly.

I had seen his kind many times over the years. Intrepid woodsmen and would-be hunters had often wandered by my cottage, though I knew in the village they warned the young men to stay out of these parts. Whenever one wandered too close, I would call on the forest—the beasts that walked its earth and the spirits that flitted on the edge of perception—to ward my house and turn their paths away. I had no use for them, their bodies, and certainly no use for their demands of me and the forest.

This one was different.

I had not heard him coming. That alone was remarkable. He walked through the underbrush with a respect for the budding leaves and rotting twigs that allowed him to travel in near silence.

Then, there was his gaze. His eyes held a willpower I had not seen in another for some time. It was not a challenge or a threat. It was only a statement: *See me, as I have seen you.*

As I stood staring, he raised his hand in a simple greeting. I hailed him in return, and when he began down the winding path to my cottage, I allowed him to approach unharmed. "You're an awfully long way from the village," I called over my fence.

"As are you," he said.

"What brings you to these parts?"

"The same thing that brings every woodsman worth his salt. Lumber, kindling, the resources only found in the forest." He paused, and cut his eyes toward me. "And a legend about an unearthly woman who stands alone against the forces of nature."

At this, I chuckled.

My response caught him off guard, but I could tell he wasn't afraid—the joke was simply lost on him. "What's so funny?"

"You put it so grandly, 'standing alone against nature.' In truth, I work *with* nature. The forest and its creatures are the only reason I survive." I offered him half a smile. "Only the village folk feel they have to lash out at the woods."

He snorted at this. "True. When my brothers chop wood or hunt, they tromp around so loudly, it's a wonder they catch anything at all."

"You're not like them."

"No, I suppose not. I enjoy the forest, and the quiet. It seems a shame to disturb the peace for a few logs for my fire."

I decided then that I liked him. He was strange compared to the other men from the village. He had a quiet intensity and self-awareness that few men possess. And he was not nosy like the others.

"Are you going to ask?"

"Ask what?"

"The question every other soul who's made it here has asked: Am I a witch?"

He appraised me then, taking in my wild curls, the dirt on my hands and knees, and the sturdy little cottage puffing out chimney smoke behind me. "I don't like to ask questions I already know the answer to."

Yes, I liked him.

Before I could say another word, he spoke again, "I do have one question."

"What is it?"

"Could you spare a cup of tea for a weary traveler?"

I brewed him a cup with herbs from my garden. He never asked to enter my home, and for that, I respected him all the more. We drank the hearty beverage, standing on opposite sides of my fence, and afterwards, I brought him some bread to bolster him on his journey home.

"What will you say of your encounter with the witch of the woods?" I asked.

"Nothing that they do not ask about directly. Your business is your own, and no one knows I was venturing this way." He stared off into the lengthening shadows of the forest.

My intuition told me he was hiding something. Had he been anyone else, made any other mistake throughout our interaction, I would have stopped him in his tracks. I would have called on a bear to eviscerate him, or struck down a tree as he passed beneath. I would have conjured up a sudden snowstorm to freeze him to his brittle core, or sent the forest spirits to drive him mad before he ever reached the village.

But I didn't do any of those things, because I liked him.

A week passed in blessed monotony.

He came earlier in the day, while I was weeding in my garden. My hare alerted me. The animal sat bolt upright, then took a flying leap into his nest under the windowsill. I looked up to see the woodsman at the treeline. He raised a hand in greeting, and waited for me to acknowledge him before approaching. Though I appreciated his good manners, I was still caught off guard by how quietly he could move.

"You're getting awfully familiar, aren't you?"

He stopped a few feet away on the other side of the fence, and shrugged sheepishly. In his hand, he held a small burlap bag. "I don't wish to intrude, but I wanted to repay your kindness the other day."

"Is that so?"

"I brought you a small token of my appreciation." He took a few steps closer, and held out the bag to me. I took it, and opened it to see two ducks—freshly killed—stuffed inside. "I won't pretend to know what a witch likes to eat, but I caught these two this morning on the lake by the village."

I glanced up at him. It made him nervous.

"I thought the lake was far enough outside your purview that you would not take insult," he said hastily. "I would never knowingly hunt your creatures."

"You have good sense, as far as the villagers go. I do like duck, and if you are content to wait, I will whip up a stew."

"That would be nice." He sloughed off his satchel, and laid his ax against my fence.

"Don't get any grand ideas while I'm inside. I will bring the food out, but take one step past the fence, and my fearsome March hare will run you back to the village."

My tone was light, but the warning was real. Though I doubted my hare could truly scare off a woodsman, this was one threshold where I would tolerate no trespasses. If he disobeyed, I would send him howling back into the woods, never to return.

Thankfully, it did not come to that. From my kitchen window, I watched him pace around the property, taking in the cottage from new angles. He never showed the slightest interest in entering the garden, and after walking the perimeter once, he returned to where his ax and satchel lay. He sat on the ground, adjusted some items within the bag, and laid his head down on it, napping until I brought out the stew.

"A chef as well as a witch," he said between mouthfuls. "It's a wonder you haven't been scooped up by a villager in need of a useful wife."

"It's a wonder I haven't picked the biggest, dumbest one of the lots to do manual labor for me." I glanced at him from the corner of my eye. He was more than handsome. It was clear his muscles were used to hard work.

"You need only ask."

"I don't need to. I can take care of myself."

"I'm sure you can, but do you really want to?" He paused, the silver spoon dangling delicately in his large hand, like a doll's accessory.

"I prefer this life. My freedom is guaranteed this way."

"It's not right for a woman to go through life all alone. I am certain the village would welcome you if you would just—"

"Bah! I have no need for those patriarchal village fools." My ire had risen, but this was his first misstep. He was allowed an impertinent remark or two. "Besides, I'm not alone, not really. I have the forest, and my garden, and the hare, and my home. These are the only things I need to find fulfillment."

He stared into his nearly empty bowl for a long moment. Finally, he scraped the last morsel from it and shrugged his shoulders, but the tension remained. I wondered if I had made him too comfortable at my cottage. I vowed to keep our next interaction brief, whenever it came.

The woodsman was wise, insidiously so. He stayed away for many days, giving me time to calm and return to routine.

It was just enough time for me to forget his impertinence. I should have known it was only the beginning of his transgressions.

I spent the days as peacefully as always, in harmony with my home and hearth. I worked small spells of protection and healing for the nearby plants and animals. I tended to the forest spirits, and brewed minor potions and tinctures for my own use. It was dull, domestic bliss.

But content as I was, even I was not immune to that all-consuming drive that takes over living things from time to time. I was growing restless, ready to sow wild oats and find sensual solace within myself and my beloved home. I wanted to feel like a woman, a fertile goddess with the world at her fingertips. I knew my home would provide for these needs, when the time was right.

Perhaps it was my impatience that was my downfall. The woodsman returned a day before the full moon, when I was hungry in all the ways one can be. I was out in my garden, running my fingers over the silky-soft skin of flower petals, mulling which components would be best for the spellwork I had in mind. My hungry hands ate up the sensation, eager for more soft caresses, eager for warmth.

The woodsman arrived just before sundown, and he hailed me, though he did not wait for my acknowledgement as he progressed down the path. His cheeks were flushed, and there was an edge to his demeanor.

He stopped on the other side of the fence, and produced a small bundle from his satchel. "You haunt me," he said simply.

I cocked an eyebrow. He was not the first to make such a statement, but rather than fear or distaste, his tone spoke of eagerness, desire.

He took my silence for what it was: permission to continue. "I returned to the village, and I tried to go about my duties, but you haunt me. I cannot walk through the woods without seeing your face, and my feet keep finding new paths to this place." He looked up at me then, and a new passion burned in his eyes. "I know you are not like the women in the village. You do not need me—or any man for that matter—but I want you."

His words sent a shiver up my spine. The urge was building up inside like a fire spreading through me. I wanted him then. I opened my mouth to respond, but he cut me off before I could say anything.

"Please, before you make up your mind, take these favors." He handed me the small bundle cradled close to his chest. "I'm not used to making overtures like this, but I know a man should always bring a gift to let his woman know she is loved."

Though I disliked his implication—for I was driven by a baser instinct—I accepted his gift. Inside, I found tokens from the forest; dried flowers, a few tawny feathers, soft green moss, fresh acorns, and a variety of seeds. I stared at the offering for a long while, struck by the thoughtfulness of it. He understood me, after so little time. For what use did jewels or silks hold for me? These were the fruits of the forest, the only treasure I truly valued.

We were cut from the same cloth, it seemed. He knew what I appreciated, how I needed to exist in the woods, how we could connect.

And so, in the molten light of the dying sun, I opened my gate and came to him. I threw my arms around his wide shoulders and pressed my mouth hungrily to his, enjoying his rough beard on my smooth face. We leaned into each other, bodies eager to entwine.

I led him away from my cottage. I could not bear the thought of straying from my one true love in sight of the walls that had so long protected me. But the call was strong, and the feeling of his body against mine was an intoxication. We scrambled out into the forest, courting like animals as we leapt between rotting logs and stoic trees, searching for a blanket of moss where we could make our stand.

The forest was neutral to our presence, and offered little shelter or threat. It was enough. Soft leaves and delicate moss became the bed where we laid. We stayed together through the long night, feeding off one another like ravenous wolves on a carcass.

When dawn broke, cold and pale through the dark branches above, I was satisfied. I was ready to return home, to put this tryst behind me and attune myself once again to my cottage and the love we shared. The woodsman would be welcome to visit in the future, but now I needed solitude.

As I rose, he seized my hand. "Don't go," he whispered.

"It is time," I replied.

"Please."

"The village will be missing you. And I have a home to tend to." I leaned down and gave him a final kiss, firm but warm. He looked like a tragic painting as he laid in our bed of moss, nude and pitiful.

"When can I see you again?"

"When the moon glows full and bright, you will find me waiting at the gate."

A flash of anger crossed his face, he was expecting to see me again in a matter of days, not weeks. But he covered it quickly by pulling on his tunic. "Fine," he grunted.

He rose and left without another word, and I returned somewhat guiltily to the home I had abandoned.

My cottage was cold and quiet for a number of days afterward. I had to restart the fire from scratch, since the coals had died while I was away. The hare jumped as though I were a stranger when I entered the garden, and for a moment I regretted my tryst with the woodsman.

But the memory of his hands on my body and his skin against mine was enough to assuage my guilt. After all, I had not invited him inside, had not violated my most private sanctuary. The house begrudgingly accepted this, and slowly I felt the flow of energy and magic return to its usual vibration. I soon forgot the hunger that had driven me into the woodsman's arms, and once again stood firm in my satisfied solitude. I was ready to embrace my home again, in the most intimate way I knew how.

On a moonless night a few weeks later, sensual howls filled the night air as wolves sought each other in the dark. I could hear the mating calls of toads from the nearby creek, and the dusky wind braced my skin and sent me shivering.

I felt alive in that most primal of ways. I finished my supper, restored order to my kitchen and hearth, and my heart began to race as I thought of what came next. I carefully banked the embers in my fire, eager to get to my bedroom.

For a passing moment, I felt eyes on me. The hairs on the back of my neck stood straight, and I froze, casting my eyes around the room.

I peered through the window, bolstered by the fact that I was in my own home and, thus, at my strongest. The darkness outside was nigh impenetrable beyond the glow of my candles. I caught movement past the fence, but it could have been anything. With the spell the night cast, it likely *was* anything. The animals, spirits and the trees themselves were thrusting toward life, and I intended to join them.

Once in my bedroom, I wasted no time undressing and leapt into my welcoming bed. My fingers knew what to do, and I stiffened, leaning into the reassuring embrace of my pillows as the cottage filled up with the sounds of my endeavors. The whole house came alive, resonating with my energy and returning it like a generous lover would. At the crescendo of my frenzied activity, my breath came in short gasps. I clutched a pillow as the pleasure overtook me.

As I lay dazed and dewy in bed, I heard a crash from outside. It was far too large and clumsy to be any of the forest's local inhabitants, and I snapped up from my repose.

I strained my eyes against the night, and I saw it—the garden gate banging shut, and the unmistakable shape of a man running into the woods.

Days passed in miserable, paranoid quiet. I busied myself around the cottage more than usual, rarely venturing into the garden.

I had been seen. The woodsman had violated my trust. He had trespassed in my garden and seen me at my most primal, my most vulnerable. It was not that I was embarrassed or ashamed—far from it.

I was furious.

Something private and inviolable had been breached, and I would not stand for it. My activities in the house were between me and it—he had no power here. Our night together meant nothing if he would not hold sacred the boundaries I set. If the woodsman could not leave me in peace, then I had every reason to suspect his motives.

He would not claim me as a wife. And I would not be burned by those fools in the village.

My workings grew dark; I drew up poisons from herbs boiled in my seething cauldron, lit black candles every night to ward off intruders, and grew thorny branches in the soil outside. My cottage oozed warning. Yet when the moon was full, the woodsman returned.

He announced himself with a single gunshot that rang out through the forest. To this day, I still associate that sound with tragedy.

The sunset left bloody tracks across the sky as it sank below the treeline. He emerged from the shadows with a jaunty smile as he swung a dripping burlap sack. He had been hunting, obviously. *So much for leaving my creatures alone.*

His pace hardly slowed as he approached, barely waiting for me to step outside before he continued his trajectory.

"I brought you dinner!" His voice was impetuous; he was proud of himself. "I think it's about time we had a proper meal together."

I offered him one last out. "I do not think that is wise."

"Why not? Can we not enjoy a civilized conversation inside for once?"

"Some things are better left unsaid." This irritated him.

He had brought me meat, and now he wanted my gratitude. "I know you want your freedom. I understand that, truly." His eyes softened. "But you don't know what you're missing. My brothers and their wives are happy with their lives in the village," he stopped, realizing how much he had revealed. When I said nothing, he pushed forward. "I have brought you sustenance, and by the laws of hospitality, you have to invite me in."

"Fine." Though under no obligation to follow such asinine traditions, I held out my hand for the bloody sack, and opened the garden gate for him. I mulled over the various spells and poisons I had on hand. Wiping his memory would be the simplest solution, but he had offended me greatly, taking my past hospitality for granted and violating the sanctity of my home and hearth. And he had spoken of me to his brothers. There would be questions when he returned. Madness seemed the more appropriate path. I would let him live—and he would serve as a testament to the others why they should stay far away from this place.

He followed me into the golden glow of my cottage, lit by dozens of candles and a well-fed fire. He tracked mud into my home, and his ax clanged where he dropped it on my kitchen floor. Each step he took was an affront, and the more space he took up, the more I felt my chest constrict with the invasion.

"You keep a lovely home," he said, turning his back to me to sit and warm his feet by the fire.

"Thank you." The words floated out of my mouth as if from another world. I placed the burlap sack on the counter and opened it to see what poor creature he had killed for his supper.

My breath caught in my throat at the sight of the mangled body. The bloody fur, clouded eyes, and stench of death could not hide what he had done.

My mad March hare had finally returned to the woods to meet his fate after all.

"Are there other witches like you?"

"What?" The question caught me off guard.

"Is there someone you learned your craft from? Clearly you know the ways of the woods, and there are plenty of other young village men who are of marrying age. With a bit of convincing, they could learn to love having a witch for a wife. They would be lucky to find a woman like you."

"Yes, there are others," I said in a daze. "We usually keep to ourselves, but we are many in number."

He laughed heartily and slapped his knee. "Excellent! Now please, the day was long, and I want to discuss our future over dinner. I think, with a bit of work, your cottage could make an excellent homestead for us." He yawned and settled more deeply into the chair.

There it was. He wanted not only me, but my home, my power. He wanted to woo himself a witch. A woman in touch with the natural world, forest spirits at her beck and call—claimed by him through the bond of marriage.

The thought churned my stomach.

Other than my home, the only companion I had ever cared for was dead, growing cold in the kitchen while his murderer warmed himself by my fire.

I would not stand for it. I caught the reflection of the flames on the woodsman's ax in my periphery.

"Yes, I will tell my sisters about the men in the village," I said. The ax handle was smooth with use, and conformed nicely to my hand. "I will remind them never to forget why we left the village all those generations ago. I will tell them to find love in themselves and their work, to stay away from men like you. I will help them build their homes strong, and their fences high." I raised the ax over my shoulder. He turned to witness the fury on my face, but it was too late. "And I will tell them to show no mercy."

The blade sliced into his neck like butter, severing bone and artery. Blood poured from the wound. His eyes grew wide and he clutched at my arm as I raised the ax for a second strike.

The cut was clean, and his head fell to the floor with a satisfying thump.

Blood pooled, threatening to overtake the fire in the hearth. A chill crept over the house. The wooden floors soaked up the blood, drinking in the essence of violence and entitlement that oozed from the woodsman's corpse. Before my eyes, the boards swelled and warped, the still-wet blood irrevocably staining my home down to the very foundation.

The hearth fire went out.

It was more than a bad omen. It was the end of my home.

No matter how hard I scrubbed, I would never remove the bloodstains. Even if I ripped up the floorboards, this house would never again be a place where only I had walked. The woodsman was everywhere, he had wormed his way inside my body and mind, and now my home. His unseeing eyes bored into me, and I imagined his severed head twisted with a gloating smile. Alone in the dark, I wept for everything I had built, and everything that was lost.

Now, I know no home but the forest.

My cottage was defiled so deeply that it could never be made right. I buried the woodsman in my garden, and planted poisonous weeds over his body. I set the cottage ablaze, and laughed as my home and lover were so quickly reduced to ash; I knew I would never feel safe there again, and now the scorched, black earth is home to nothing but rubble and poison.

The forest provides everything I need to survive. Shelter from the rain, food when I am hungry, even occasional companions in the form of small animals or spirits. But the forest does not love me. It does not breathe with me the way my home did. We simply co-exist.

We do not love.

I spend my restless nights haunting the village for the sins of the woodsman. He was a product of this place, and so it is the village's fault that I am without hearth and home. I curdle milk and blind cows. I set dogs barking in the dead of night and pilfer cheese and other goods from the villagers' pantries. Sometimes I steal a babe, and leave behind a hare in the crib. The irony is lost on them. The hares usually escape. The babes do not.

I become everything I was once accused of being. I live up to my legend, so the villagers will leave my sisters alone.

I plague this village, tormenting them so they know how it feels to have the sanctity of their homes violated. The women make the sign of the cross when a cold wind blows and nail iron horseshoes to their doors, as if that could stop me. They cry out in the night and ask the clergy to rid the village of this pestilence.

They pray for mercy.

I pray for retribution.

CHAPTER TWELVE

LISSANDRA
A.L. GARCIA

Oh, patroness of my soul
Benefactress of all things lunatic
Oh, celestial goddess of my darkest nights
Bring me back to life
Under the blood moon at the witching hour
Imbue me with the power to devour
The souls of all those enemies and cowards
That watched me writhe in vain
Let them learn to fear my name
As requiem of hell descent upon their spineless breaths
Sink bloodlust revenge deep into feeble necks
With fangs the color of midnight
Eyes flickering viridian in undead candlelight
Turning swords and stakes to rust
They'll soon lose faith in all the gods and saints they trust
When Lissandra comes

Lissandra paces the garden, nervously running her fingers along the petals of crimson peonies as her mother speaks with Dr. Froelich in the parlor. She has been under the care of his staff at the San German Institute intermittently over the past year. Dr. Froelich visits Lissandra more frequently in her home than the other patients on account of her mother's sizable donations to the Institute. Lissandra's mother spares no expense when it comes to her health, and there are few doctors more notable than the illustrious Wilhelm Froelich, particularly at dealing with women's psychological disorders. Her mother assures her she will be relieved of her mental afflictions soon, as she requested private services. Lissandra's mother is confident she will rid her daughter of the evil magic and sapphic desires the ungrateful Vadoma Grey cursed her darling daughter with, as well as the subsequent parasomnia and hysteria they caused.

Vadoma Grey arrived at the estate on a cold autumn night begging for cover, soaking wet beneath a raging thunderstorm. Vadoma stayed the night and was so helpful the next morning, Lissandra's mother offered her employment. She had not noticed the indigent was with child at the time. A few months later, the child was born on the estate, a beautiful baby girl she named Beatrix. Many years passed, as Beatrix grew alongside Miss Lissandra, building an extraordinary bond, much to Mrs. Beth's dismay. It was not until she discovered Vadoma teaching Lissandra and Beatrix her sorcery in the forest that things took a turn for the worse. Mrs. Beth accused Vadoma of being a gypsy witch and had her taken away. After the removal of her mother, Beatrix became increasingly scornful and brooding. Other than to fulfill her duties at the estate, she spoke only to Miss Lissandra. Then, one day, she also vanished without a trace. It was as if the earth had swallowed her whole. Miss Lissandra was inconsolable for months.

Lissandra looks over to a row of lion's tooth growing at the edge of the woods and recalls exploring the lesser-known corners of the grounds with Beatrix. They'd spend hours searching for distinct species of mushrooms to take home using her father's copy of *Linnaeus' Systema Naturae*, content to snack on wild berries as they frolicked barefoot, daydreaming of impossible futures, laughter dense with mirth. Flashes of their last day together assault her senses in waves. Beatrix's berry-stained lips upon her own, their breaths forming fog in the frigid breeze. She stands frozen too, paralyzed by the bittersweet memory, an odd statue adorning the otherwise unblemished garden. Tongue-tied tears pool in her bright turquoise eyes, oceans of nostalgia threatening the delicate features beneath them.

She doesn't notice Dr. Froelich approaching from behind her until he speaks. "Today, the sun-kissed earth grows green again, and flower buds slip out silent tongues to taste the morning dew, and yet we struggle to renew our faith in the sun's sweet rays. What a glorious morning, wouldn't you say so, Lizzy?"

His broad, stern voice jolts her out of the memory, and she turns and replies, "Pardon?"

He furrows his brow, pulls a cloth from his right pocket, offers it and continues. "Oh, I was just commenting on this lovely weather. How are you feeling today, Lizzy? You are all right with me addressing you as Lizzy, no?"

She takes the handkerchief with a sigh. "I prefer Lissandra actually, if you don't mind."

He smiles, and places a hand on her waist, guiding her towards a nearby marble bench adorned in her mother's haughty fashion, with an imposing winged lion on each side. "Not at all. Lissandra it is. Shall we take a seat and talk for a while? Your mother called me here for your benefit, and I have some suggestions for your treatment that she has approved. I would like to make you aware of them, out of courtesy."

Lissandra scoffs. "Oh, is that so? How kind of you and mother. She is such a darling, isn't she? Always so concerned over my health; always so aware of everyone's state of well-being." She laughs with contempt. "Go on, Dr. Froelich. I would be honored to hear your suggestions for my apparent condition."

Dr. Froelich clears his throat. "Well yes, we will get to that, but first, let's talk a little about these apparitions you have been having since Beatrix disappeared. Were you seeing something just now? In the woods over there?"

Lissandra sighs. "Oh, I just thought I heard some birds cooing. I like to watch them, you know?"

He nods. "Hmm, I see. They must be special to bring you to tears. What can you tell me of the apparitions that come to you at night? Your mother claims you are waking from your sleep to walk the grounds."

Lissandra's gaze widens, fixating her eyes on his. "Yes, this shadow figure. It comes to me in blackened dreams, pulling me down with it into a deep abyss with phantom hands. It started in the corner of my room, three months I think, after Beatrix went missing. It lies in wait for me, glistening teeth gleaming in the dark, inching closer to my bed each time I try to find relief by shutting my eyes. Just yesterday, it remained hovering over my knees watching the screams lock in my throat until they turned to gasps. It smiled at my fright, then vanished." She stands, pacing nervously and wringing her hands. "I go for a walk in the woods to clear my mind afterwards. Nature, the trees, the grass beneath my feet, they always seem to soothe the…the demon." She laughs. "Well, that's what mother calls it. I'm not so sure of what it is. Beatrix's disappearance put a fear in me I am unable to escape from, I assume, or she is haunting me, who knows." He pulls a small notebook from his breast pocket, scribbles some notes, and replies with a smile, "Well yes, mourning the loss of a friend can have some quite undesirable side effects, particularly one with such a troubled past. I have faith my treatment will cure you of these specters. I'd like to invite you to stay at the hospital for a fortnight. You will be directly under my care, and I promise you will have the freedom to roam the grounds, just as Vedoma did, respecting treatment conditions, of course."

She stares at him in disbelief. "Vedoma? She was at the hospital?"

Dr. Froelich clears his throat. "Well yes, of course. She was at the hospital for quite a while before her passing. I didn't know you were unaware. Your mother informed me she was a friend and that you remain in a state of perpetual anguish over her. However, it's best to keep her medical history undisclosed for the duration of your treatment. She is the reason for your…hmm, current condition, would you not agree?"

Lissandra frowns and backs away. "The cause? Of my condition!" She grabs him by the lapels of his jacket. "What did you do to Vedoma? When did she pass? Tell me, do you have Beatrix there as well?"

He grabs her wrists. "Unhand me, child, you are not well. Vedoma was not well and I know nothing of Beatrix's whereabouts. I am trying to help you. Your mother is trying to help you. These people were not good for you. Look at the state you are in? Is that not proof enough?"

She shoves him away from her, tears of rage filling her eyes, "Oh God, help me. Who knows what treatments you subjected Vedoma to? Oh God, I am to blame as well, to leave my Bea unprotected, at the mercy of the likes of my mother—oh God, mother. Leave! Leave now! I can't bear to look at you. I want you to leave! Now!"

Her mother and two nurses run out to the garden upon hearing the commotion. The nurses tend to the fallen doctor as Mrs. Beth chides her daughter. "Lissandra, what is this nonsense you speak of? Have you lost your manners along with your mind?" Lissandra's mother turns to the doctor, "My sincerest apologies, Dr. Froelich. As you can see, my daughter is not well. She has gone mad. You must help her."

Lissandra retorts, "Yes, help me, so I may see my grave soon too, like Vadoma, or vanish like Beatrix. Do you think I have lost my memory along with my mind? What did you do to them, mother? Where they rest now could not be any worse than being here. Yes, go ahead and send me away. Send me to the grave. Surely, I will be more content there than I have ever been in this god forsaken prison you call a home." Suddenly, an apparition appears before her eyes, drowning out the world around her. She is speechless as the vision of a ferocious panther prances towards her then evanesces, calming her. Somehow, she knows it is a sign. *She must go with Dr. Froelich to the Institute. She must discover what happened to Vedoma. She must find Bea. This is the way.* She turns back to face them. "I'm sorry, I don't... I don't know what has gotten into me. Mother is right, perhaps, I am not well. I will pack my bags and be off to the hospital in the morning. Is that all right?"

The doctor nods, though he is suspicious. "I look forward to seeing you then, Lissandra." Her mother takes his hand and thanks him again, and they walk away, leaving Lissandra in the garden.

Lissandra watches them leave and becomes a statue again, a contrived smile fading into the hollow look she tends to bear these days. Her chambermaid, Augustina, finds her in the garden, and beckons her to her room. "Come on now, come up to your chambers, Miss Lissandra. It seems we have some packing to do."

She finally releases her sobs. "Oh Augustina, I can hardly bear to be away from my darling woods, so far from Bea's memory. Why did she leave me here Aggie, why?"

Augustina holds her lithe frame in her arms, stroking her auburn hair as she whispers, "Oh, Miss Lissandra, she didn't choose to leave of her own free will. She would never leave you. You must know that."

She pleads, "Tell me, Aggie, did mother send her away to the institute, please tell me the truth."

Augustina bites her lip, appearing conflicted. "Oh, I don't know, Miss Lissandra. There's some evil looming over us all. I can feel it. You should be careful over there in that hospital. I wouldn't trust that doctor with a single hair on my head if I were you."

She gathers Lissandra to her bosom and lets her sob until she hears approaching footsteps. "Come now, Miss Lissandra, let's get you upstairs."

Augustina helps Lissandra bathe and prepare enough belongings for a fortnight at the hospital in relative silence. Lissandra sits at her desk writing letters for Augustina to send out while she is gone, giving her instructions and sharing memories as she goes. "Aggie, you do remember Sebastian from Governor's Square, don't you, at Cecilia Northam's townhouse, the dark-haired fellow that came to my aid? I'd like you to deliver this letter to him personally. I have been meaning to repay his kindness for some time now and I am not certain it will get to him if you post it."

Augustina nods. "Yes ma'am, I remember him well, pretty looking fellow, wouldn't you say so?"

Lissandra giggles. "Oh stop it, Aggie."

Augustina smiles, watching the moment of levity fade from Lissandra's features. "It's always so lovely to hear your laughter, darling. It is such an odd occasion nowadays. I know you miss Bea, but she is gone, and you are still here. Do promise me you'll take care of yourself and come home for good."

Turning her head away, Lissandra replies, "I'll do my best, Aggie, I promise. Would you mind fetching me some soup? I won't be joining my mother for dinner tonight."

Augustina nods. "Alright sweetie, I'll bring some up." When she returns, Lissandra is gone. She has taken to the woods again. Augustina places the tray by her bedside, whispers a prayer her mother taught her, and heads to the garden to look for her.

Lissandra passes through a narrow clearing in the pines, breathing in their citrusy scent, the dirt beneath her feet shifting into a familiar moss. She looks down, noticing the circular mound protruding from the ground. *The tunnel.* Her slender fingers scan the perimeter of the door, memories flooding her mind. She stops when she hears Augustina calling to her from a distance.

"Lissandra, child, are you out here? Come dear, it is far too late, you'll catch your death out here."

She stands and leaves the clearing, moving towards Augustina's voice until she finds her. "I just wanted to take one more stroll through the pines, Aggie. You didn't have to come for me. I won't be disappearing anytime soon."

Augustina smiles sadly. "Come, Miss Lissandra, let's get you inside."

In the morning, Lissandra bids her mother farewell and is taken to the San German Institute. She looks up at the looming structure she has come to know well, its stark white facade bidding her welcome once again. She shuts her eyes and takes a deep breath, preparing herself for what lies ahead. Dr. Froelich greets her at the steps, a frail young nurse and a burly orderly on each side of him. "Welcome, Miss Lissandra. I am so pleased to see you here." She nods, then lowers her gaze and follows them into the building. Dr. Froelich pulls the young nurse to one side as Lissandra gazes around the haunted halls of the asylum, the tile floors reflecting the fractured sunlight pouring in through the gates on the large, ornate venetian windows. The nurse returns to her side and they guide her to her quarters.

The moment she enters her room, the nurse and orderly close in on her and administer a sedative. She wakes strapped to a gurney in Dr. Froelich's operating room, the bright white light from the overhead lamp blinding her as she opens her eyes. She shuts them again, turning her head to the side and blinking repeatedly in an attempt to see. She writhes against the straps holding her to the gurney, noticing her nakedness. Dr. Froelich walks in and stands over her. "*Tsk, tsk, tsk,* Ms. Lissandra, you must calm down now or I will have to administer another sedative. You wouldn't want that, now, would you?"

She glares at him, "What do you want with me? Why do you have me here?"

He clears his throat. "For your treatment, of course."

She scowls. "What kind of treatment requires me to be sedated from the moment I walk in, and strapped to a gurney so indecently? Did my mother approve of this?"

He chuckles. "These are simply protective measures. We have all seen your wrath, Miss Lissandra. For as much beauty as you possess, there is also a beast in you. We cannot have you hurting yourself or the staff. Trust me. It is for your own well-being. Your mother knows that and has approved any and all treatments necessary to cure you of your evil afflictions. No harm will come to you so long as you cooperate."

"Cooperate with what?" Lissandra growls.

He ignores her question. "Very well, since you seem so eager, let us begin."

Dr. Froelich leaves and returns with a frail young nurse hauling a medical trolley of skillfully placed toxins and surgical tools. He places a hand in between Lissandra's breasts, feeling for her heartbeat. He orders the nurse to undress.

Lissandra panics. "Please stop. What are you doing? Stop touching me, you *charlatan.*"

He turns to face her. "Do not forget yourself—I am a professional. This is an approved treatment for your condition. There is nothing indecent occurring here." He motions for the nurse to continue undressing, keeping his hand firmly placed over Lissandra's heart. "Look at the nurse or I will clamp your eyes open," he orders as she winces and turns her gaze.

She turns her eyes back to the nurse in fear.

He orders the nurse to come closer, to caress her, to kiss her. The nurse complies as Lissandra wails, agonized at her powerlessness. He moves his hand down, over her navel, then in between her thighs, "You are a lecherous evil woman. Your body betrays you despite your protests, but I will cure you."

He cranks the gurney up to a sitting position, takes a tonic from a tray on the trolley, grabs a fistful of Lissandra's hair, and orders her to drink. He pours fetid liquid into her mouth. "Drink it."

She chokes as she thrashes, spitting the vile concoction out at him. *"Go to hell! Help me! Someone, help me! Please!"* She pleads with the nurse, still standing stark naked in silence, motionless.

The doctor grabs her by the throat. "You will learn, one way or another, you will learn. You will not be my failure."

She struggles to breathe, gasping when he lets her go to grab another tonic and a metal mouth gag. "I warned you not to be uncivilized, Lissandra. Why do you women choose to do things the hard way?" He forces the metal gag into her mouth and pours the second rancid tonic down her throat. She heaves in disgust as it slithers down her throat, and he calls the slender nurse back to her. The nurse resumes caressing her as the tonic makes her sick. Lissandra retches over and over again, but the nurse continues her task undaunted, massaging her even though she is covered in regurgitation. The doctor looks on in approval, then orders the nurse to stop. He unbuckles the gurney straps and watches Lissandra crumble into a defeated, curdled heap. He orders the nurse, "Clean her up and bring her to my office. I am sure she will be more compliant now."

The nurse nods as he walks away, notably pleased with his work. She leads a shivering, traumatized Lissandra to a large shower room where she bathes her.

"You did so well in there, darling," the nurse attempts to assuage her. "You will be cured in no time. I'm sure of it."

Lissandra dresses in the plain white linen nightgown the nurse gives her and follows her in silence to Dr. Froelich's office. She glares at the doctor as she enters but sits compliantly in the chair the nurse pulls up for her.

"You may go now," the doctor instructs the nurse dryly. She nods and leaves. Lissandra sits in a catatonic state until the doctor addresses her. "Do you know why you received this treatment?"

"Yes."

"So, you are ready to admit you and Beatrix were having sexual relations, and that this evil is the cause of her death and your decline in health. Correct?"

Lissandra replies emotionlessly, "Yes."

The doctor sighs. "Good. Exceptionally good. It is such a pleasure to see you responding so well to your first treatment. I have full faith we shall have you restored and ready to rejoin society shortly."

Lissandra nods. "Yes, doctor, thank you. I am so thankful for your faith in me. I will not be any more trouble, I promise. You do believe me, don't you? Wilhelm? May I call you Wilhelm, doctor?"

He kneels beside her, touched. "Why yes, yes, you may, Miss Lissandra. May I call you Lizzy?"

She giggles. "Sure. I'm sorry I was so much trouble before. I was under a sort of spell, I think. I don't know. You see, Beatrix practiced the dark arts, magic, well, sorcery. I'm almost certain it had something to do with my obsession with her. I feel better now. I don't think I need more treatment. What I need...no what I want is...is...someone like you, to understand me, to listen."

His face lights up. "Oh Lissandra, you don't know how happy it makes me to hear you say this. I have fantasized about this day for months. However, I cannot stop your treatment. What would happen if you regressed?"

She stands, wrapping her lithe hands around his broad shoulders. "I won't, not with you by my side. I want to show you something that will make you trust me, but you have to take me back home, to the grounds, then we can return before morning. I will show you everything."

The gleam of mischief in his eyes lets her know she has him hooked. He grins, "I knew you were special, Lizzy."

She giggles, pressing her bosom to his chest and kissing his cheek. "Let me show you just how special I am, doctor."

He shudders at her touch, then composes himself. "We can use the old entrance behind the east wards. No one will see us leaving." He walks over to his wardrobe closet and retrieves a long, thin trench coat. "Here, put this on." He pulls his jacket from a nearby hook and beckons her to follow him. They use an old staircase at the back of the hospital only he has access to and walk outside into the evening breeze. Lissandra takes a deep breath; a breath of freedom she knows she will not lose again.

When Lissandra enters the grounds with the doctor, she does not even need to see to know the way. She breathes in the scent of the woods, thinking: *Our footprints remain buried in this earth, our paths hidden in the soles of my feet, every detail of our history seared into my heart. Still, my heart grows harder with every passing minute spent wondering why you chose to take your final breath. It won't be long till all the blood's replaced with frigid water cascading over stone. I am alone. Come back to me, Bea. I am here. Come back to me.*

She falls to her knees, hands searching in front of her for a break in the surface of the ground. She digs her fingers into the earth to find familiar grooves, then pulls up a small wooden door covered in moss and slips inside. The doctor looks on in amazement. By the scant light filtering through the trees, Lissandra retrieves a small satchel from a hook built into the makeshift shelter. It holds three small candles, seeds of black mercy, a tin matchbox, a sewing pin, and a tiny portrait of Bea. She lights one of the candles, calls the doctor to follow her, then continues her descent, rediscovering the tunnel. Mesmerized by the mystery of it all, the doctor scans the walls of the underground lair, completely ignorant of Lissandra's plans.

She sets to work quickly before he notices, hatred for him burning through her veins. She sets Bea's picture down on the earth and lights an onyx candle atop it. She pricks her finger with the sewing pin and holds her finger over the flame, dripping blood onto the candle, then throws the mercy seeds towards the opening of the tunnel, chanting, *Beatrix... Beatrix...Beatrix.*

The doctor turns towards her, bewildered. "What are you–are you doing–what did you say?"

As she utters the final vowel, a colossal demon appears at the mouth of the tunnel. As dark as the shadows surrounding it, except for glistening teeth, its wide, sharp grin is made more macabre by the flicker of candlelight. Dr. Froelich stands paralyzed, mouth agape. He releases a petrified shriek as the demon digs its claws into the sides of his head and holds him up in front of them, as if inspecting a putrid specimen.

Lissandra can't help but smile. The demon slams Dr. Froelich into the walls of the tunnel like a rag doll, crushing his bones with blunt force until he is a bloody sack of pulp held together only by his skin. It drops him to the side and faces Lissandra, licking its lips.

Lissandra stands, concealing her own terror and feigning bravery. "You are the one who wakes me from my rest every night, the one who torments me. If you are the Devil, or something akin to it, if you are as powerful as you seem, then prove it. Am I to be afraid of you? I, who have lost the only person in the world I have ever loved? Well, I am not afraid of you. At the very least, I have not been alone when you come to me and if I am damned, then so be it. They say my Beatrix was damned too. If that is so, is she with you, my Bea? I would give my life for her. I would give my soul, I swear it. Return my Bea to me and I will be your willing servant until the end of time."

The shadow beast cocks its horned skull at her and growls, "It is I that stands at your command, your grace."

Lissandra shuts her eyes, breathes, and recites the words of an ancient spell she thought she had forgotten, one Bea's aunt taught them when they were children, before she was taken away from the estate. Her mind flashes back to memories of rituals performed under the light of countless moons, to tales of immortals, of eternal loves, of incantations that reverse the impossible when repeated thrice. *"Ego creo quad ego loquar, I create what I speak, moderari tempore sum, I control time, amor venit ad me, I command my love to come to me, somnia verita sum, my dreams come true, sacrificabo cor meum pro ea, I sacrifice my heart for her, anima mea ad eum, my soul to him, factum est, it is done…"*

Upon hearing the final words, the demon lunges forward as thunder roars in the distance, grabbing her by the waist, and falling with her to the earthen floor. It greedily inhales her scent, a grotesquely long tongue slithering over her bosom in search of its prize. It gnashes at her nightgown, ripping the trenchcoat and delicate linen gown to shreds. Lissandra groans in ecstasy at the supernatural touch of the beast, its magic assuaging her with memories of Beatrix. They race through her mind, assaulting her senses, feeling as soft as the fingertips of her lost lover even as the creature's claws scrape her skin raw. Its vicious assault buries any remnants of the human girl she once was, imbuing her with a power she had never known. Plunging its teeth into the soft tissue of her breast, the demon devours her as she still moans with pleasure, drinking her blood, and chewing through skin, muscles, bone, until it reaches her heart. There, it pauses, and the transformation begins.

First the beast transforms, then she. Light overpowers theshadows revealing smooth tawny skin, shapely thighs–oh, how she knows those thighs–a scowl fades into a smile, the smile of her lover…whose coarse demonic features now turn angelic…horns exchanged for the soft, bouncing black curls she remembers. Lissandra stares, not noticing her own metamorphosis, her unblemished alabaster skin intact once more, her auburn tresses burning brighter, more the color of wildfire than ever before, and her nails long and dark, as black as the shadows that consumed her. They lie in their nakedness for just a moment, in awe of each other's forms. Then, they fall into one another's arms, Lissandra cupping Bea's warm bronze face in her hands. "I thought I would never see you again. I thought you were gone."

Bea chides her lovingly. "You are wrong to assume I would ever let you live in peace. I would have tormented you for eons, my love, if you did not come to me."

Tears stream from their eyes as they embrace, covering each other in caresses. Their lips lock in a kiss ripe with need, pausing only to protract sets of gleaming ebony fangs that they hastily sank into each other's necks. They feed on each other's accursed inky blood, becoming the same, as the darkness of the warm, wet, earth envelops them in its safety, transporting them to another world; their world.

Lissandra looks around, eyes wide with wonderment. "Where are we, Bea?"

Bea smiles. "We are home."

They walk along a brilliant lake surrounded by enormous canyons of ice under a sky as red as the blood moon, its crimson light tainting everything it touches. Beatrix takes Lissandra's hand, kneeling before her, and scooping some of the water up with her free hand, tells her, "If we drink from these waters, we will never forget our time on earth or each other."

Lissandra joins her, and Beatrix brings her hand to her lips. She sips, then Lissandra returns the favor. She pulls Beatrix into an embrace and whispers, "Now, time for more revenge."

Beatrix pulls away. "Lissandra, I cannot return to earth without the ritual, for my spirit passed before my demon emerged. I am tethered to our home."

"There must be something we can do," Lissandra pleads. "Bea, please."

Bea replies sternly, "No, there is not." She softens her voice. "Go, Lissandra. I will be with you in spirit always, and ever await your return."

Lissandra shakes her head stubbornly. "No, I'm not leaving you."

Bea growls, "You must." She pulls Lissandra into an embrace again, muttering an ancient spirit binding spell. They writhe in pain as their spirits become one, Bea's corporeal form turning to dust within her grasp.

Bea's voice chimes in her mind, "Now, nothing can part us. Go Lissandra, the night is yours."

"Ours," Lissandra echoes.

Lissandra shuts her eyes, and transports back to the tunnel. They slip out of the earthen hideaway into the chill evening air, through the forest, glide through the halls of the peaceful manor, into Mrs. Beth's room so silently, she does not even stir. Lissandra kisses her mother on the cheek, ever so tenderly, then sinks her midnight fangs into her neck.

Mrs. Beth gasps and thrashes for a short while before succumbing to blood loss. Then all is quiet again. They return to the tunnel, traveling in the opposite direction once inside. Bea's voice assures her it leads to the dungeons of the hospital where they kept her mother. Lissandra descends upon San German with unbridled fury, their demonic powers unfurling before their eyes. Those spared flee into the darkness towards uncertain freedom.

It is nearly noon the next day, when authorities finally arrive to assess the carnage left behind at the San German Institute for the Clinically Insane. The detectives exit their carriages to see the bodies of dozens of orderlies, nurses, and doctors strewn about, dismembered, beheaded, their eyes crushed into their skulls. The only clue left behind for them to decipher the events that transpired is a name painted on the stone steps in cruor. *Lissandra.*

ACKNOWLEDGMENTS

As with all our publications, Eros & Thanatos would not be possible without the help of some dedicated Crows. I would first like to thank my co-editor, Damon Barret Roe, for her tireless help putting this anthology together. This was our first project besides Quill & Crow's monthly literary magazine, *The Crow's Quill*, and I'm hoping it will become a more common occurrence. I would like to thank the rest of the editing team for their assistance, including K.R. Wieland, Tiffany Curry, and the irreplaceable William Bartlett. I am always so honored to work alongside the Quill & Crow Editing Team and this project was no exception.

Back for a second anthology, Marie Casey once again led the creative design efforts, from the darkly romantic cover to the beautiful interior details in the ebook. This book would not be possible without her, and I hope you appreciate the unique artistic touch she brings to Quill & Crow projects.

Lastly, I'd like to thank all the authors who contributed their stories. I wasn't sure what to expect with an anthology based on death and desire, but I was not disappointed. After the submissions were selected, Damon and I quickly realized we'd compiled a collection with stories that represent the inclusive nature of our company. This brought us both a lot of joy and we are so honored to bring these poignant, diverse stories to life.

Putting this anthology together was a truly enjoyable experience, through and through. I appreciate everyone's efforts and look forward to seeing what more we can come up with as a publishing house. I hope you've enjoyed these stories as well.

Dreadfully Yours,
Cassandra L. Thompson

AUTHOR BIOGRAPHIES

ALEXANDRIA BAKER is a Seattle-based writer and editor with a passion for wordsmithing and a mild caffeine addiction. She earned her Master's from the University of Washington and has worked on everything from foreign policy research to travel magazines. Baker has previously published with Mason Jar Press and HellBound Books Publishing; she is currently working on her first novel. Her work can be found online at alexbakerwriting.com, or you can follow her on Twitter.

MEGAN BONTRAGER is a recent graduate from Johns Hopkins University's MA in Writing program, and previously received her BFA in Creative Writing from the University of Central Florida. She lives in Ireland with her husband and three four-legged children, where she works as a fiction editor. In her free time, she volunteers with animal rescue organizations in the Dublin area.

MADDIE BOWEN-SMYTH is perpetually, endlessly tired. She's an avid tabletop role-player, spends hours hunting obscure historical facts, and all her characters wind up bi until proven otherwise. After working in Japan for several years, she now lives in Australia with her wife and their growing menagerie. Maddie holds a Bachelor's in journalism and writing, and is currently studying psychology. Her work typically explores mental health, sexuality, gender identity, the relationships we have with our bodies, and the lasting echoes of trauma. All of this work is animated by a spirit of bull-headed hopefulness—despite all obstacles, hope can endure.

DAN DOLAN first crafted imaginary worlds as a young child as his escape and now has turned that passion into his life's work. As a creative writer he's been published multiple times, not just prose works but also selections of his poetry. His short stories, rooted in the myths and fables that were his youthful obsession, range from urban fantasy to Gothic to sci-fi often using magic and the paranormal to tell stories about the human experience and the unsung lives of misunderstood people.

A.L. GARCIA lives in Massachusetts with her loving husband, two spirited children, and new addition to the family, fur baby/tender hellhound, Mo. She began writing poetry as a youth as a way of coping with abusive family dynamics. She joined the writing community in August of 2020, after independently publishing a personal narrative, *Broken Things*, detailing the abuse she endured as a child. She is a veteran of the U.S. Army and studied Sociology/Social Science at Towson University. She handles marketing/public relations for Quill & Crow Publishing House. She also has an independent poetry collection, *Broken Heart Mosaics*, is featured in all the *Crow Calls* volumes, and *Ravens & Roses: A Gothic Women's Anthology*.

REBECCA JONES-HOWE is a neo-noir writer from Kamloops, British Columbia. Her short fiction has appeared in PANK, Dark Moon Digest, and The New Black anthology of neo-noir fiction, among others. Her first collection of short fiction, *Vile Men*, was published in 2015. Her gothic horror has appeared in the Anomalies & Curiosities anthology, as well as the *Ravens & Roses* anthology. She regularly writes for *The Quill's Crow* and also scathingly reviews V.C. Andrews novels on her writer blog at http://rebeccajoneshowe.com.

JEREMY MEGARGEE has always loved dark fiction. He cut his teeth on R.L Stine's Goosebumps series as a child and a fascination with Stephen King, Jack London, Algernon Blackwood, and many others followed later in life. Jeremy weaves his tales of personal horror from Martinsburg, West Virginia with his cat Lazarus acting as his muse/familiar. He is an active member of the West Virginia chapter of the Horror Writers Association and you can often find him peddling his dark words in various mountain hollers deep within the Appalachians.

NEWTON is an author, artist, and oddity who spends an inordinate amount of time diving into the depths of his overactive imagination in an effort to dredge up original stories of both wonder and terror. He currently resides in St. Louis, MO.

ASHLEY VAN ELSWYK is a queer Canadian writer of speculative fiction and poetry with works in From the Farther Trees, Green Ink Poetry, Idle Ink, and several anthologies from Ghost Orchid Press including *Dark Hearts* and *Chlorophobia*. She enjoys collecting old postcards, field-walking, and spoiling her cat.

MELANIE WHITLOCK is a writer, historian, and poet hailing from Cumbria. With supernatural roots from her grandparents, her life is steeped in magic and folklore. Her work is featured in the previous *Crow Calls* poetry anthologies and national newspapers, and she uploads short pieces daily to Twitter. Gothic short stories and her first supernatural/romance novel are expected late next year and you can also catch her hosting Crow Spaces for Quill & Crow. You can summon her upon the witching hour, between the moon and stars.

KAYLA WHITTLE works in marketing and social media for a medical publisher. She has previously had a short story published in Luna Station Quarterly. When not writing, she's usually busy reading, embroidering, or planning her next Disney vacation. She currently resides in New Jersey.

PERRY WOLFECASTLE hails from the Staffordshire Moorlands where he spends his time writing, tweeting absolute nonsense, exploring nature, and disliking writing about himself in the third person. All his life, he would have stories brewing in his head. Perry has spent most of life wanting to write, and finally, in 2019, he began pursuing that dream. Author of the dark fantasy novella, *Promised Land*, Perry holds a BA Hons in History, which he's used exactly once.

Discover more titles from Quill & Crow Publishing House
www.quillandcrowpublishinghouse.com

CPSIA information can be obtained
at www.ICGtesting.com
Printed in the USA
BVHW060857110222
628683BV00001B/58